NAIL BITER

ALSO BY SARAH GRAVES

Triple Witch
The Dead Cat Bounce
Wicked Fix
Repair to Her Grave
Wreck the Halls
Unhinged
Mallets Aforethought
Tool & Die

NAIL BITER

A
Home Repair Is Homicide
Mystery

SARAH GRAVES

BANTAM BOOKS

NAIL BITER
A HOME REPAIR IS HOMICIDE MYSTERY
A Bantam Book / January 2006

Published by
Bantam Dell
A Division of Random House, Inc.
New York, New York

Library of Congress Cataloging-in-Publication Data

Graves, Sarah.
Nail biter / Sarah Graves.
p. cm. – (A home repair is homicide mystery)
ISBN-13: 978-0-553-80310-5
ISBN-10: 0-553-80310-7
1. Tiptree, Jacobia (Fictitious character)–Fiction. 2. White, Ellie (Fictitious character)–Fiction. 3. Women detectives–Maine–Eastport–Fiction. 4. Dwellings–Maintenance and repair–Fiction. 5. Eastport (Me.)–Fiction. I. Title.

PS3557.R2897N35 2006
813'.6–dc22

2005050368

Printed in the United States of America
Published simultaneously in Canada

www.bantamdell.com

10 9 8 7 6 5 4 3 2 1
BVG

NAIL BITER

Chapter 1

Cursing the wild raspberry brambles that snatched at his hands and the cold mist drifting in off the salt water a hundred yards distant, Eugene Dibble made his way clumsily through the overgrown brush and weeds behind the old McSorley place on Long Cove Road.

It was already midmorning, much later than he'd expected to be hanging around here. But he'd had to wait until the tenants went out.

Short-term tenants, only visiting for a few weeks according to what he'd heard. So wouldn't you think they'd have better things to do than sit around inside all day, delaying his plans? But finally their white van had backed from the driveway and pulled off down Long Cove Road.

About time, he grumbled inwardly. Stupid tourists going on another one of their stupid outings, he thought, plucking a thorn from the skin of his left hand as he pushed forward.

Cursing, he stumbled on an old broken-out section of picket fence hidden beneath the matted weeds. Damning his luck as he licked fresh blood from his wounded finger, he tried shaking the fence piece off his boot while eyeing the house again.

It was a small, cheaply built bungalow overlooking Long Cove, on Moose Island seven miles off the coast of downeast Maine. With faded red paint, sagging gray shutters each with the shape of an anchor cut into it, and a tumbledown attached utility shed at the rear, the house was one of dozens of such dwellings hurriedly put up by the Navy for its station here during World War II.

Yanking his boot from between a pair of rotting fence pickets, Eugene found himself remembering back when he was a kid, visiting the house for Cub Scout meetings. The fence had stood tall and proud then, painted white every year by Mr. McSorley, a retired Navy man himself.

Eugene wondered idly whether horse-faced old Mrs. McSorley ever figured out which Scout was pilfering her purse while he was supposed to be busy earning yet another of her half-assed merit badges.

Then the feeling of being jammed into the cramped house with a dozen other Cubs flooded back, the noise and little-boy smells. One week the meeting might be about butterfly collecting; this he had enjoyed because he liked sticking pins into the insects even though they were already dead, courtesy of a homemade gas chamber devised from a canning jar and a clump of alcohol-soaked cotton.

But the next week the troop's agenda might involve learning to make butter by shaking jars half filled with cream (and only recently emptied of butterflies, he'd suspected) until the boys' arms nearly fell off.

Eugene scowled as he recalled the yellow clots taking shape in the cream, which he'd tried to drink afterwards only to find it had turned to buttermilk. Stupid woman, he remembered thinking at the time; why wasn't there a merit badge for something useful like making beer?

The memory fled as another wave of his current mood, which was anxious resentment, washed over him again. The tenants *were* gone, off to experience the delights of this remote and undeniably scenic part of the Maine coast. And that–the empty house just sitting there waiting for him–was a good thing.

Still, nobody ever took *him* on an outing, did they? That was for sure. Instead he was out here risking life and limb in this decaying backyard jungle, the very sight of which would've given Mr. McSorley a heart attack even worse than the one that finally did carry him off.

And all for a paper bag that might or might not contain what Eugene had been promised that it would.

No, he corrected himself as another bramble snagged his pants leg. Not just promised: *guaranteed.* And if by some chance that guarantee didn't pan out in spades, Eugene thought as he kicked fiercely at the offending vegetation, it wouldn't be his neck that got broken. That was for sure, too.

His foot caught again, this time in a loop of bittersweet vine tough as rope, sending him flailing until he came down hard on his left ankle, twisting it painfully.

He bit back a yelp. No one could see him. The houses here at the west end of the island were too far apart and the intervening weeds and scrubby saplings too thick and tall, up over his head.

But it wouldn't do to have anyone hear him, would it? Some nosy idiot whose presence absolutely hadn't been planned on, who might hear him cussing and wonder what the dickens he might be up to, stumbling around out here in the brush and trash.

And remember it later maybe, too. No, Eugene definitely didn't want any of that. Wincing, he hobbled the last few yards to the edge of the thicket and peered again at the rear of the house.

No one in there. The whole plan depended on it. *And on me,* Eugene reminded himself with a fresh surge of annoyance as he scooted from the cover of brush to the broken back door.

Never mind that there's two in this plan, he thought darkly as he tried the old door. Two splitting the profit.

But only one taking any of the risk. *Yeah, and what else is new?* he thought irritably. *If there might be a dirty end to the stick, just call Eugene. He's dumb enough to grab it.*

Which had happened before, and was pretty much what he was

doing this time, too, while his partner sat safely in the car up on the road, on the other side of the back lot.

So much for fairness. So much for sharing the work equally. But this time at least there was *guaranteed* to be a fine payoff.

One hard yank and the door to the falling-down little shed popped open. He glanced around furtively, then ducked inside and pulled it solidly closed behind him again.

And paused. No sound from within the house. He could hear his heart pounding but his breath came easier, though his ankle now felt like the fires of hell had been ignited inside his boot.

Reassured by the silence, he examined his surroundings. An old washing machine, some broken flower pots, cans of used motor oil... things had sure changed since the McSorleys lived here.

Man, and people said *his* place was a dump. Which it was, but at least he had an excuse. When you never got a break, just more struggles and disappointment, when the others got moonlight and roses and all you ever got was a kick in the face, then maybe you just didn't have the resources to keep everything all spiffed up and la-di-dah all the damned time.

He looked around some more, conscious that even with no one in the house he had better hurry. The bag should be right here somewhere. An ordinary brown paper bag, folded over and stapled at the top.

A bag with a couple of hundred illegal pills in it. Eugene felt his heart lift buoyantly just at the thought. Two hundred pills, twenty or even thirty bucks' profit on each: best case, and if his arithmetic was right, the score added up to a whopping six thousand dollars. Divided by two...

Which Eugene grudgingly admitted to himself was probably necessary, since someone had to sell the pills and he was not in a position to do it, especially not now with a bum ankle.

It was still a good payday for a relatively simple outlay of work, he told himself, even if he did have to split the cash. So all right, then, where the hell was the damned bag?

With a scowl of distaste–for in his heart and despite the disorder of his own personal living situation, Eugene Dibble felt himself to be a fastidious man–he began picking through the many items left here to decay by some long-ago occupant.

The shed's old double-hung windows, gone awry in their weather-beaten wooden frames, shivered in the wind as he searched, his hands stinging and blood-streaked from thorn scratches and his boots sliding on the mossy, uneven red bricks that formed the floor of the rickety structure.

Under old magazines: no. Behind a laundry hamper half buried in a pile of yellowed venetian blinds that clattered and fell as he touched them: *nada.* Under a heap of old ice-fishing gear...

The bag was supposed to be right out in plain sight, but of course *that* was too much to hope for. *That* would be way more luck than Eugene Dibble, at the relatively young age of forty-six a seasoned expert in the many varieties of ill fortune, had any right to expect.

Or so he griped to himself as he went on searching, now beginning to feel real worry along with the flares of anguish from his ankle each time his weight came down on his left foot.

Had something gone wrong? Even after all the assurances he'd been given, could the bag possibly *not* be here?

Then he froze, one hand on the top drawer of an ancient, veneer-peeling bureau with a broken mirror and the other on the lid of an old toolbox. A *sound,* somewhere in the house...

Guilt overlaid by a spine-tingling thrill of superstitious fear overcame him as he stood very still, listening for the sound to come again. Because the tenants were rumored to be...

Witches. That, anyway, was the story around town. A coven, Eugene had been told that it was called, and once he'd heard this rumor he'd done as much to spread it as anyone.

Not that he believed it. He'd never even seen them. But he figured the tale would help keep anyone else from burglarizing the place before *he* did, someone who might accidentally find the bag before he got to it.

Although finding it at all was turning out to be more of a chore than Eugene had expected. *Just my luck...*

When after a few more moments nothing else happened, though, he relaxed, even laughed a bit at himself. Some burglar he was; one funny noise and here he was getting all spleeny about it.

Spleeny; now there was a word he hadn't thought of in a long time. What his mother, a downeast Maine girl born and bred, used to say when she meant *anxious, unreasonably nervous.*

Still, he'd been in here too long. Irked at the amount of time the job was unexpectedly taking, he returned to his search.

Witches, that was a hot one, he thought as he poked beneath some old seat cushions. Four grown-ups and a kid from down south in Massachusetts, he'd heard; from the practical standpoint they couldn't have picked a worse time to occupy the old place.

Which wasn't surprising. It was how his luck always went. He unrolled a dusty rug; nothing in it. On the other hand, having the whole town all excited about a witches' group kept people from paying attention to any of Eugene's activities, didn't it?

Which *did* work out just fine. So like most things in his life, it was a trade-off. Damn, where *was* the bag?

Just then the sound came again, louder.

Footsteps. Soft but purposeful, coming steadily toward him.

Panicky, Eugene looked out through a shed window and spotted the crown of a dark blue baseball cap peeping through the weeds out back. Wondering what could be keeping Eugene, his partner in crime had apparently gotten out of the car, which they had *both* agreed that his partner would *not* do, would not have any *reason* to do.

And furthermore would not have time to do, because this was going to be such a piece of cake. Uh-huh, and look how well *that* worked out, Eugene thought, readying himself for a hasty exit.

So now his partner had come anyway. Gotten out of the car, pushed his way through the thorns and bittersweet, and hunkered down in the weeds at the back of the yard with his hands shading his eyes, probably, so he could try to see what was up.

Yeah, well, a *complication* was up, Eugene thought savagely, heading for the door. But when he grabbed at it the knob stuck and it was too late now. The footsteps were nearly in the shed.

And then they *were* in the shed. Feet clad in a pair of new, obviously pricey white sneakers appeared in the doorway.

Eugene stared at the expensive sneakers with a pang of his usual resentful envy, then let his gaze move upward to the things this utterly unexpected person held in each hand.

This person who was not supposed to be here, but was. In one hand: a paper bag, folded and stapled at the top. Eugene licked his lips as he caught sight of it.

There, only a few tantalizing inches away from him, was his six thousand dollars. Then very reluctantly he turned his attention to what his surprising visitor held in the other hand.

Oh, in the other hand.

Staring, Eugene thought about bad luck, reflecting that in spite of all his earlier mental whining he'd never really had any such thing, never in his whole life. But now...

In the other hand was a gun.

Aimed at him. Again he considered running. But the shed door was jammed, so to do it he'd have to get *closer* to the gun.

Nope. Better try to talk his way out of this. Eugene opened his mouth but no sound came out. Or maybe he couldn't hear it through the sudden, impossibly loud explosion happening *inside* his head.

Abruptly he was looking up at the ceiling. Hell, he thought. Here a gun was aimed right at him and he couldn't even summon the breath to say anything about it. Those mossy bricks were cold and uncomfortable on his back, too, and the window had become drafty all of a sudden.

On the other hand, his ankle didn't hurt anymore.

Which was exactly the kind of dumb thought that hit you, Eugene

Dibble realized with a stab of regret, when you were about to die. Plus a whole laundry list of irrelevant stuff like how amazingly much of the world there was, and how very little you had managed to experience of it in what had turned out to be your too-short life.

And how big the sky was, the sky outside if you'd only managed to make it there, and how high and bright the moon would be tonight if only you were still around to see it.

If only. Contrition pierced him suddenly. For the pocketbook pilfering. For all of it.

"This what you were looking for, Eugene?"

The paper bag, held up right over him, inches from his face. But it wasn't important.

Not anymore. A couple of the old windows reached all the way down to floor level. Eugene turned his head to somehow signal his partner in the weeds at the back of the yard.

Signal for help. But the baseball cap had vanished.

"Look at me, Eugene."

He looked, still not quite comprehending how everything had gone so suddenly sour.

"I... I don't get it," he managed. Because he was *supposed* to be here, he was *supposed* to find the–

"No, of course you don't. I guess it was too much to hope for that you would. But it doesn't matter. In the end it doesn't matter at all."

Eugene thought about this in a series of moments that seemed at once to pass in a flash and yet to go on forever, deciding finally that it was true. Nothing mattered: not the paper bag or the gun, or where the baseball cap had gone to.

Or who'd been wearing the cap, which by now Eugene could no longer quite remember. From the corner of his eye he caught sight of a small movement behind his assailant.

A white, shocked face, a pair of frightened eyes.

But they didn't matter either. All that felt the least bit important now was how wide the world was, how vast the sky.

Wonderingly he noticed too how swiftly and effortlessly he seemed to be sailing right up into it, leaving his body stuck to the earth like a dead bug impaled on an invisible pin.

Going up, he thought in surprise, in the last few sparkling broken-mirror shards of awareness that remained.

Now there's a piece of luck I wasn't expecting.

Chapter 2

I **said goodbye to my ex-husband Victor Tiptree on the day** our divorce was final, back in Manhattan, and hello again to him nearly every day thereafter for the next ten years.

Because he wouldn't let go. He didn't want me, but once I'd dissolved our legal connection Victor clung to me with the desperate tenacity of a selfish three-year-old, unwilling to let even his shabbiest, most unplayed-with toy be taken away.

A three-year-old being in many areas exactly what Victor was. On the other hand he ended up showing some pretty impressive maturity, all things considered.

But that was later. On the bright autumn morning when he walked into my big old house in Eastport, Maine, made a beeline for the refrigerator and located the last slice of blueberry pie, then sat down at the kitchen table to devour it without so much as a word to me, he was the same old Victor.

Rude, inconsiderate. And somehow proud of it, as if in his head he was hearing the applause he always felt he deserved.

Although now when I think of it I wonder whether applause was really what he was hearing, or if even then it was more of a slow, deliberate drumbeat.

Victor finished the pie, licking his fork before dropping it onto the stained plate.

"Coffee?" he asked, peering around as if the pot were not on the kitchen counter as always, and as if he didn't know perfectly well where the cups in my house were kept.

I'd been out target shooting before breakfast–bleak skies and chilly mist always made me feel like shooting something, and the early-morning weather had been dreary–and his tone made my trigger finger feel itchy again.

The .45-caliber Bisley six-shot revolver I'd been practicing with at the target range wasn't even stowed away in its lockbox yet, I mused as he went on eyeing me expectantly.

But instead of pursuing this thought I fixed coffee for him without complaint, dosing it with cream and sugar just the way he liked it, because I needed to talk to him and I knew from experience that waiting on Victor was a good way to soften him up a little.

Giving him, I mean, what he believed was really only his due. At the time, I felt that I was merely kowtowing to his ego as usual, in that moment of simple service when I set the white china mug, steaming and fragrant, on the table in front of him.

But these days I am grateful for it. Anyway:

"Victor, I do wish you'd stop spoiling Sam the way you have been lately."

Sam was our son; bright, charming, and dyslexic, he was a twenty-year-old boat-school apprentice and student at the nearby community college.

Victor went on stirring his coffee with his fork. Apparently I hadn't gotten the sugar dissolved quite perfectly. He frowned briefly at the tiny crumb of piecrust floating on the surface of the coffee, picked it out with a fork tine.

"What do you mean, spoiling him? He needed school clothes," my ex-husband said innocently.

Victor always tried innocence first. Next came shouting and sulking. But not this time, I thought determinedly. It was October and Sam had just recently started classes again, his time divided between the campus in Calais—the next town to our north, thirty miles distant on the mainland—and the boat school here in Eastport.

I kept my voice even. "Yes, I appreciate your taking care of that for him. But he didn't need the four-hundred-dollar leather jacket, did he? Or the hand-sewn leather loafers."

If Sam ever starts loafing I will take him to the hospital for a battery of blood tests. By harnessing half the energy that boy generates on a slow day, you could light up the East Coast.

Victor smiled a little, sitting there in my big barnlike kitchen with its high, bare windows, scuffed hardwood floor, and tall wooden wainscoting surrounding the old soapstone sink.

"Or," I went on, "those hundred-dollar-plus work boots from the Eddie Bauer catalog."

From her usual perch atop the refrigerator, Cat Dancing opened her crossed blue eyes and yawned expressively, then stood and stretched.

"All Sam's friends . . ." I began.

Mmrph, the Siamese uttered, leaping down onto the washing machine and across to the kitchen table. There she deliberately walked around Victor's plate three times, twitching her tail in his face while he tried swatting at her before she streaked from the room.

". . . dress out of the sale bins at Wal-Mart," I finished; good old Cat Dancing. "He'll have to scuff up those boots with a wire brush just to seem normal."

Victor grimaced, brushing fastidiously at the area around his plate.

He was a good-looking man in his forties with long-lashed green eyes, a lantern jaw, and lots of dark, curly hair just beginning to go a little gray at the temples.

"...and as for that cowhide book bag you bought him..."

Also, Victor was a cleanliness nut. Today he wore a spotless white V-neck cardigan over a white turtleneck, cream slacks, and a pair of ten-year-old driving moccasins that looked as if they'd just come out of the box.

Irritably he plucked Cat hairs off the cardigan. "Hideous beast," he muttered, and it was a good thing Cat Dancing didn't hear him; tail-twitching was the least of what that animal could accomplish when somebody riled her.

I pretended I hadn't heard him either. "...it's ridiculous," I persisted. "Donald Trump should be carrying that book bag. And Sam surely didn't need season tickets to the Boston Celtics."

We were getting to the heart of the matter now, the thing I objected to way more than any of the rest of the stuff Victor had been treating Sam to during the past few weeks.

"It's six hours to drive there and he still has his weekend job, so during the school year–which may I remind you is mostly when professional basketball is played–he can't even *get* to the arena to *see* the games," I said.

No reply from Victor. Encouraged, I went on. "There's not a thing he can even *do* with those tickets except sell them, so..."

But then I stopped, alerted by something even sneakier than usual in Victor's expression.

"Oh, no. Tell me you didn't."

Victor put his cup down, spread his hands placatingly. "I know it's extravagant. But you're right, the tickets are useless if he can't get to the games. And since I'm planning to use one of those tickets myself–"

"You're chartering down," I said flatly. "To Boston, out of Quoddy Airfield and back."

When I first moved to Eastport I thought our little island airport, with its wooden sign, bright orange wind sock, and metal quonset hangars, was charmingly quaint. Then I learned that it is (a) big enough for a Learjet and (b) so well maintained that it is regarded as a safe haven by pilots for hundreds of miles in all directions.

Also, you can get on a plane there in the afternoon and be in Boston by evening.

"Victor, that's outrageous. It's out of the question. What do you think he is, a movie star?"

"Jacobia, it's not–"

"No," I said flatly. "It's just way too out of line for his financial circumstances. I mean, I know *you've* got the money to do it, but..."

Before following me here to Maine in order to drive me crazy and incidentally also (he maintained) so that he could be nearer to Sam, Victor was the kind of brain surgeon you would go to when the other surgeons had all washed their hands of you because your neurological situation was so ghastly, it terrified even them.

And Victor's take-no-prisoners brand of scalpel-wielding chutzpah–not to mention his win-loss record on the operating table, which wasn't half shabby, either–hadn't come cheap.

So he could afford this stuff. But I couldn't, and neither could Sam. "Victor, I just don't want him thinking he can–"

"What?" he demanded. "Have something that not everyone else can, once in a blue moon? Something special?"

He narrowed his eyes at me. "Or is it only a big problem for you when the something special happens to be supplied by me?" His tone had turned waspish.

I opened my mouth to explain very specifically and in detail why he was wrong, which would have turned the conversation into a verbal slugfest. But I was saved from this by the arrival of my friend Ellie White.

"Hey, everybody," she called out cheerfully as she swept in lugging two brown paper bags in one arm while leading my two huge dogs on their leashes with her other hand.

Although "leading" was a gentle term for what those dogs were like, clipped to the ends of leashes. "Are you ready for the big storm?" she asked, not even out of breath.

Ellie was tall, redheaded, and so slender that she could wear green sweatpants, a big yellow sweatshirt, and a turquoise fleece top without impersonating something that has been inflated with a bicycle pump. Also, for today's three-mile midmorning dog-jog she wore white sneakers with thick pink socks puffing up over her pants cuffs.

"Going to be a humdinger," she added; Ellie liked what she called big weather.

"Because," Victor continued, glowering at me and ignoring her, "I notice that when Wade takes Sam hunting, they charter a seaplane right into the hunting camp up in the Allagash. But *that's* fine."

Wade Sorenson, my current husband, was a gun-repair expert, prizewinning target shooter–he'd taught me the basics and given me the Bisley .45 as a wedding gift–and devoted outdoorsman when he wasn't too busy being Eastport's harbor pilot, guiding huge freighters in and out of our deep-water port.

"The Allagash is different," I said. "It's nature, it's..."

I waved my hands inadequately. In fact Wade had intended to go deer hunting today, at his camp on Balsam Lake with a few buddies. But instead he was on a tugboat headed out to a big vessel diverted here for repairs.

"...character building," I declared, and Victor grimaced.

The freighter's diversion was bad news for Wade, but not for local truckers, since the repairs required offloading the cargo with cranes and land-hauling it elsewhere: good money for all the stevedores and drivers.

"*That's* just great," Victor fumed. "Whatever *Wade* does..."

The dogs snuffled eagerly at his pants legs, causing him to pull his feet sharply up like a man whose toes are about to be nibbled by alligators. Prill the red Doberman turned away at this gesture of unwillingness to socialize, but Monday the old black Labrador went on nuzzling him; she figured he was just playing hard to get.

"... out*doors* with a *gun*," he groused...

Down in the cellar my father went on hacking away at another part of the massive old stone foundation, which he was replacing section by section. The rhythmic *chunk! chunk!* of his mason's axe rang metallically as it ate its way through the antique mortar.

"... is always just ducky," Victor concluded in disgust, and made another attempt to shove Monday's head out of his lap.

Ellie hauled the bags full of quinces she carried across the kitchen and deposited them on the counter where they promptly fell over. The quince bushes grew in her yard and we'd been waiting for them to ripen enough to pick.

"You know, you just wouldn't believe what they put on kids' TV ads," she announced, speaking over the sound of Victor's voice.

We were used to speaking over the sound of his voice. "The sheer mind-bending audacity of them," Ellie went on indignantly.

Her own daughter, Leonora, was now nearly a year old. "I mean, it's almost as bad as all those dreadful political ads I've been seeing lately."

It was an election year and the candidates were busy trying to convince us they were saints, while their opponents had horns and forked tails. "Look, Victor," Ellie said. "Quinces."

Victor eyed the round greenish fruits spilling out of the bags. "Oh," he said, sounding pleased. "That means quince jam."

The thought of which was enough to sweeten even his prickly nature for the moment. Then he apparently heard the rest of what Ellie had said and switched into lecture mode; this was one of his favorite subjects.

"Ellie, TV advertisers can't sell goodness, you know that. No one would buy. TV sells fun, toys, things that taste sweet and so on."

He took a breath, warming to his topic. "So the politicians, knowing people feel guilty about glutting themselves and their kids on what the TV ads sell, offer to let people off the hook in their own ads."

He waved an expressive hand. "That way you can buy, say, an expensive gas-guzzler or bucket of chicken wings, and just *vote* for a good energy policy, healthy food, or whatever."

Enjoying himself, he went on. "By which I mean, and I'm sorry to have to tell you this..."

He wasn't. "... but it's worse than you think. *They're all in it together.*"

I'd come to Maine after a career of managing money for Wall Street honchos so corrupt that the Devil probably sold his soul to them. Thus I shared Victor's opinion, but you can't go around saying it or people will start thinking you're nuts.

Which we already knew Victor was; this time, though, his words resonated strongly with Ellie, fresh from watching her baby daughter's eyes widen at the sight of an ad for a toy makeup kit in a glittery pink plastic pouch.

"Jake," she said, angling her head at Victor, "sometimes I actually understand why you married this man."

He smiled self-importantly, missing the dig. "And when I pick Leonora up in a little while, I'm going to tell the day-care lady to keep her away from the TV from now on," Ellie added.

Leonora saw no television at home but went to the day-care place for four hours each morning without fail. If she didn't she got cranky, refusing to take her naps and howling inconsolably to communicate her craving for infant society.

Pleased with her decision not to let the baby become a TV addict, Ellie shoved the quinces back into the bags, then set the bags upright again.

"Have our tenants called yet?" She peeked into the cabinet under the sink to see if I had enough jelly jars, tops, and jar rings for about a dozen pints.

"Twice," I said, sighing while mentally counting the jars myself. Owing to Wade's habit of appropriating them for use in storing small gun-parts, we were probably a few short. "Once for an electrical problem, once for a leaky faucet," I added.

Victor pushed his chair back and got up, since if we weren't going to make the quince jam right that minute and he had already eaten the pie, he saw no reason to stick around.

"I thought I'd wait for the third call," I went on to Ellie when he had gone. The dogs returned from following him to the door. "It'll probably be coming any minute now and I thought I'd go out there after lunch and get all the chores done up at once."

Two months earlier Ellie and I had bought a small house on the waterfront in Quoddy Village, which was the nearest thing to a suburb that the tiny island city of Eastport had. We'd planned to fix the place up and rent it long-term or maybe even sell it.

But while we were still working on it, a set of temporary tenants had descended, referred by a local real estate agency. And an actual income from the beat-up little bungalow had been the height of good luck.

Or so we'd thought at the time. Income, it turned out, was only a small part of the overall landlady experience. "Better go soon," Ellie said with a glance out the window.

The day's early fog and mist had cleared to reveal a bright blue sky. "Storm tonight," she repeated.

Wade had said so, too, although I didn't believe it, nor did the weather report. So I paid no heed to Ellie's warning, sitting down instead with my own cup of coffee at the kitchen table.

Ellie had already poured some for herself. "You know, it's not that I'm sorry the place is rented," she began.

Me either. We'd picked it up for pennies, mostly because it hadn't had any real maintenance in decades. The foundation under my house was as solid as the Rock of Ages when compared to the slurry of shifted earth, rotted sills, and gritty powder that we'd discovered under the Quoddy Village property.

"And they seem like okay people, even if they are a little weird," Ellie went on.

"Weird," I agreed, but the term did not cover the unusual nature of our tenants. It's not every day you rent a house to a coven of witches, five of them if you counted the teenaged girl who I guessed must probably still have training wheels on her broomstick. And especially with Halloween coming so soon, news of their unorthodox religious views was causing enough local comment to raise the dead.

Or anyway I supposed you could call it a religion. They'd been here only a week and responding to their repair requests had kept me so busy, I hadn't had time to bone up on the subject.

"Deke Meekins from down at the boatyard stopped me on my walk this morning," Ellie went on. "He particularly wanted to know if they wear black pointy hats and sacrifice small animals at midnight."

"Oh, dear. Did you set him straight, I hope?"

The part about the animals I knew for sure wasn't occurring, since even before I found out about the witch portion of the program, I'd put my foot down: no pets.

"Yes," Ellie replied, "but I'm not sure he believed me."

Gregory Brand, leader of the coven and the one who signed the rental agreement and wrote the deposit check, had looked at me as if I were the one with the funny hat on when I warned him against noisy, bad-smelling, or otherwise objectionable occult nonsense. But he'd made no comment, merely assuring me that his group fully intended to be clean, quiet, and responsible.

"And yesterday at the IGA, Esther Deedy was complaining that her neighborhood has been invaded by black cats. Two or three dozen of them, and she was staring right at me when she said it," Ellie continued.

I happened to know that if Esther Deedy spotted a pair of grasshoppers in her backyard, she reported a plague of locusts.

"Ellie," I said helplessly, "their check cleared. We asked top dollar and they're paying. And other than repair calls, there hasn't been a peep out of them. No complaints from the neighbors about loud parties . . ."

Which if they'd had any you could be sure someone would be

calling the police to say it was a Black Mass. "And considering the shape it's in..."

Wade and my father had gone underneath the house and set up a dozen pump jacks to level it enough so the drains would run. Until then, the result of toilet-flushing had been unfortunate.

"...we're lucky to be renting it at all," I finished. "And anyway they're only going to be here another week. We can handle the gossip until then. And the repairs," I added resignedly.

Ellie brightened a bit. In the beginning she'd been the one who was most gung-ho about renting the place. But Ellie was born and had lived all her life in Eastport. She was more sensitive to local talk.

"I guess," she conceded. "Just because they call themselves witches doesn't mean they really are. Or that Greg Brand is, at any rate, because for one thing I don't think any real witches sell their powers, or whatever it is they have. Do you?"

According to Brand, the little group was paying him for a seminar he was giving. "No idea," I told Ellie. But it sounded right.

"And in a way they're doing us a favor, too, by finding all the things that need fixing," Ellie remarked.

"Hmm," I said, finishing my coffee. "Maybe."

Before they'd moved in we'd made certain that the house was both safe and sanitary, all nuts-and-bolts plumbing and wiring situations up to code. But the number of problems the tenants had discovered, at the rate of two or three a day for the past seven days, had begun to make me feel I was being nibbled to death by ducks.

Just then my father came upstairs, covered in concrete dust. He was a tall, wiry old fellow with a graying ponytail tied back in a leather thong, wearing coveralls, a flannel work shirt, and battered boots.

"Phew," he sighed, crossing to the sink for a drink of water. "I don't know what somebody thought he was doing, building that northeast corner of the foundation over by the cold room."

The cold room, back in the early 1800s when my old house had been built, was where they stored meat: sides of beef and slaughtered half-pigs, whole deer and turkeys, bacon and hams, hung from big iron hooks fastened into the massive beams of the cellar ceiling.

Great chunks of ice cut from lakes on the mainland a dozen miles distant had been packed into sawdust and brought here on barges and trundled into the cellar for refrigeration in summer; in the winter, the northeast corner of the house was plenty cold enough all by itself.

"That one whole area's built like a brick sh–" my father began.

But then he caught himself, washing his throat clean of concrete dust with a gulp of water. "It is," he amended judiciously as he went back downstairs to hack at it some more, "a very strong corner."

Before being cleared of all charges against him, my father had for years been a federal fugitive suspected of, among other things, murdering my mother. So hour upon hour of demolishing a stone wall with a pickaxe was his idea of a peaceful morning, as long as he didn't have to wear a set of leg irons while doing it.

Ellie looked out the kitchen window, where a couple of newly appeared clouds on the horizon made the otherwise blue sky seem even bluer. "Going to blow a gale," she remarked.

On second thought, even I decided the clouds looked ominous, long and white like the fingers on a skeletal hand. But their presence hardly marred the unusual perfection of the autumn day, warm and humid as if a last bit of August had been saved over for us until now, when we would really appreciate it.

"Ellie, why do you keep on insisting? It's like summer out there." I leaned down to pat the two dogs who had romped back in from the parlor when my father came upstairs, and were now searching for him with canine determination.

"No storm is coming and I don't see why you and Wade keep on saying there is," I said.

Monday butted her squarish head into the side of my leg. It was noon, which was when the gray-faced canine began anticipating an evening meal. Seeing that I was taken, Prill sniffed around for other sources of treats, fixing at last on Ellie.

"Okay," Ellie said, patting the big red dog's smooth flank and smiling at me. "Have it your way, Jacobia. The weather's terrific."

Green-eyed and even-tempered, Ellie was as fine-featured and delicate-appearing as an antique cameo, with small pale freckles like a dusting of gold flecks scattered across her nose.

She was also as tough as a steak carved from one of those old deer haunches in the cellar. "But," she finished as she got up to depart, "if you do go to the rental house, bring your umbrella."

With that she headed out to pick the baby up at the day-care place. Minutes later the phone rang and just as I'd expected it was our tenants again, calling for yet more help in the fix-it department.

Only this time the repair they wanted was a doozy.

• • •

Rain slashed the windshield as I squinted past the flapping wipers into the gathering darkness, driving out of town toward the Quoddy Village place about four hours later.

Ellie had been right; the weather was deteriorating into a squall. Someone's trash can, propelled by the wind, tumbled from a driveway and bounced wildly through the gloom, directly across the rain-slick road in front of me.

I hit the brakes, feeling the tires make that awful weave-and-a-bobble slither that means they are losing traction. Then the can rolled away into the darkness and the tires caught again, my heart pounding as the truck straightened.

"Haunted," I'd repeated disbelievingly into the phone when the tenants called. "You want me to come out there and make the house sound less . . ."

Yep, that was it: a low, mournful *woo* noise alternating with a high, overexcited *yow-wow!* It had started a little while ago and could I please do something about it, they'd wanted to know. Because it was driving them crazy.

Biting my tongue, I'd refrained from replying that in the week since they arrived I'd learned all about being driven crazy and as far as I was concerned, a *woo* noise was small potatoes.

Instead I said I'd be over shortly. But after hanging up the phone I'd taken a moment to stow the Bisley away in its lockbox in the cellar, then stepped out to inhale some sanity-restoring breaths of fresh air while gazing at my own house.

It was a massive 180-year-old white clapboard Federal with three full floors plus an attic, forty-eight old double-hung windows flanked by dark green wooden shutters, and a rotten front porch. In fact, that porch was so decrepit I feared that on Halloween night some trick-or-treater might crash through it under the added weight of even a single Snickers bar.

So over the past few days I'd been demolishing it board by board with a crowbar and sledgehammer, preparatory to building a new one. And after glancing again at the sky I decided that before I left I'd better put the tools indoors, just in case the weather did decide to throw me a curve.

But then the truck with the lumber for the new porch pulled up; I had forgotten it was coming. The lumber had to be stacked so it wouldn't warp and then covered with a tarp, and that meant a trip to the hardware store. Also the tarp needed to be weighted down with bricks, and I knew I had some, so I scavenged dutifully around the yard for... well, you get the idea.

Thus it wasn't until four in the afternoon that I'd left a brief note on the kitchen table, got Wade's pickup truck started and muscled it out of the driveway, and headed for the rental house.

And now I wished I hadn't. Wet leaves plastered themselves to the windshield like dark flattened hands and were swept aside; headlights glared smearily yellow through the rain, then vanished behind me.

As I reached the Long Cove Road turnoff, a tractor-trailer came barreling out of the rain, its massive tires spinning silvery gouts that blinded me for a long moment while the pickup shuddered in the bigger vehicle's backwash.

But I made it through the turn and a few grateful moments later pulled up in front of the rental property. The tenants' white van was in the driveway, so I backed the truck onto the lawn and dashed for the front steps.

From behind me as I knocked and then struggled as usual with the sticky door knob, one of many in the house that needed repair–*screwdriver, chisel, new can of 3-In-One oil,* I recited mentally–waves crashed wildly onto the shore of what was ordinarily a quiet cove just across the road.

Suddenly the door jerked inward, yanking me along with it.

"Goodness!" exclaimed Marge Cathcart. She backed away hastily as I stumbled inside.

It was the kind of remark Marge tended to make. At fifty or so, she was plump, plain, and motherly-appearing, with washed-out blue eyes, soft blurry features, and a habit of wearing a cotton housedress with a droopy cardigan and fuzzy blue slippers.

In reply I made the kind of remarks I tended to make, none of them having to do with goodness. Marge supposedly had some old family connections in Eastport, and this ordinarily would've made me more careful about how I spoke in front of her; after all, who knew who her cousins might turn out to be?

But at the moment I was soaking wet, worried about the drive home, and thoroughly annoyed, mostly at myself for coming out here at all in the middle of what was turning out to be a major weather event.

And as if all that weren't bad enough, while I was standing there scandalizing Marge with the number of naughty words I knew, a huge crash sounded somewhere nearby and the lights went out.

"Oh, dear," Marge said into the darkness.

Yeah, no kidding. Eastport has its own local generator for emergencies, but that crash had sounded irresistibly like a tree going over, probably taking down a power line along with it. Then while I stood there cursing and dripping, a pale greenish glow began brightening eerily in the living room, to the right of the entrance.

As the hairs on my neck rose it occurred to me that I was (a) alone,

(b) at the height of a raging storm, and (c) in a house occupied by a bunch of self-proclaimed witches, with no way to call for help because (d) by now the phones were almost certainly out, too.

Then more greenish lights blazed up, revealing themselves to be the small propane lanterns Ellie and I had left here in case of emergency.

Too bad they were all being operated by the other witches. On the other hand, at least I could see them as opposed to their flitting around me invisibly. . . .

Oh, get a grip, I scolded myself, brandishing my toolbox. "So what actually is the problem here?" I demanded.

And then I heard it.

"Ow-owwow-ow-*ooooohhh!*" came the sound.

Ye gods.

"Ow-w*oooooh*-wow-wow!" Holding his lamp at chest level so it lit his face from below, which I heartily recommend as a strategy for illuminating every single one of your nose hairs, a man stepped forward. It was Greg Brand, the leader of the group.

"Sorry to bring you out in such bad weather," he said.

"No problem," I replied curtly. Dressed all in black–shirt and tie, slacks, black leather belt and wing-tips–Greg was tall, fortyish, and dark-haired with deep-set eyes and sharp features. His thin mouth tightened, probably registering my annoyance, but I wasn't about to make nice with him–or anyone–at that moment.

"I'll just go find whatever's causing the noise and fix it," I added, unwilling to trust myself to say more.

Because the sound was ungodly, that was for sure, but it was also flat-out obvious what was making it: wind leaking in through some small crevice in a door or a window frame.

Behind Greg Brand the other tenants gathered around the glass-doored woodstove which none of them had managed to light even though there was kindling and a big basket of firewood ready to hand.

"How long do you think it'll take?" inquired Hetty Bonham in a snippy I-want-it-now tone that I felt was entirely uncalled for.

Like Greg Brand, Hetty was forty or so, dressed too young for her age in white pedal pushers and a tight, low-cut pink sweater that put her considerable cleavage on display. She brushed back her long blonde hair impatiently. "Because it's quite annoying, you know," she added.

"It'll take as long as it takes," I replied, counting to ten in my head. Along with rings, bracelets, and huge hoop earrings, Hetty wore an eye-catching silver pentacle pendant on a silver chain positioned on her chest like a flashing road sign: *This way to my two best features!*

"Anyone want to come and help me?" I asked. I didn't expect an answer. The tenants had already proven they weren't big on do-it-yourself projects.

But to my surprise, the woman standing next to Hetty Bonham spoke up. "I will," Jenna Durrell said agreeably.

A slender brunette in her mid-thirties, she wore slim blue jeans and a crimson turtleneck with a pale blue sweatshirt. "It's coming from somewhere in the back of the house," she added.

According to the real estate agent who had referred this group to Ellie and me, Jenna was an ex-cop. But as she stepped forward I noticed the collection of items spread out on the coffee table behind her. The array included a deck of Tarot cards, incense cones, and what appeared to be a real, no-kidding crystal ball mounted on a black base.

You'd think somebody accustomed to dealing with physical evidence would make the connection between the blowing wind and an eerie howling sound. On the other hand, the coffee-table items reminded me again that Jenna was here as a member of a witches' group. Maybe logic wasn't her strong point.

I was about to turn away when I noticed Marge Cathcart's daughter Wanda peeping shyly from behind the others. She looked to be about fifteen, wearing baggy khaki cargo pants and a gray sweatshirt with a pocket on the right sleeve. Her long dark hair was pulled messily back with green plastic barrettes, and she stared at me with a frightened expression in her eyes.

"Wanda doesn't speak," Marge cautioned before I could try to say anything to the girl. "Not at all."

I'd known this; the real estate agent had told me. And to me it was just another strange fact about a strange group. But then I spotted something moving inside the gently curved fingers of Wanda's hand. Something alive, small and furry, like . . . a mouse?

No. It was a bat. A small, brown, wickedly bright-eyed little bat with its wings folded up tight, so it resembled at first an ordinary household rodent.

"Um, Wanda?"

Bats carried rabies. "Honey, aren't you worried that bat's going to get startled or something, and bite you?"

Wanda's face lit up. *Silly woman,* her look said, but not in an unpleasant way. *It won't hurt me.* Tenderly she tucked the tiny creature into the pocket on her sleeve, from which refuge its eyes went on staring unblinkingly, shiny black and expressionless.

I broke from its gaze at last, unsure why the girl and her unusual pet had captured me so thoroughly. "Come on, Jenna. I can't fix electrical things until the power goes back on, and the pump's on the power, so I guess that means I can't do much with the leaky faucet either."

Ellie and I had left flashlights here, and once Jenna had produced them we went together toward the back of the house, where the howling seemed loudest.

"But I'll get rid of the noise, if I can," I said. Probably the broken window or whatever it was just needed a rag stuffed in it to stop the sound.

"Ow-wow-wow!" Howling when the wind blew and fading when it subsided, the noise seemed to come from everywhere and nowhere. But at last we followed the flashlight beams out to the small attached utility shed, where we hit pay dirt. The volume jumped as soon as I opened the door.

Jenna waved her flash around. Its beam reflected off the windows and picked out the shapes of a lot of useless, unrelated junk. The area had become a catchall for the things Ellie and I had found too heavy to remove by ourselves, or that we couldn't find other places for: an old wringer-style washing machine; big rusty pieces of weight-lifting equipment; an ancient, massive automobile engine nailed into a wooden crate.

The air was sharp with the smell of old potting soil spilled on the brick floor, mingled with the faint sweet scent of motor oil. In a corner lay a heap of ice-fishing equipment including an ice strainer and an auger, which was the tool you used to drill down through the ice to where the fish were.

If you liked going ice fishing at all; I'd been meaning to take that bit of gear home for Wade, who actually did. But now as the autumn storm hurled itself darkly against the windows, I figured I had time; with luck, it wouldn't be ice-fishing season for another few weeks.

"There," uttered Jenna, aiming her flashlight at the base of the wall where a puddle reflected the beam.

Drat, it meant water was coming in somewhere above. But that was odd. Ellie and I had worked in the house through a couple of August storms, removing what old stuff we could. And although the shed was ramshackle we hadn't discovered any sizable leaks then.

Maybe one of the tenants had shifted some of the junk out here, I thought as I stepped carefully between the washer and the auto engine. The window frames were warped, and if you bumped one of them its sash might move enough to...

I reached down, touching the wet spot, then yanked my hand back with a visceral little shudder. *Uh-oh.*

"What?" Jenna asked. "You okay?"

"I'm fine. Go back with the others, all right?"

But something in my tone alerted her; at once she was right beside me.

"What is it? You don't sound so good... Oh."

Because the puddle wasn't water. It was blood, its surface sticky and darkly gelatinous.

Ow-ooh! the wind howled unhappily.

Also there was a pair of leather boots lying near the puddle, and unless I was mistaken the boots were being worn by someone.

A dead someone.

Chapter 3

My **name is Jacobia Tiptree and when I first came to** Maine I thought "old paint" was a nickname for somebody's favorite horse. But then I bought a massive old rambling fixer-upper of a house with a lot of old rooms, a lot of old woodwork, and a lot of old windows, each equipped with a pair of emphatically antique wooden shutters.

In other words, a *lot* of old paint. Which was why soon after I moved into the house I came to realize that I might have preferred horses. At least when you clean up after animals, you don't risk poisoning yourself to death.

Not that paint-stripper fumes are the only dangerous part of old-dwelling repair. Death by falling (from a ladder, off a roof, or most annoyingly through a collapsing floor) ranks high on the hazard list, too, right up there with electrocution (bad wiring), blunt trauma (those floors again), and the sort of silly mishap in which you mistake your own arm for a two-by-four, then shorten it swiftly and, alas, irrevocably with a power saw.

But your biggest risk of all will be in getting out of bed in the morning, since that's when you'll choose between (a) facing yet another endless day of home repair, or (b) climbing the damned ladder and hanging yourself from one of the rafters just to get it over with.

That last option was one I'd already rejected when I bought my old house, however. If I'd wanted to die I could have stayed in Manhattan, where the way things were going I had six months, tops, before I took a header off the roof of my building.

Because look: I had a crazy ex-husband who hated me because I'd gotten the divorce, a drug-abusing son who hated me because it took me so long to go after the divorce, and a long roster of clients who'd made pretty much all the money in the world by the simple method of following my financial advice.

For which they paid fifteen percent. And fifteen percent of all the money in the world is a lot, but there was nothing that I wanted to buy with it. Sure, I had clothes, jewelry, furniture, and an address so swanky that you practically needed to have your retinas scanned to get past the guards in the lobby.

But I didn't care. All I wanted was to go into Sam's room each morning–I'd given up trying to stay awake until the wee hours when he usually came home, and anyway if I was still up he would only swear at me or threaten me–and not find him dead.

Victor, meanwhile, contributed the helpful information that our son's problems were all my fault, a mantra he recited at me by phone or e-mail when he wasn't busy boffing the latest in a line of pretty nurses, and sometimes I suspected even when he was.

So one way and another that rooftop had begun looking fairly attractive. But then I visited Eastport, a tiny village on the downeast Maine coast, and noticed that many of its houses were in even worse shape than I was, a comparison I found heartening.

One in particular caught my eye: vast, paint-peeling, and neglected, with shimmeringly empty rooms, three tall red chimneys whose bricks were in the process of toppling onto the lawn, roof leaks galore, and plenty of windows, several of which still even had intact panes of glass in them.

Two weeks later I'd sold my apartment; by that time I already owned an almost-two-hundred-year-old house in Eastport plus a cheap pair of pliers, a screwdriver, and a claw hammer with which I immediately removed my left thumbnail while trying to hang a picture.

I remember the moment clearly. Sam lay on the floor, rigid with the misery of not having been able to find any drugs in this new town. At his insistence I was ignoring him while also keeping the phone number of the local ambulance service close to hand, since if he went into clinical withdrawal I might have to rush him to the hospital.

"I hate you," he said as I fumbled with a hammer, a nail, and a pencil with which I was trying to make an X-marks-the-spot. The task was made particularly difficult by the fact that every time I touched the old plaster wall, more of it crumbled and fell to the hardwood floor.

"You agreed to try Eastport," I reminded him.

"Uhh," he replied.

I held the nail to the X mark and tapped it tentatively with the hammer. The hammer knocked the nail sideways, bounced off the plaster, and clattered to the floor, barking me on the shin as it went by.

"Ouch!" Next the hammer landed hard on my sneakered foot while the nail first nicked my finger, then fell *inside* the wall through the hole the hammer had opened.

Whereupon as blood welled redly up from my finger I decided to tiptoe from the room, believing that if I went into hysterics in front of Sam it might be too much for him.

Although by then I was feeling a little ragged myself. After our aforementioned swanky digs in Manhattan, equipped with a staff of concierges who would pick up your dry cleaning and overpriced Thai take-out right along with your theater tickets, this wasn't what either one of us was used to:

Primitive bathing arrangements, windows that rattled like castanets in the slightest breeze, and a silence at night as endless-seeming as the dark sky stretching over our heads, full of unfamiliar stars.

When I got back from the kitchen with a bandage for my finger, Sam had turned onto his stomach again with his face pushed into the crook of his arm so I couldn't see it.

"Hey," I said, but he didn't answer.

I'd have nudged him with my foot but I felt too sorry for him. He was only here with me because I'd threatened to send him to a teenaged boot camp if he didn't agree to come–

"Threaten" was a nice way of describing the coercion I had applied, complete with four-color brochures depicting hard labor, spartan meals, dormitory living, and a Cyclone fence topped with razor wire and electronic monitors.

–and because his father wouldn't take him, another thing I felt bad about. But there wasn't anything useful I could think of to do for him, so after a moment I returned to the hammer, the nail, and the disintegrating plaster.

Outside it was dusk, lights coming on in the big old houses around us and mist creeping softly uphill from the bay, smelling of sea salt. A car went by on the street. A dog barked, and a foghorn sounded.

A door slammed, cutting off the sound of a radio playing the country hits. Then silence, as night fell and people went inside; people who laughed and gossiped together in the grocery store and at the gas station, places where I still drew studied politeness to my face and curious stares behind my back.

Reaching up to reposition the new nail on the X mark, I had never felt so alone in my life.

But one thing at a time, I instructed myself: nail, X mark, hammer. The problem, I realized as Sam tossed and turned on the bare wooden floor behind me, was that I had not hit the nail hard enough.

Not by a long shot. So *this* time I steadied the nail with my left hand, then reared back with the hammer and gave that nail a no-holds-barred smack, missing the nail entirely and bringing the hammer head down full force onto my left thumbnail.

What I said then really doesn't bear repeating.

Sam turned over. "Mom?"

I dropped the hammer, careless of whether or not it hit my foot. The pain in my thumb was blinding, exploding into my hand and paralyzing my whole left arm.

Tears sprang to my eyes but I bit them back; the pain would subside.

It would, damn it. It would.

"Mom, are you okay?" Sam sounded frightened. He was used to me cursing, a bad habit I'd acquired in the financial district in Manhattan.

But not like this. He sat up.

"I'm okay," I managed to whisper through gritted teeth.

The hammer had indeed slammed down onto my foot again, then bounced off and hit the other one, but that was nothing compared to the booming anguish still coursing up from my thumbnail, which was already turning purple.

Then, as the pain faded gradually from excruciating to only agonizing, I caught my breath. It was going to be all right; I'd made the right decision. We weren't really alone among strangers, miles from anywhere and without anyone to help us.

It just felt that way. Sniffing, I managed a smile for Sam's sake. "See?" I held out my thumb. "It's only..."

And then it happened: that foghorn again. Low, mournful, and even more sorrowful at night and from a distance, as if all the peril and uncertainty of the ocean were somehow distilled in it.

And the loneliness; oh, that most of all. I felt my lower lip quivering, warm salty tears brimming and running down my face uncontrollably.

"Oh, Sam," I said, sitting down on the floor beside him. I just sat there and bawled my head off. After a moment Sam leaned over and wrapped his arms around me, sobbing too, neither one of us really knowing exactly what we were crying about.

Pretty soon we'd cried so hard, we had to get up and go back out to the kitchen and find some tissues, we were both so snotty and messy. And it was while we were standing there sniffling and blowing our noses that a huge piece of the kitchen ceiling let go without warning, crashing down onto the kitchen table and missing Sam by an inch.

After a moment of shocked silence and seeing that he was apparently not meant to die, or at any rate not that evening, Sam began laughing. And once he got started I did, too, hysterically, weeping with hilarity, staggering with mirth.

"Nearly... *killed* me!" Sam guffawed, small grayish-white bits of plaster littering his hair and shoulders.

"Only... not *quite!*" I agreed, gasping and wiping my eyes.

Later, when we had both calmed down again: "Listen, what do you say we go out for an ice cream?" I asked.

We hadn't had any dinner. "Yeah, okay," Sam said, shrugging. "Why not? I mean, seeing as we're both not," he exaggerated the final word theatrically, "*dead*."

Now, I won't pretend that the events of that evening cured matters between Sam and me, or anyway they didn't completely. But we did go out, and it was good ice cream, too, made even better by the knowledge that we were–by some grace neither one of us yet wanted to explore too carefully–still walking around able to eat it.

And that's how I've approached life in Eastport ever since, even while enmeshed in situations much less pleasant than confronting a kitchen ceiling that's decided to find out whether or not it can commit murder.

Such as for instance coming upon the body of someone who's *really* been murdered.

Recently.

• • •

"Do you know him?"

I jumped about a foot. In my shock over finding the dead guy in the shed at the tenants' place, I'd forgotten Jenna Durrell was even there.

"No. You?" I moved my flashlight a little so she could see him better.

She shook her head, her dark hair moving softly against the strong lines of her face. "How'd he get in here?"

"No idea," I said. "But when he fell he must've jostled one of those old windows out of its frame."

I moved the flashlight again. "See that gap? It's where the wind is coming in, and..."

Stepping past me, Jenna seized the corpse by its shoulders, shifting it away from the wall. As she did so she brushed against the knocked-askew window, which fell back into place with a thud.

The howling stopped. "Oh," I said doubtfully. "Jenna, are you really sure you should...?"

Move the body, I'd been about to say. But the absence of the awful noise was such a relief, I didn't bother finishing.

"I guess we'd better call the police," I said instead.

Jenna laughed without humor. "Good luck. Phone's out. Guess the storm must have knocked a line down."

As I'd feared. "Cell phone?" I suggested.

"Already tried. When the weather started getting wild I was going to call, tell you not to come. But all I'm getting is a 'no signal' icon."

Have I mentioned that Eastport is three hours from Bangor and light-years, or so it often seems, from everywhere else? Cell-phone coverage around here could be spotty at the best of times.

"Maybe it'll clear up later," I said, but not with a lot of hope. Then I looked down at the body again. The blood from his head wound was like a mask over his lumpy features, disgruntled even in death, and the clothes could've been anyone's: old jeans, gray long-sleeved undershirt, and over that a flannel shirt so faded it was impossible to tell what color it had been.

But there was something about those lips, so thick and blubbery looking... then I had it. "I do know this guy," I said.

"Yeah, great," Jenna said carelessly. "I'm going back in the house."

"But... hey, wait. What're we going to do now?" I thought that as an ex-cop she might at least have a clue about a standard operating procedure for a corpse plus no phone.

And she did, but it wasn't one I liked. "Watch our backs, for one thing," she replied. "Unless you'd like to try driving in this. I wouldn't."

She waved at the windows, still deluged by rain. Outside them raged a storm so nasty that all the animals on the island were probably lining up two by two, waiting for the ark.

"What do you mean?" I asked her. "Why should we have to be worried?"

But she didn't answer, instead returning to inspect the body again. "Who is he, anyway?"

"Eugene Dibble. Kind of a jerk," I told her, though there was more to him than that. Among other things, he'd been a bully and a self-styled preacher of fire and brimstone.

These latter materials always being aimed at others, of course. But there was no sense speaking ill of the dead in front of Jenna, who hadn't even known him. "Sad story," I added.

No real church would go near him but he had a small, ragged following of hard-luck cases. The point of his sermons–often delivered on street corners with firepower provided by beer–usually being that all their troubles were the fault of someone else.

"Poor dope," I said, remembering how angry Eugene's hate-spewing mouth had made me. But it was his hands that interested me now, and the area around them.

Because speaking of things being somebody else's fault... "Help me a minute, here, will you?" I bent over the body again.

My first thought had been that he'd come in here thinking the house was unoccupied, and shot himself. From what I'd heard he'd had plenty of reasons: chronic pain from an old work injury, no money, and a wife who treated him like something she'd like to have scraped off her shoe, for starters.

But if he'd done that, there should have been a gun. And as Jenna had seen–and already understood, I now realized–there wasn't one.

"It's not going to be here," she said as we lifted Eugene's shoulders.

My earlier qualms about disturbing a fresh crime scene had vanished; hey, we'd already moved him once. And at the moment I was a lot less worried about the cops being mad at me than I was about how Eugene's body had gotten into the shed in the first place.

Specifically I wanted to be reassured that Eugene really had put it there himself. Versus for instance someone else having done it, as Jenna had implied; someone who might still be around.

After all, if Eugene had found his way in here, anyone could do the same...

"People who shoot themselves don't fall on the weapon very often. For one thing they usually sit down first," Jenna remarked as we hauled on him.

Criminy, he was heavy. But we got him rolled over and as she predicted no gun was underneath him. I aimed the flash all around just to be sure.

"Nope. No sign of it."

So: someone else. I said the next thing that came into my head. "Where was everyone before I got here? Earlier today, I mean."

She thought about it. "Well, we were all here first thing in the morning, of course. The others were going out before lunch, I think. But I left before they did, for a bike ride when it first started to look as if the sun might come out."

She paused thoughtfully. "Then I came back here, had my own lunch, and took the boat out. I was on the water, saw the clouds come up again, and got in just as things were getting rough."

My boat, she meant. When Ellie and I bought the house, Sam bought a wooden dory last year's boat school students had built and brought it out here for me as a surprise. I kept it across the road, pulled up on the beach in the cove.

"You tied it up after you used it?" If not, by now the dory would be halfway to Greenland.

"Oh, sure. Everyone else was back when I got in. Hetty was complaining about the noise," she added wryly. "I think Marge had already called you, in fact."

It sounded right, timing-wise. "Anybody come out here? Of the other tenants, that is, after you got in from the water and before I arrived?"

She shook her head. "Don't think so. I didn't, I know that much. But I wasn't really paying attention to what everyone was doing."

Sure, why should she? I had the sense Jenna didn't find the other tenants in the house particularly congenial, and I wondered again why she'd come here with them.

But now wasn't the time to get into it. Eugene's eyes gazed sightlessly up at the shed's low ceiling, rain still beating hollowly on it.

"Come on," I told Jenna. "We'd better tell the others what we've found."

"I guess." Then, "Listen–you don't think one of us did it, do you? Because when I said watch our backs, I didn't mean..."

"I can't imagine why any of you would," I replied as we went back into the darkened house.

"Plenty of locals probably wouldn't have minded putting his lights out," I added, shining the flash ahead so we could find our way through the kitchen. "Overall, he was what my son calls a crude dude. But I doubt anyone in your group ever met him."

And at that stage I hardly cared if anyone had. I just wanted two things, the first being to get back home as soon as possible.

In the living room the others had finally gotten a fire going in the stove and were gathered around it as if attempting to soak up its feeble cheer.

"You tell them," I said to Jenna. "I'm going out to try the phone in the truck, just in case."

Because the other thing I wanted was the cops notified, and as swiftly and efficiently as possible, too, since it seemed now that an evil deed might have been committed and not just a sad or foolish one.

Pushing my way out the front door I met a battering ram of rain and wind-driven debris, sticks and leaves whipping into my face and getting tangled in my clothing and hair.

Gasping, I hauled the pickup's door open, barely catching it before it could fly back in the wind and spring the hinges, then scrambled up onto the seat. I sat there catching my breath while turning the headlights on.

As I'd feared, the dark hulking shape of a fallen tree lay a few hundred feet away, downed power lines gleaming in the truck's high beams. But the tree didn't seem to be blocking the road.

Hallelujah, I thought, shutting the lights off; no sense wasting the battery. Sudden darkness closed in, broken by distant gleams from the eighteen-wheelers moving over the causeway on the far side of the cove, headed for the freighter in port.

Next I tried the phone wired into the dash. *No signal,* the blinking icon reported. But I'd expected that, too, and I *could* just call the police from home; Jenna's doubts notwithstanding, I'd been out in far worse, and the phones might be working there. Driving back would be a hellish chore, I thought resignedly, but not an impossible one.

But then over on the causeway a row of orange running lights came around ninety degrees from behind one of the moving truck cabs, dimly visible in the others' headlamps. From where I sat it appeared that the truck's lights were swerving in slow motion.

To the driver, though, what happened next must've felt nearly instantaneous. The cab itself moved oddly, its headlights shining upward, creating bright nearly-vertical bars in the night sky....

The cab lights vanished. I felt my fingernails biting into my palms as I imagined the trailer slammed by a wind gust on the rain-slick road, pulling the cab out of control until it and the trailer toppled over together.

Blocking the one road to town . . . oh, fiddlesticks, I thought, still hoping against hope.

But already more headlights were lining up on the causeway, nothing moving in either direction. So even if the cell phone had been working it was useless to me now.

No one could get here past the crippled rig. Worse, until it was cleared, I couldn't get home. Instead, I was stuck with a dead guy, five witches, and–

I checked around the dark interior of the truck. A hunting jacket of Wade's, a pair of his old boots, two sticks of Black Jack chewing gum, and a paperback price guide to American rifles, its pages dog-eared to mark the most important and/or valuable of the weapons.

But–drat, no magic wand.

• • •

Inside, the tenants had found the utility candles Ellie and I had left in one of the kitchen drawers, and lit them in the kitchen and living room. All the flickering flames made the place seem ready for an impromptu funeral, which considering the body out in the shed I supposed was appropriate.

But Greg Brand's reaction to my return from the great outdoors wasn't. "What's the idea?" he demanded. "What's going on, and what if anything are you doing to take care of this situation?"

It was the "if anything" part that got me. I was soaked to the skin, not to mention a little shaky from discovering the late Eugene Dibble, and Brand's attitude wasn't improving my state of mind.

"Mr. Brand, I have no idea what 'this situation' even is," I retorted. "All I know is, there's a dead guy in the house. Somebody shot him and I gather that you all are the only other ones who've been in the place recently."

Their eyes widened at the implication; only Wanda seemed unmoved, silently tending the fire with her back turned.

"Oh, now wait just a damned minute," Brand replied. "None of us is even from around here, we wouldn't have any possible motive to–"

"That shed door doesn't lock right," Hetty Bonham pointed out with a toss of her blonde mane. "You should've repaired it before you rented this place. Anyone could have gotten in," she added accusingly.

True; the door from the shed to the outside was so crooked in its frame that it was a struggle to get it to latch, though once you did, you couldn't get it to open again. Besides, as I'd told Jenna, Eugene Dibble was such a scuzz that he might as well have lived on another planet from any of these people.

And finally, with the exception of Jenna herself–although considering the company she kept I was having my doubts about her, too–my tenants had pretty well proven they lacked the ability to change a lightbulb, much less kill a guy.

"Okay," I conceded grudgingly. "A lot of things could have happened. And you're right, it probably has nothing to do with any of you, so there's no need to get upset."

I pulled my wet jacket off. "The police will be able to get it all figured out. But," I added cautioningly, "not tonight."

I explained about the truck on the causeway. "So we'll just have to wait until the authorities can clear the road," I finished.

"You mean," Hetty asked, "the body has to stay *here*? With *us*?" She touched her long scarlet-tipped fingers to her crimson lips in a theatrical gesture.

Greg narrowed his eyes at her. "He's not going to get up and pester anyone, Hetty. Your virtue is safe."

Her answering tone was bitter. "Yeah, Greg, with you around, everyone's is."

Jenna rolled her eyes; from her expression I gathered this kind of bickering went on between Hetty and Greg pretty much nonstop.

Then she went to kneel by Wanda, putting a gentle hand on the girl's shoulder. But Wanda shrank from the gesture.

"Oops, sorry," Jenna said. "I forgot you don't like being touched by people."

Great, a neurotic teenager; just what we needed to give this witch's brew of an evening another stir. Meanwhile Hetty Bonham and Greg Brand were already healing their quarrel at the drinks cabinet.

Watching them, it struck me suddenly that their interaction wasn't at all what I'd have expected from a teacher and a newly recruited student. Their arguing, for one thing; it sounded too personal. Then there was the way she seemed to know without asking what to put in his glass, and the easy gesture she used to hand it to him. . . .

"Not that I expect it will be, but *is* the name Eugene Dibble familiar to anyone here?" I addressed the group.

Because if Hetty and Greg did know each other, maybe I had other things wrong about them, too. Maybe one of them *had* known Eugene.

Stranger things had happened. Like for instance his corpse out in that shed.

"Not to me," Jenna said; Marge nodded agreement, and though Wanda said nothing her blank face was answer enough.

But at my question Brand's highball glass tilted abruptly, spilling some of its contents.

"Jesus, Greg," Hetty protested, brushing angrily at herself. "You clumsy–"

"Shut up, Hetty," he replied, crouching to retrieve fallen ice cubes.

Only not so fast that I didn't get a chance to see the color draining out of his complexion. Even by candlelight the change was striking, and when he stood again the ice chattered in his glass.

Oho, I thought as he gulped down the contents; the plot thickens. Because not much was clear about this horrible night, but one thing was. Greg Brand had heard Dibble's name before.

• • •

"Will your family at home be awfully worried about you?" Marge Cathcart asked kindly a couple of hours later.

The power was still out but she had put together a dinner of packaged things and canned goods heated on top of the woodstove, and Jenna had lent me some dry clothes.

"I hope not," I told her. "I left a note and my husband will know about the jackknifed truck. He'll figure out where I am pretty quickly, I think."

In fact Wade was probably out there now helping to clear the mess. But it could take hours for a big enough wrecker to arrive and make the road passable.

"All right, then," Marge said. "You try to sleep." Carrying a flashlight, she went away, closing the door and leaving me in the makeshift bed she and Jenna had helped me make on the floor of the upstairs spare room.

Outside, the wind went on howling. Rain thrummed on the roof slanting a few feet from my head. A wave of homesickness swept over me as the rest of the house grew silent, the others gone to bed, too.

But even as tired as I was, no way would I be able to sleep. Instead I lay there in the dark, eyes open and ears alert for the slightest sound.

Tap, tap. I sat up suddenly. The sound came from the window.

Rain dripping from the eaves, probably. I lay down again. Just a few more hours, I told myself. By morning the storm would surely pass and the wreckage of the truck would be hauled away.

Tap, tap. I pulled the blankets over my head, then checked my watch once more. In the dark, the radium-green numbers said it was 12:31 A.M.

Scuff-scuff.

I popped out of the blankets. Something crept quietly just outside the door to the spare room. But before I could react...

Tap! Another sound came at the window. A *purposeful* sound. But I was upstairs and so was that window, and I happened to know there were no ladders at the Quoddy Village house. So *how*...?

Grimly I scrambled across the room and shoved the window open, stuck my head out, and squinted into the streaming night.

"Wade!" His rain-slick face grinned up from the darkness at me. "What're you doing here? And how'd you get here?"

Not that I cared. I'd have ridden a flying carpet home by then if that's what it took.

"Come on down," he whispered back. "No sense waking the rest of them." He dropped the handful of small stones he'd been tossing one by one at the window.

"Got the ATV, you can ride behind me. Come on, Jake."

Moments later I'd flown down the stairs and out the door, barely pausing long enough to pull my shoes on, and was seated on Wade's oversize-wheeled all-terrain vehicle, affectionately known around our house as The Beast.

"Hey," he said, "don't I get a hello kiss?"

Oh, did he ever. "How'd you know I was up there?"

He shrugged. "Process of elimination. I knew which rooms the tenants had, didn't think you'd be bunking in with any of them."

Just the thought made me grimace. "That's for sure. But didn't they need you for . . . ?"

"The wreck?" He shrugged. "Yeah, probably they did. But I did my share, and after a while I had a feeling maybe you needed me worse."

And that in a nutshell was Wade. "Thank you," I said.

Wade smiled back at me, a tall, broad-shouldered, craggy-faced knight in rain-soaked armor, riding a squat, four-wheeled steed that belonged in a heavy-artillery battle.

Then he fired up The Beast with a roar loud enough to wake everyone in the Quoddy Village house, including possibly Eugene Dibble.

"Hang on," he yelled, his voice snatched away by the wind as we turned into it.

The trip home was a wet, noisy, bruising assault on every muscle and bone in my body, The Beast howling as it powered through flooded gullies, swerved around huge uprooted trees, and muscled its way up steep embankments, only its small yellow headlamps glaring ahead of us until we'd bypassed the causeway.

So it wasn't until the lights of town spread welcomingly before us that I thought again of the sound I'd heard coming from just outside the spare room, back at the tenants' house.

The deliberate sound, soft but unmistakable, of footsteps oh-so-stealthily approaching my closed but unlocked door.

Chapter 4

Ellie and I had a sort of game we played back and forth sometimes, called 1823. In it we took turns coming up with facts related to the year in which my old house was built.

For example, "In 1823," Ellie said early the next morning after the fiasco out at the rental property, "Edgar Allan Poe was fourteen years old."

We were on my front lawn contemplating the porch wreckage; I'd already brought her up-to-date on all that had gone on at the tenants' place.

"Nice," I said of her game contribution. We'd used up the easy ones: the Monroe Doctrine, the invention of Santa Claus, and the patenting of roller skates, for instance.

So we'd gotten a little loose on the rules for what made an acceptable entry; later I would learn that 1823 was the death-year of Edward Jenner, developer of the smallpox vaccine.

But I didn't know it yet. So when Ellie made a challenging little "your turn" gesture at me, I was about to offer the start of construction on the British Museum in London.

Just then, though, Eastport police chief Bob Arnold's squad car pulled up to the curb across the street.

I'd talked to him already, too, and I wasn't particularly eager to do it again; the whole episode was like a nightmare I just wanted to shake free of as soon as possible.

But now here he was. "Morning, ladies," he said, getting out of the car.

A stout, round-faced fellow with a ruddy complexion, pale thinning hair, and small rosebud lips that didn't look as if they belonged on a police officer, Bob wore a gray cop-uniform shirt, blue serge slacks, and black utility shoes.

His belt was loaded with many items of professional policing gear: sidearm, baton, radio, pair of handcuffs, and so on. "Got yourself quite a project," he added to me with a glance at the front steps.

Which was an understatement. Then he said what he'd come to say and I just stood there wondering if I'd heard him right.

"Oh, you've got to be kidding," Ellie said finally, but Bob just shook his head.

The storm had blown through with the speed of a freight train, leaving behind a washed-clean morning sky bright with sunshine and crisp with the threat of early snow.

"You're saying Wanda Cathcart is *missing*?" Ellie demanded.

"Ayuh," Bob allowed unhappily. " 'Fraid so."

The trees in the yard were stripped, their branches turned skeletal overnight and the lawn beneath them an autumn patchwork of orange and red. For a moment I thought about raking up a pile of the leaves, then just burrowing under it and staying there.

Instead I dragged my attention unwillingly back to Bob, who pulled a toothpick from his shirt pocket, stuck it in his mouth, and spoke around it.

"Girl's mother called in a panic about an hour ago, said the kid's gone," he said.

I put down my sledgehammer. Around me lay more wreckage of the old porch, broken planks and rusty remnants of the cast-iron railings. A few yards distant, out of the way of possible flying debris, Ellie's baby daughter Leonora slept in her stroller.

"Wanda wouldn't just happen to be around here by any chance, would she?" Bob asked, chewing on the toothpick.

"Huh?" I replied intelligently.

With the coming of day the stealthy sounds of the night before had simplified in memory, the mystery draining out of them until they were no more than a bit of loose wallpaper rustling in the drafty hall.

"Around *here*?" I repeated, still not getting it, and Ellie looked puzzledly at him, too.

Down the street a big orange town truck moved slowly along in front of the other old houses, its grinder roaring as the men alongside it shoved fallen tree limbs and other storm debris into its hopper. From its rear spewed a thick gout of yellowish wood chips, which the workers shoveled into enormous piles for later collection.

"So I guess she's *not* here, then?" Bob yelled over the sound of the truck.

"No," I shouted, my voice too loud as the racket faded all at once. "Why would you even think that?" I added in more normal tones.

"Her mom said she must've gone sometime during the night," he replied. "And since you also went missing from those very same premises, at about the same time..."

"Oh, for Pete's sake," I said when I finally understood, or believed I did. "Marge thinks I *took* Wanda?"

I'd called Bob when I got home and found the phones *were* working here. So he knew all about Wade coming to get me.

"I can see why Marge Cathcart might jump to conclusions if she's worried," I added, "but..."

Bob shook his head. "No, she doesn't think you took the girl. I was just hoping for a nice, simple coincidence, that's all. Like maybe Wanda knows where you live and showed up here."

But his face said there was more to it than that. Sighing, he gazed down Key Street toward the old redbrick Peavy Library building on the corner, and Passamaquoddy Bay beyond.

In 1823 Eastport's harbor was so busy, people said you could walk across the bay on the decks of ships waiting to come in. Now a single scallop-dragger motored on it toward the Canadian shore.

Bob turned to me again. "Crews cleared the jackknifed truck about two this morning, I met the state cops in Quoddy Village 'bout an hour later."

He went on, chewing the toothpick. "They got photographs, asked the tenants some questions, transported Dibble's body out of there, and took a walk through the house," he finished.

"Was Wanda there then?" Ellie asked reasonably.

Bob scratched his head. "It isn't real clear. I guess this kid's a little, um . . . unusual?" he asked.

"Yes," I told him, and went on to describe shy, speechless Wanda.

"Yeah, that makes sense," he said when I'd finished. "She wasn't in the house but Marge told the state police she probably got scared, decided to hide when she saw all the flashing lights show up in the middle of the night. Wind had gone down a lot by that time and the rain had quit," he added.

I already knew when the storm had passed. "So?" I demanded, beginning to be impatient. "Then what?"

I was sorry about Wanda but it was none of my business and anyway, I wanted to get the porch torn down and the wreckage cleared while the sun was still shining.

"So the staties figured they'd talk to Wanda when she showed up," Bob went on, "which Marge kept insisting she would do sooner or later. That's when they took their walk-through."

Bob removed the toothpick and tucked it back into his shirt pocket. "That," he added, "is when they found a paper bag full of pills. Oxycontins, big stash in a bag in the utility shed."

Oh, brother. Oxycontins, or "oxies" as they were called by illicit users, were the latest and most horrendously addictive drug of choice in two areas of the United States: rural poverty-stricken Appalachia, and here.

"They're sure?" I asked, and he nodded.

"Pharmaceutical stuff," he confirmed. "But you didn't see anything like that?"

I shook my head. "No, but it was dark, and..."

And anyway, why would I? I'd had the little matter of a dead guy distracting me.

Leonora had slept through the din of the town truck but now she woke and began bouncing energetically in her stroller, her small arms and legs waving as if being pulled up and down on strings.

"I put a word in for you two, by the way," Bob added, "so no DEA guy'll start thinking maybe one of you hid 'em there."

"Thanks," I said sincerely. Paunchy and faintly comical-appearing draped in all that cop paraphernalia, Bob didn't resemble a fellow who could vouch for you with anyone much higher than dogcatcher.

But over the years, he'd been quietly involved in some law enforcement matters whose reach extended far beyond Eastport, Maine. So his character reference was golden; right away I felt a little better about the situation.

"I'll bet the body and the pills are connected," Ellie said, crossing the lawn to retrieve one of Leonora's kicked-off pink booties.

That was a reasonable idea, too; Eugene Dibble was just the kind of loser to whom a stash of oxies would look like a winning hand.

"I still don't get what that's got to do with Wanda Cathcart being missing, though," she went on, replacing the bootie.

The baby grinned, showing nubbins of new front teeth, then let out a squall they must've heard across the bay. Ellie picked her up and began walking around with her, as Bob went on to me.

"Maybe nothing," he said, pushing some wet leaves around with the toe of his own boot. "Trouble is that when the cops left, Wanda didn't come back. Marge is pretty scared, which is why she decided to confide in me at all, I guess."

That was the plus side of Bob Arnold's unthreatening looks: people talked to him. Once they did they often found out mild appearances aren't everything, but that's another story.

"And," I thought aloud, "she's also afraid if Wanda doesn't show up soon they'll think maybe she *is* involved somehow with the drugs?"

"Yeah. Or even the murder. Or both. Hey, they don't know the girl," he said as Ellie returned with the baby, "so why shouldn't they think that? Anyway, the long and short of it is, Marge asked me to ask you two to help try finding her daughter," he finished.

"Preferably before the state boys come around again wanting to complete their interviews?" I suggested.

"Wouldn't hurt," he agreed amiably. "They're all over this thing like fleas on a yard dog. They find out the girl's gone, they're going to draw some conclusions."

Just the thought of the state cops trying to make heads or tails out of Wanda Cathcart made me feel like taking that sledgehammer to my own head. But so did what Bob Arnold was asking Ellie and me to do.

"Criminy," I said helplessly. "How did Marge even find out we might be any good at it, anyway?"

"Yeah, Bob," Ellie said, stepping forward with the baby in her arms. "How did she?"

Surprised, Bob took a hasty half-step back. "Now, Ellie," he began placatingly.

"Don't 'now, Ellie' me." She advanced relentlessly on him. "Girl vanishes, cops are on the scene, but the mother wants *us*?"

She put a hand on her hip. "So, Bob," she persisted, "would you care to explain to us how *that* little eventuality happened to happen?"

Here I should perhaps make clear that in the past Ellie and I had cleared up a number of fairly grisly Eastport crimes. Obsessed stalkers, murderous embezzlers, and in one truly horrid instance a corpse dangling upside down from a graveyard gate had helped form our unwanted reputation as . . .

Well, as snoops. Emphasis on *unwanted* reputation; what we *wanted* was normal life. But if wishes were horses, one of my dogs would be winning the Kentucky Derby right this minute.

Bob gave in at last. "Actually the reason Marge asked for you two is that I told her to."

"And that would be because . . . ?" Ellie appeared stern, which on her was quite a trick.

He held out his hands. "First of all, the state cops've got a murder and felony drug weight to keep them occupied. I mean, you should've seen their eyes light up."

I could imagine it. "So all by itself, if it's just a simple teenaged runaway case . . ."

Bob nodded briskly. "Yep. Oh, they'll do everything that's in the procedure book. Everything necessary," he emphasized. "I'm not sayin' they'll sell it short. Put out the word, bulletins, the whole nine yards. But even after all that, in the end I figure there's two ways it could go." He raised an index finger. "They'll decide maybe Wanda's got something to do with the felonies, and when they do find her, that'll be a mess."

Another finger. "Or . . . hey, kids run off. The girl didn't know Dibble. How could she? Only fifteen years old and a *young* fifteen, from what the mother told me."

I caught the drift. "So maybe Wanda won't show up *and* they won't find her. Because they *didn't* make a connection when maybe they should've."

A connection that might help find her, he meant. Because despite my impression of her, I supposed it wasn't impossible for Wanda to have known about the illicit pills. After all, Sam was a lot younger than fifteen when he first learned how to skin-pop cocaine using the TB syringes he'd stolen from his father's medical bag.

And if such a link existed, recognizing it might be the key to finding her. But I could think of a third way things could go, too.

A worse way. "Wanda Cathcart," I said slowly, "couldn't fend for herself in a roomful of kittens. Drugs or no drugs, if she ran off on her own–or worse, if someone took her–she could be in a lot of trouble."

"Yeah," Bob said. "There's that. Don't know why anyone would take her, though. She didn't see anything out there, did she?"

"You mean like who dunnit? Bob, she's timid and she's speech-impaired but she seems perfectly normal intelligence-wise. Seeing a murder... I think she'd have been trying to tell us about it."

True, there had been her frightened expression. And even now that I'd dismissed them I supposed the sounds I'd heard last night *could* have been made by someone creeping stealthily to the door. But...

"Anyway, if she had seen something, why wouldn't she have tried telling her mother?" I asked.

I knew one thing for sure: When I opened that door on my way out of the little room, I'd found no one. And it was still none of my business. Stubbornly I hefted the sledgehammer.

"Maybe what happened," I suggested, "is that Wanda just got tired of the witches of Eastport."

I went on to describe the scene at the Quoddy Village house, a mixture of New Age mysticism, old-world superstition, and Gregory Brand's patronizing style, which he'd displayed both during and after the canned-goods dinner we'd all... well, "enjoyed" might not be exactly the right word for it.

"Greg's like one of those how-to-empower-yourself gurus that used to be giving thousand-dollar seminars all over the place," I said, "before people with money got tired of mingling with the great unwashed in seedy hotel banquet halls and started hiring individual life coaches instead."

I turned toward the remnants of the porch, readying the hammer. "And kids can spot a phony a mile away, you know that. Wanda might be trying to give her mother a scare, so when she does come back Marge will agree to take her home."

"Yeah?" Bob said, interested. "So you think the witch stuff is fake, do you?"

I blew out a skeptical breath. "Bob, if they were real witches, why not just cast a spell to bring Wanda back? Anyway," I added, "tell Marge the answer's no. They paid for rent, not human bloodhounds, which Ellie and I are out of the business of being, anyway."

Saying this, I waited for Ellie to jump in and back me up. But she didn't; instead she gazed thoughtfully down at the baby and as she contemplated her offspring I could practically hear her thinking: *What if it were Lee?*

"Girl's a diabetic," Bob said suddenly.

I hadn't known that. "Not the shots kind," he added. "Pills. Kinda holds off the diabetes from settling in, from what I could gather. She's okay as long as she takes 'em. But if she doesn't, she could get real sick, real fast."

He looked straight at me. "Marge says Wanda's got the idea she can *think* the diabetes away, by the force of her mind or some such foolishness. If she can just get off those pills long enough to try, that is. Course Marge wouldn't allow it," Bob added.

"But the pills are still at the house?" I asked.

Bob nodded. "Little orange bottle. None missing."

Which could either mean that Wanda didn't want the pills, or that someone else didn't know that the girl needed them. Or just didn't care. . . .

Stop that, I instructed myself sternly. "Bob, I really don't want to get involved in this. And you'll be looking for her anyway, so why–?"

"No I won't," he interrupted. "State guy in charge of the investigation, he made that real clear right from the get-go. I'm to keep right out of the whole situation, Wanda included. His turf, y'know."

I raised an eyebrow.

"Yeah, yeah, I know. It isn't like that kind of thing's ever stopped me before, is it?" he replied.

"But I got this guy," he explained, "young fellow here in town with two little kids, the state's trying to decide whether or not to take those children away from him. Which," he added, "I know they absolutely should not. Take them away, that is."

"Where's their mother?" Ellie asked, embracing Lee.

"Ran off," he answered, "with some other guy, she thought he was a better bet. Now she's in the women's prison, check forging and assault with a deadly."

Weapon, he meant. "Which is how your state guy found out about the whole situation?" I guessed. "He was involved in *her* arrest?"

Bob nodded unhappy agreement. "Yeah, and he's already busting my shoes about it. Knows the story, and he's the kind of guy if he's got something he can use on you, then right away he's got to use it. He can't just wait and see how you're going to behave."

Bob made a face, commenting on what he thought of that kind of tactic. "Anyway, I screw up and my detective pal starts taking an interest, communicating with social services and so on, bottom line is that right or wrong my boy is gonna lose those kids. Which're doing just fine where they are, besides bein' all that's keeping him on the straight an' narrow himself."

He took a deep breath. "So I'm out. I don't want to be, but from now on I'm local support as requested and not a thing more. Only if you could just ask around," he added persuasively, "maybe see if Sam's friends have heard anything, it'd mean a whole lot to Marge Cathcart."

And to him, he didn't add. But he had two young kids of his own and I knew the tough family cases always bothered him most.

Still I said nothing, staring at the thick, dark mat of leaf mold that had accumulated under the front porch over the decades.

"It won't take long for the news about all this to spread," he added warningly. By then the silence had lengthened enough for him to know I wasn't just going to cave right in on this, despite his feelings.

On the other hand, if you spilled red wine on a tablecloth at one end of the island, ten minutes later people were arguing the relative merits of bleach versus lemon juice at the other end, and by the way had anyone else noticed that you were drinking a lot lately?

And it was *my* house the drugs were found in. Well, Ellie's too, but Ellie was so well liked around Eastport that no one would accuse her if she were selling the stuff from a pushcart.

So I'd be getting the blame, and never mind that the story would be far-fetched in the extreme; on the Eastport grapevine an ounce of *colorful* beat a pound of *believable*.

"You've made a few enemies in town lately even on top of that," Bob observed. "Bad-mouthing Gene Dibble, for example."

"Yeah," I said sourly. "Couldn't have happened to a nicer guy."

Because despite the way I'd soft-pedaled my opinion of him after finding him at the rental house, in my opinion Dibble had been a troublemaking son of a bitch.

And I'd said so recently, out loud and in public. "Bob, he was outside the fish fry at the Congregational Church last Friday night. Up on his soapbox, loaded to the gills and spouting his nonsense."

The gist of it had been that the Quoddy Village tenants were summoning up the Devil. "So what was I supposed to do, just stand there and keep my mouth shut?"

As I was saying this, my son Sam drove up and went into the house with a laundry bag over his shoulder. Ellie looked at me; *What if it were Sam?* her expression said.

"No, no," Bob replied placatingly, "I know what a royal pain he was, Jake. Thing is, though, a lot of other people heard you. His people, who go–went–to those street-corner Sunday sermons of his."

"Sermons," Ellie spat. "That's a laugh. Gene Dibble made a hobby of getting people riled up about anybody who was different. And you know it," she added to Bob.

"Yes, I do know it," he responded evenly. "Eugene approved of white, Protestant, and male, and he had the tar and feathers out for everybody else."

He hitched up the utility belt. Bob rarely used any of the items on it, but he said the one time he ended up needing any of them, he wanted them handy.

Even more, he wanted Eastport's few bad guys to know they were handy. "But that's neither here nor there," he went on. "The thing is, his pals include some pretty vindictive personalities."

"And they talk," Ellie conceded quietly, having sussed Bob's point, too. Drugs in my house plus Dibble being found dead in it, and now a missing girl...

If you wanted, you could base a fairly effective character-assassination program on all that. Which Eugene's pals *would* want; in short, in the let's-make-a-meal-of-her department it was a pretty good bet that I was about to be served up hot.

Suddenly that porch wreckage looked like a lot more fun than it had half an hour earlier. For one thing, there were no killers in it, and for another I doubted any missing girls were hiding among the rotted planks, busted support posts, and rusty railings strewn gaily over my front lawn.

But in Bob's mind Ellie and I were the town busybodies, and I supposed he figured that for once he might as well get some use out of us. I sighed.

"Okay," I said. "I'll poke around a little, see what I can find out about where Wanda might have gone."

Bob looked satisfied. "Good. She's pretty sure to be here on the island. State guys put a checkpoint on the causeway to try to pick up any known drug dealers, soon as they found the bag and got the truck wreck cleared. So even if she tried hitchhiking, no one could've taken her off in a vehicle."

I thought a minute about Wanda hitchhiking, then put the idea immediately into the category of *when pigs fly*. That along with the checkpoint at least narrowed things down a bit. And the island was only seven miles long by two miles wide.

"And I guess we could put a few feelers out, ask around. But that's all," I cautioned Bob Arnold.

With any luck Eugene Dibble's killer would be identified and arrested quickly, along with his partner in the drug deal–for that surely had to be why Dibble had ended up dead–and the murder part of this fiasco would be over, along with any rumor of my own participation in it.

"We can ask Sam to let us know if he hears anything. Check some of the places the kids hang out here on the island, too," I finished reluctantly.

Woodsy secluded areas, private little coves, reachable only if you clambered down steep, loose-shale cliffs . . . these had been the places Sam and his friends spent time in as young teens.

"Me too," Ellie put in loyally. Because she was right; if Lee were ever missing *we'd* want someone to help *us*.

But there was another reason that I was agreeing to look for Wanda Cathcart, and Ellie probably sensed it. Personal and complicated, it boiled down to the number of people who really do need assistance in this world versus the number who ever get any.

Young female people, especially. I wasn't up for facing that thought directly, though; not yet. Firmly I shoved away the clammy feelings memory summoned up at the idea of Wanda somewhere alone right now.

Or worse, not alone. "So okay," I told Bob again. "But as for Dibble and the drugs, and whatever else people might decide to say I'm involved in–"

Gossip fodder or no, it was Wanda who interested me, not some mouth-breathing slime toad whose drug deal, predictably and I thought deservedly, had gone south–

"The rest of this whole mess," I finished to Bob, "is up to the Maine State Police."

Even as I spoke I think I sensed the emptiness of my remark, the foolishness of insisting to myself that in this instance, as in no other, bad things might not lead irresistibly to other bad things.

Or to worse ones. But at the time I thought I could limit my own involvement. Curtail, as they say, the collateral damage. Because the real reason I'd agreed to Bob's request had nothing to do with my vulnerability to local rumor, Bob's problem, or my feelings for Ellie's daughter Leonora, who might someday need assistance herself.

The reason was in me, and in the still-fresh, incineratingly shameful memory of my own narrow escape from the kind of trouble I hoped Wanda *wasn't* in, right this very minute.

That is, if you could actually call what happened to me an escape.

I could.

Mostly.

• • •

After Bob Arnold left and Ellie took Lee to day care, I went inside, where Sam wanted to explain to me why plane chartering was Really No Big Deal Whatsoever.

"Mom, I'd like to hang out with him more, okay? He's my dad, I want to spend time with him, and he picked this. So is that so strange?"

"Of course not," I replied. "I just don't see why you can't do it here in Eastport. I mean he *moved* here to be near you, so you *wouldn't* have to spend zillions of dollars just to–"

Sam frowned briefly into the washing machine, so heavily loaded it might as well have been trying to mix concrete, then closed the lid and turned to me.

"Mom," he said patiently. "I knew you wouldn't approve. But it's all arranged, so try to be cool about it, all right?"

Outlined against the tall, bright windows of my old kitchen, Sam was tall, dark-haired, and muscular, graceful in the way men are who are comfortable on boats. Today he was wearing dungarees, old deck shoes, and a white T-shirt that said "I'll try to be nicer if you'll try to be smarter" in black letters on the front.

"How can I be cool about you and your dad turning into a pair of jet-setters?" I demanded.

It wasn't a jet. From what I'd heard it was a small twin-engine turbo-prop, and I wasn't all that comfortable about Sam getting onto one of those, either. But the real point was that Victor seemed to be buying Sam's affection, and by doing so getting Sam used to things he couldn't afford and would yearn for later, when he should be thinking about practical matters.

Achievable goals like finishing school, getting a job, and staying off substances. Or anyway I hoped they were achievable.

"What's up with all the spend-time-with-Dad stuff anyway, all of a sudden?" I asked.

Sam opened the washer again, stuffed a few more socks into it, tipped his head consideringly at the result, and added some T-shirts. The way he overloaded the thing, you'd think I charged him a quarter for using it instead of only threatening to.

Closing the lid, he replied, his face troubled, "It's just . . . I don't know, Mom, but I'm kind of worried about him lately. The way he talks to me, the way he acts . . ."

The washer began rumbling loudly as it labored; for Sam's laundry anyway maybe we'd have been better off with a cement mixer. Over the sound, he finished, "I think he doesn't feel very good, or something."

A snort of unkind laughter escaped me. "Victor? Are you kidding? Sam, the only time he doesn't feel good is when girls half his age turn him down for dates. The rest of the time he's a man of steel, you know that."

And especially when it came to his heart, I added silently. Victor was older now and his conquests were fewer, but just as when I was married to him they lasted about as long as the bloom on a fresh-cut rose.

After that, whammo. But I'd long ago decided not to subject Sam to any more of that kind of information. For one thing, Sam still thought the swath his father cut through the world of women was remarkable, even somehow admirable.

It was a further reason I thought Sam should spend less time with Victor, rather than more.

"Probably he ate a bad clam," I said. "And you'd better look out, he gets even sicker on bouncy little airplanes."

But I could see I was getting nowhere. Sam's face closed the way it always did when his mind was made up.

"Hey," he said quietly, taking a banana from the fruit bowl. "Mom. I've thought about it, and I'm doing this. I'm sorry if you don't like it, but–"

Right, message understood. Where chartering a plane down to the Celtics games was concerned, I could stand at the end of the runway and wave as they took off.

But otherwise I should keep out of it. *Maybe,* I thought in a final little burst of last-ditch optimism, *something else will keep them from going.*

I turned to another subject. "Sam, do you know anyone–or anyone who might know anyone–who deals in oxycontins?"

Sam paused in the act of feeding half a banana peel to Monday. The old Lab loved them, even scarfed up shriveled ones from the side of the road when she got the chance.

Next he fed the other half to Prill, who didn't care for them, but if Monday had something, the big red Doberman had to have it, too. Finally his face turned toward me, grinning.

"Yeah, actually I do. Why, d'you want some?" my son teased.

I gathered that during the pause he'd been deciding what to say and how to say it. A recovering alcoholic as well as an ex–drug user, he'd had a bad slip the previous winter. He knew I was touchy on the topic.

"No. There's a girl missing," I said, and filled him in on Dibble's murder and Wanda's disappearance.

Sam frowned thoughtfully, and in that moment he looked just like his father when his father was twenty. Right about then the whole world is a fellow's oyster if only he knows it.

Victor had known. "There's someone," Sam said carefully, "I used to hang out with. She might be able to tell you something."

Used to. I kept my face still, determined not to press him for details: when? how? and how well had he known this person?

He waited until he was sure I wasn't about to come down on him like a ton of bricks, then went on.

"Luanne Moretti. She lives here in Eastport. You want to make sure the missing girl isn't hooked into the drugs somehow? Is that it?"

The name wasn't familiar, but there was no particular reason why it should be. "Mmm, not exactly," I replied.

I still couldn't believe Wanda was connected to the pills in the house. Something else Bob Arnold had said, though, was still bothering me: whether she might have *seen* something.

"Mostly I'd just like to know who else *was* involved," I told Sam, "in that stuff being there at all."

A lurker, I imagined, someone besides Gene Dibble hanging around the place, whom Wanda might have seen. Someone who'd seen her, too, and once Dibble was shot might've decided that a witness to his unexplained presence was too dangerous a loose end to leave untied.

"If anyone was," I amended hastily. "I'd just like to cover all the worst bases first; that way I can rule them out. Um, anything else I should know about Luanne?"

He scribbled an address on a scrap of paper. "Like does she have a mean boyfriend you might have to deal with? No, Luanne's on her own."

Handing me the paper, he added, "She's kind of high-strung." As if either one of us had ever met an addict who wasn't.

"But just don't try to talk her into rehab and you'll be all right," he said, aware I'd be tempted; he knew the spectacle of a young girl in trouble pushed my hot-buttons.

Then, after agreeing to keep an eye open for Wanda himself, he grabbed another banana and left to go home to his own place on Liberty Street. He'd been there a few months now and except for me still drying and folding his laundry it was working out well, I reflected as I sat back down thoughtfully at the kitchen table.

By now it was midmorning and from downstairs my dad's pickaxe went on chinking patiently at the mortar between the granite blocks of the old foundation, the sound forming a bright, sharp counterpoint to the low rumble-thump of the overstuffed washer.

My dad always said you only got one chance to take a thing apart without destroying it. After that you'd never have another opportunity to understand how it had worked or what someone might have meant by putting it together just that way. And though he didn't quite know what, he did seem convinced now that something was hidden in the cellar.

Just as I already felt there was some element of Wanda's missing-girl status that I hadn't quite tumbled onto.

Yet.

• • •

With Lee settled for the morning, I could've picked Ellie up and we could have taken a ride around the island, scouting for Wanda. But instead I kept seeing the bat the girl had cradled in her fingers the night before.

Small, soft, and easy prey for anything bigger or stronger, the animal reminded me way too much of Wanda herself. So instead I took the address Sam had given me and headed out solo.

"Yeah?" Luanne Moretti's place was a small battered house crowded in among a half-dozen similarly unfortunate frame dwellings on Patron Street. An old car with four flats hunkered in the driveway, a faded green air freshener shaped like a pine tree dangling from its rearview mirror.

"I'm Jake Tiptree," I said. The front door knob was loose, hanging out on its metal stem.

Screwdriver, plastic wood-goo, electric drill, wood screws, I recited mentally; it was the opposite of the problem at the tenants' house. "I need some information and my son Sam said you might be able to help me," I went on.

Her bony face, haggard in the light of midmorning, looked low-level hostile and a little paranoid at first. But when she heard Sam's name a light went on behind her eyes, and she let me in.

Though I got the sense she'd have eventually done the same for just about anyone who knocked. In her late teens or early twenties and rail-skinny under a thin blouse and dungarees, Luanne gave the impression that she thought everything was pretty much inevitable anyway, so why argue?

She led me through a cramped living room whose plasterboard walls were scarred with evidence of parties that had gotten out of hand–

Razor knife, patching compound, wallboard tape, latex paint, my mind listed stubbornly–

–but whose thrift-store lamps and yard-sale furniture were primly arranged on a spotless though threadbare carpet.

"In here," she said, moving away from me. "I'm just having a cup of coffee. You want some?"

I followed her into the kitchen, where she gave it to me in a chipped pottery mug. The faucet, I noticed at once, was dripping.

"So how is he?" she asked.

All it needed, probably, was a faucet washer. "Sam? He's good," I replied. "He's doing really well."

The kitchen floor, old and badly worn in the traffic areas, glowed with fresh wax, and the countertops were militarily tidy. But Luanne's furious attempts at domestic order didn't fool me a bit.

Back in the bad old days Sam used to get high, then go on a cleaning binge. Once I found him at midnight detailing the grout between the bathroom tiles with a toothbrush and a jug of bleach.

"Sam's a nice kid. I hope he makes it," Luanne said flatly, lighting a menthol cigarette. "So what do you want, anyway?"

It was all I could do not to drag her home and force a glass of orange juice on her. In the light of the kitchen window her dark, wavy hair was bristly with split ends, her arms so thin you could see the tendons and her wrist bones jutting sharply out of her frayed cuffs.

Behind her on the fake-wood-paneled wall hung a puppies-and-kittens calendar that hadn't been changed since August. *Not with a bang but a whimper*, I thought.

Drip. Drip. Drip. "Just some facts," I said.

The faucet was already driving me crazy. And astonishingly I'd remembered to get washers for the tenants' place at the hardware store when I went there to get the lumber tarp.

So they were in my bag. But no. That wasn't what I was here for.

"Facts, huh?" Luanne chuckled tiredly, rubbing her bare feet together on the linoleum. "Most people I meet, facts're the last thing they want."

I could already see she was too far gone to be buying drugs in quantity; that is, dealing in them herself. She couldn't have raised the needed capital to go retail.

"So what're these facts you want worth to you?"

Drippety-drip. Water collecting in the trap under the sink began adding its own annoying contribution to the mix: a hollow, musical-sounding *blurp-blurp.*

Ignore it. I took a twenty-dollar bill out of my pocket and laid it on the table between us. She snatched it and it vanished into her pants pocket.

"Okay, who d'you want the dirt on?" Her tone let me know the money'd put her on board, not to waste her time with small talk.

Drip-blurp. I'd read somewhere that in a couple of weeks a leaking faucet could fill an Olympic-sized swimming pool. With effort I managed to banish this fact from my consciousness.

"I'm not sure," I admitted. "That's what I'm hoping maybe I can find out from you."

She said nothing.

"I need to know who might've been in on a deal with Eugene Dibble, for a whole lot of oxies. Somebody who might have been Eugene's partner," I said.

I didn't even know if there was anybody like that. But at my question, caution flickered again in Luanne's dark eyes.

Big-time caution. She got up, filled her mug once more from the coffeemaker even though she'd hardly drunk any of what she had.

Playing for time. "Why d'you want to know? The kind of thing you're asking, if it got around I was telling it..."

So she did know something. Which was good for me, maybe not so good for Wanda Cathcart. "Right, somebody moving volume. Who isn't scared of it. Which means you *should* be scared of him."

Luanne looked down at the iridescent green nail polish on her fingertips. Around her the shabby kitchen gleamed dully like a stage set of poverty, all the cheap things rubbed spotless.

"Yeah," she said almost inaudibly.

The faucet kept dripping. I clasped my hands together on the oilcloth-covered kitchen table. The texture on the tablecloth had little lines of solidified gray grime deeply embedded in it, the kind wiping doesn't remove; you need a scrub brush to get it out.

"Yeah," Luanne repeated, "I'm scared of him, all right."

The tablecloth was the first tiny chink in her denial-fueled armor. Near the end, Sam had quit brushing his teeth.

Impatience seized me. "Luanne, I know I'm probably putting you in an uncomfortable situation–" I began.

Her harsh laugh interrupted me. "Uncomfortable! That's a hot one. You come in here, start asking questions... you don't care what kind of trouble I could get in," she accused, picking at a hangnail.

Emotional seesawing being just another nifty part of the show. She wasn't getting high anymore on whatever she was using–God, I knew way more about this than I'd ever wanted to–merely keeping herself from getting sick.

"I'm no hard-core junkie, you know," she said resentfully when the silence got to be more than she could stand. "I'm just chipping a little now and then, it's under control. And don't get me wrong, I can take care of myself in case you're wondering."

Her glance strayed to her purse, a black fake-leather affair slouched on the counter. Plenty big enough for, say, one of those cheap little Korean-made .22s you can buy in a pawnshop.

It wouldn't have surprised me; I didn't even disapprove. If I'd been Luanne I'd have carried every kind of protection I could get.

But it was feather-smoothing time. "Luanne, I never said you were a junkie, and I surely didn't come here to heavy out on you about your personal life," I told her.

God, that faucet was like Chinese water torture. I got up and crossed to the sink, feeling her eyes follow me. The faucet handle was your standard cap-pressed-on-over-a-screw deal.

And I had a Swiss Army knife in the bag with the washers. "But I need a name," I said, crouching down.

"What the hell are you doing?" she demanded when I opened the cabinet under the sink.

Yep, there were the two shutoff valves, right where they belonged; one for hot, one for cold. Reaching in past a truly impressive collection of household cleaning agents I turned both valves off.

"I'm fixing the damned drip," I answered, pausing to find another twenty and fling it at her. "There, I'm paying you to let me do it, all right?"

Bemusedly, she picked the money off the floor.

"And... Ouch!" I'd bumped my head getting up out from under the sink. Rubbing it, I straightened grouchily.

"And I'd appreciate it if while you're sucking up my twenties like a vacuum cleaner you could also try helping me out a little," I snapped.

Note to self: While getting out from under a kitchen sink, remember to wear all the appropriate safety gear. Like possibly a motorcycle helmet; I was going to have a nasty goose egg later.

"Whatever you say to me, it didn't have to come from you and I won't ever tell anyone you told me," I promised, leaning over the sink again.

The leak had stopped. Popping the shiny round caps off the faucet-handle tops with the pry tool on the Army knife, I set them aside. In the recessed area beneath each cap was a slotted screw, and under each screw–I'd done this before–lay a small black utterly essential rubber washer.

"When you turn off a water faucet what you're really doing is tightening this screw down onto the washer beneath," I told Luanne conversationally. Just talking, trying to establish some rapport.

As if. "Once the washer disintegrates you can't tighten it anymore. So you have to replace the washer," I went on, "and to do that, you have to remove the screw."

And of course one of the screws was rusty. "Damn," I said, trying and failing to de-rust it with the corkscrew on the knife; none of the blades would fit into the small round space. "You wouldn't happen to have something small and sharp around here, would you? Something with a little point on it?"

Luanne got up and rummaged in a drawer, came up with a metal shish-kebab skewer and handed it wordlessly to me.

"Perfect," I said, digging rust out of the screw slots with the skewer's tip. After that I backed the screws out.

"Anyway, I'm kind of up a creek, here," I prattled on as I worked. Digging the washers out of the holes, I found that one of them had already crumbled to brittle pieces and the other was about to. "That's why I came to you."

Luanne snagged the hangnail, pulled till the bright blood welled up. Wincing, I turned back to the faucet assembly.

"A girl is missing," I said. "I'm trying to find her. Please."

When I looked back at her again a faint sheen of sweat had broken out on her brow. At first I thought maybe she was late for her dose of whatever, that I was keeping her from fixing.

But then I saw the desperate expression in her eyes and knew she was really scared.

"There's this guy..." she began reluctantly. "A local guy. I used to party with him."

I shook the rubber washers from their packet onto the sink's drainboard.

"But not lately," she added.

"What's his name?" I turned back to my task. Two washers were required; only one of the proper size was in the packet. Typical.

"I shouldn't even be talking to you." She lit another cigarette. "This guy, he's not funny. You really don't want to mess around with him." She dragged on the cigarette. "I'm sorry I let you in here," she said, exhaling a stream of smoke.

I was starting to be sorry also, but for a different reason. Probably only one of the faucets was actively leaking. But which? I should have checked before I took the handles apart.

"Luanne, I'm not going to mess with him," I began. "I just need to know..."

She was turning out to be like every other addict I'd ever met. Just when you thought you'd gotten a little traction, they went passive-aggressive on you and slipped through your fingers.

On top of that, I could only fix one faucet handle. Common sense said to replace the washer that had already disintegrated. But that wasn't the one whose screw had been rusty.

And rust + metal = leak. Coming to a decision, I dropped the new washer into the cold-water handle receptacle, put the old-but-so-far-undisintegrated washer in the hot-water side, and tightened down both screws. Crawling back under the sink, I turned both valves on and straightened again, careful this time not to clobber myself on the way out.

Bingo. No leak; I dusted my hands off. Then motion flashed suddenly in the corner of my eye and I jumped startledly. With it came a humming sound, loud in the quiet kitchen.

"Christ!" Luanne uttered at my sudden movement, lurching up.

But it was only a fish tank, half hidden by the refrigerator on a far corner of the kitchen counter. The tank, I now saw, was inhabited by a dozen or so of the cheaper kinds of tropical fish: neons, small angelfish, others I didn't recognize.

"Sorry," I said, sitting again. "I didn't notice the fish when I came in, that's all."

"Damn aerator's on the fritz." She crossed the room to reach down into the tank and jostle the mechanism in it. "You don't know how to fix those, do you?"

The hum faded as bubbles began rising; she dried her hand on a dishtowel. And no, I didn't know how.

"My mom sends food and stuff for them," Luanne said, watching the brightly colored fish for a moment before turning to me again. "She says I ought to have some kind of pet."

I pulled out another twenty, then a fourth, laid them on the kitchen table but kept my hand on them. "Last chance," I said.

Luanne stared at the money. Then: "Mac Rickert. Don't ask me for his places, though. I don't know any. He won't deal to me anymore for some reason, I don't know that either. And I've heard he moves around a lot."

Yeah, well, for eighty bucks you don't know much, do you? I thought sourly as the phone rang in the front room. But at least I had the name. Tearing herself from the twenty-dollar bills on the table, Luanne went to answer.

"Yeah," she said into the phone. "Sure, tonight. You want to come to my place, or . . . okay. But I can't talk now, so I'll see you later. No, I really can't talk. Sure, I remember you. I do, but . . . Okay, bye."

She returned, trying to appear nonchalant. "Friend coming by?" I asked mildly.

This was what it came to when you had no skills and a habit as big as a house. "Yeah," she said casually. But her hands shook as she lit yet another of the menthol cigarettes.

Dragging on it, she snatched up the twenties. "So've you got what you wanted? Are we done?"

Across the room the fish darted brightly among the plastic toys in the aquarium water, the tiny waterwheel rotating and the miniature frogman bobbing up and down as the aerator burbled.

"Mac likes animals," she said irrelevantly, glancing at the tank. "Only thing ever softens him up. Or used to. I haven't seen him lately."

I pushed my chair back. A dead neon tetra was snagged in one of the green plastic aquarium plants, but she hadn't seen it yet.

"Yeah, we're done. But Luanne, if you ever need any help..."

Her expression hardened; she'd heard it before, and she knew I didn't mean assistance with home repairs.

"...with the fish," I finished as her eyes narrowed. "I mean sometimes people want to go away," I improvised. "On vacation, or if they have to leave town for a little while for some reason..."

Like to a rehab facility, I thought. But Sam had warned me. And anyway it wouldn't have done any good.

"...and leave their pets," I added. "I'm just saying I could come over and feed them for you, is all."

She wasn't deceived and she didn't intend to take me up on my offer. But as she listened her mood softened grudgingly.

"Yeah, okay," she said. Then, "So Sam's doing good, huh?"

"Yes, he is. Well," I amended, not wanting to shame her, "he has his ups and downs. Like everyone."

"Uh-huh." She thought about that. "Um, listen, say hi to him for me. And...thanks for the money."

"Sure, Luanne. Take care," I said, leaving her there in the kitchen with the aquarium bubbling and the faucet fixed.

Right; everything hunky-dory, including a pocketful of extra money. She already had a date for tonight, too.

Or at any rate that's what Luanne was still calling it to herself, probably. And as I went out into the cold fresh air I knew the eighty bucks I'd given her wouldn't make tomorrow night any different.

Still, like everyone else who knocked on the door of her spotless little trick pad and asked or demanded to be let in, I'd gotten what I wanted.

And like most people who left, I supposed, I was satisfied but not particularly proud of the transaction.

Or of myself.

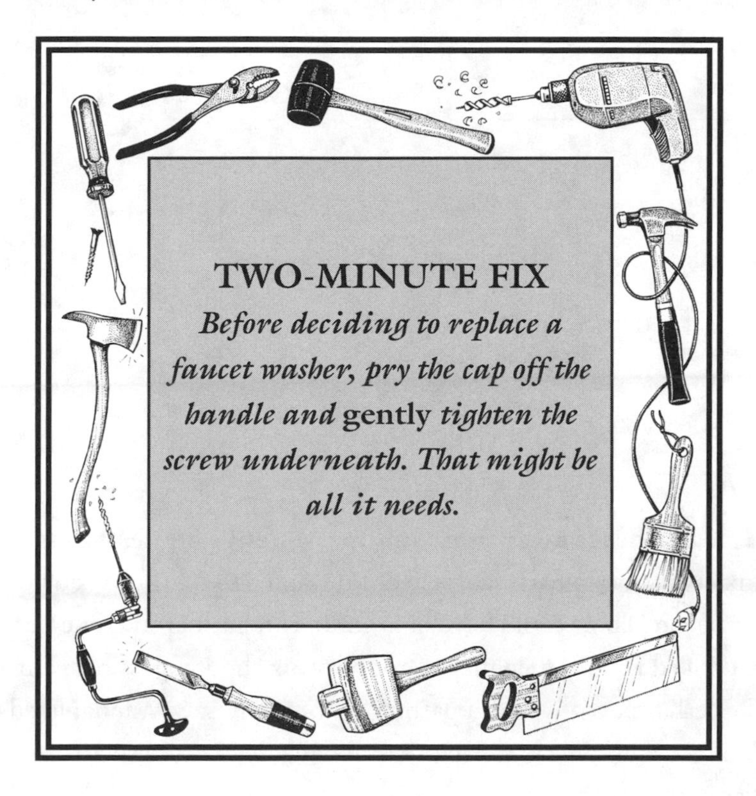

Chapter 5

As I drove away from Luanne Moretti's house, the gnawing of anxiety in my stomach sharpened. I'd wanted to rule out a bad notion, that Eugene Dibble could have had not only a partner in crime but one who'd killed Dibble, then maybe got nervous about a possible witness.

Or perhaps even worse, a partner who simply saw Wanda, liked the look of her, and came back later to grab what he'd taken such a fancy to earlier in the day.

But instead of eliminating this suspicion, Luanne had supplied me with a candidate. So next on my to-do list was a chat with the tenants, to find out if any of them had noticed anyone hanging around.

And to check on my boat. When I arrived at the rental property, though, no one was around, and in my annoyance at this I forgot all about the rowboat until I was halfway back to town.

Next time, I resolved, and continued on home, where I found my housekeeper, Bella Diamond, already busy at the stove though dinner was still hours away.

"Mmm," I said, sniffing appreciatively. "That smells like shrimp casserole."

She'd already made the quince jam, the jars glowing jewel-like on the kitchen windowsill and the jelly pan clean and upside down on the dish rack. Now she turned from stirring the fragrant sauce of sautéed scallions, mushrooms, and garlic.

"That's right. Better'n a restaurant dinner, for sure." She spoke with deserved pride.

Several generations of bad childhood nutrition showed in the bone structure of Bella's face, and she'd apparently decided to try making up for all of it by cooking for us. "I'm sure," I told her inadequately, "it will be lovely."

From the ingredients ranged out on the counter, I gathered that clam juice, chicken broth, oregano, and cream also featured in today's creation. The shrimp she'd peeled were in a bowl and the angel-hair spaghetti was out, ready to be dropped into the olive-oil-tinctured boiling water.

"With green salad and garlic bread," Bella agreed. "Just the thing for a chilly fall day. And this nice dry raspberry wine to go with it."

All of which spelled Bella's special brand of dinner-table heaven, as usual. I'd never meant to have a housekeeper but I'd won a week's worth of Bella's services at a church raffle, and after I helped clear her of the charge of bonking her ex-husband to death with a cast-iron skillet, her devotion to me became complete.

"Here, you strike me as if you could use cheering up," she said, and poured me a glass.

I sank into a chair at the table. "Thanks. So what have you been doing besides working your fingers to the bone as usual?"

With skinned-back dyed red hair, big buck teeth, and pale green bulging eyes that reminded me of a pair of peeled grapes, Bella also kept Wade and me in pristine surroundings five days a week.

"Oh, not a lot," she said, gesturing at the kitchen, which was so clean, Victor could have done brain transplants in it. She'd have come to work the other two days, too, if I'd let her, and now that I'd trained her to let Wade finish his beer before grabbing the bottle out of his hands to rinse it, she was working out just fine.

Also, Bella was a reliable Eastport information resource; in other words, a gossip.

"Have you ever heard of a local guy named Mac Rickert?" I asked as she returned to tinkering with the shrimp sauce.

Her eyebrows went up as she stirred. "Um, yeah. Kind of like I've heard of the boogeyman, though."

The wine was cold and delicious. I let it roll around my tongue for a while before swallowing and taking another sip, then pressed the cold glass to the side of my forehead.

Only then did what she'd said sink in. "Wait a minute, the boogeyman? You mean he's not real?"

A pang of irritation hit me. Had Luanne taken my cash and told me a fairy tale just to get rid of me?

Bella dumped the bowl of cleaned shrimp into the sauce. "No. It's just that no one much sees him," she replied.

Cat Dancing watched from the top of the refrigerator as the morsels disappeared, then pronounced a disappointed cat-syllable and went back to sleep.

"Mac's an outdoors type," Bella went on. "Lives in the woods, knows how to catch wild game to eat, make a fire by rubbing two sticks together. Build a shelter, keep you from freezing to death in the winter, just out of pine boughs and such."

"I see." But guys like that weren't really rare around here, so I still didn't understand the boogeyman reference.

She poured another dollop of olive oil into the boiling water, then opened the spaghetti. "Funny thing about that, though. The hunting part, I mean. Few years ago when Mac still lived in town, he was the animal control officer."

Extracting the spaghetti, she broke it all in half and began feeding it into the water. "And he was death on people who were mean to their pets, Mac was. He caught you tyin' 'em in the yard out in the cold, he'd take 'em right away from you."

She tossed the spaghetti box out. "Take 'em home himself, he would, and if you complained he'd threaten to tie *you* out in the snow. Which people believed he *would* do, too. He's an imposing man, Mac Rickert is," she added. "Mountain-man type of fellow."

It was the second time that day that I'd heard of Rickert's supposed fondness for animals, or at any rate for ones that were under human protection.

"But if you shot 'em clean–game animals I mean, not folks' pets–well, I guess Mac thought that was different."

The sweet perfume of olive oil wafted into the room. "Later on he had a business guiding hunting trips. Only the deal was, he would take you into the real backwoods, teach survival skills while you were bagging your moose. Or deer or bear, or whatever."

"Uh-huh." The wine had unlocked a kink in the back of my neck. I finished the glass and set it aside, touched the tender bump rising on my head where I'd banged it coming out from under Luanne Moretti's kitchen sink.

"But I gather Rickert's in another business now?" I asked, then related what Luanne had told me about him.

Bella dumped the cooked spaghetti into a colander, stepping back from the cloud of steam. "Drugs? That I didn't know about. Interesting, though," she said, putting the drained spaghetti back into the pot along with a lump of butter half the size of my clenched fist.

"What is?" Oh, what the hell, one more glass of wine wasn't going to kill me any more than that butter would, or anyway not immediately. So I poured it.

"Well, it probably doesn't mean anything," Bella answered. "But Jenny Dibble mentioned Mac Rickert this morning when I stopped in at her house on my way here to work."

I sat up straight. Jenny Dibble was Eugene Dibble's recently bereaved wife. "Really. Why did you visit her?"

Bella sniffed as if the answer to this question ought to be obvious. "Girl's a grievin' widow, ain't she? Christian thing to do, stop by an' see if she might need anything."

Of course. And to pick up any interesting facts that might be floating around while she was there, too.

"Which, by the way, she's already moving out of." Bella tasted the sauce with a spoon. "The house, that is."

"That didn't take long." From down in the cellar came a low grinding sound, like a dentist's drill being run on slow speed.

"Nope. Getting her clothes together, leaving the furniture and so on. All junk, Eugene was an awful slob. I don't think that place holds many happy memories for Jenny," Bella remarked.

She took a second taste, larger and more thoughtful than the first. "Married him on the rebound from her first husband, had a daughter already then. Girl's out of the house now, though, has been for a while. I don't know her at all."

She shook salt into the sauce. "Anyway, there was a brace of partridges in the kitchen, all ready for the oven, along with the casseroles and other things people had been bringing on account of Eugene, and when I asked her where they came from she said she thought them partridges was from Mac Rickert."

She pronounced it the Maine way: *pah-triches*. "Really," I said, and then because she'd been so informative so far, I decided to tell her the rest of what I'd been up to for the last twenty-four hours.

"So does all that plus a bag of pills smell like partnership to you?" I asked when I had finished. "Because it does to me."

Bella turned, spoon in hand. "Well, I wouldn't know for sure. But I can tell you this much–Mac Rickert wouldn't be caught dead within a mile of that goofball Eugene Dibble unless he had *some* reason."

At my questioning look she explained, "When Mac was out an'

about more he only hung around with the hunting guys, loggers, some of the commercial fishermen. 'S all you'd ever see him with, not fools like Eugene."

Cat Dancing stood up, peered around for possible stray shrimp, and settled herself once more with a soft thump. "And now he's not around at all?"

Bella shrugged expressively. "That's the other thing. He's around, all right. Once in a while you'll hear a boat, no running lights on a foggy night, or some hunter'll catch a glimpse of somebody a long ways from the road, slippin' 'mongst the trees."

She paused, thinking. "Or a car will go missing out of some driveway, stay gone for a day or so, then show up again like it was never gone in the first place, 'cept the gas tank's empty."

"So not a bad boogeyman, exactly?" Unless he'd taken Wanda. "Because from what you're saying, shooting people and kidnapping girls doesn't sound like Rickert's M.O.," I added.

Bella nodded agreement. "Mac's more the type to go out and shoot a turkey, dress it all out, and leave it on somebody's back doorstep. Like them partridges."

I raised my eyebrows.

"Somebody who can't afford to buy a bird for Thanksgiving," she explained. "That's the rumor, when it happens people say it was Mac."

"A Robin Hood boogeyman, then." Only in Eastport, folks.

"Jenny Dibble said one other strange thing," Bella continued. "She said Gene'd been real cheerful lately. Which I imagine was unusual. As if something was going right for him, she said."

Which was pretty unusual, too, I supposed. Picking up the garlic press, Bella broke half a dozen cloves from the garlic head, removed the peelings, then put them through the press into a bowl that already held another stick of butter.

So maybe our arteries would harden but at least we wouldn't have to worry about vampires. "I'd like to talk to this Rickert," I told her.

She tipped her head doubtfully as she mashed the garlic into the butter with a fork. But before she could answer, my dad stomped up the cellar stairs, a string of profanities issuing from his mouth.

Stopping when he saw us. "Oh. Sorry about that," he said. He crossed to the sink and drew himself a glass of water, guzzling it down without pause, then let out a sigh.

"But I've just discovered there's a *box* hidden in that wall," he added. "Or at any rate I think there is. And I don't mind telling you two it's driving me plumb nuts."

He ran more water. "A big box. At least two feet long and a foot wide from what I can tell." He held his hands out to indicate the item's dimensions.

They were big, work-gnarled hands, knuckles grimy and joints knobby with early arthritis. "A *wooden* box. But–"

In every old-house task there is always a "but." You can depend on it.

"...I can't get the box out without taking apart a lot more wall," he went on. "And I don't know what they used for mortar, but here we are almost two hundred years later and it's still harder than the stone."

He drained his glass again. "So what I need is to find out the true size of the thing," he said, his frustration easing somewhat as he aired it out by talking to us. "Just start outwards and work in till I get to its edges, so I don't have to take down more old mortar and stone than I need to."

"And you'll find out the true size," I asked, "by...?"

"Drilling," he replied firmly. "Drill some test holes with a mortar bit, I don't hit wood, then I haven't hit the box."

Frowning, he went on. "I already nicked it once, wood chips came out on the pick edge. Mahogany, it appears, which is why I think it's a box and not just a structural part of the house."

Indeed, I thought; let's not damage any of those. The place already had an alarming tendency to fall down at one end faster than I could prop it up at the other.

"I want to preserve the thing whole, if I can," he said.

I wanted it, too. A mysterious box dating from when the house was built...

"But it's not going to be easy." He wiped his forehead with his bandanna. "There's an old pipe of some kind in the wall. I'd rather not hurt that. And like I said, some old-time builder put that box in there to stay."

He eyed the counter where Bella stood spreading thick slices of a French loaf with the garlic butter. "Course," he added, "some other old-timer might just manage to get the jump on the situation, he's well fueled enough."

Bella sniffed. "Go on with you, shedding grit an' grime all over my clean kitchen. Supper ain't for hours, yet."

But then her face softened, which on Bella was really saying something. She was no oil painting but when she looked at my dad she was almost pretty.

"Here," she added, reaching into the cookie jar and coming up with a couple of homemade date bars. "Wouldn't want it to be said I turned my back on a starving man."

She thrust them gruffly at him and when he'd departed with them she turned back to me. "Missus," she began; one thing I hadn't been able to train her to do was call me by my first name.

"Missus, here's what I think. Eugene Dibble's brains had about enough powder to blow him to hell, which I'm guessing is what happened one way or another. And from what I've heard, Mac Rickert is exactly the man Eugene would've needed if he was all involved in some kind of drug deal and it was too big to handle by himself."

"But would Dibble be smart enough to realize that?" I asked. "I mean that he needed someone else, with experience in this kind of thing, badly enough to consider sharing the profit?"

Which he'd have had to do and from what I knew of Dibble myself, I felt confident it would've half killed him. Bella shook her head, sliding the casserole into the oven.

"No, I wouldn't expect so. But you never can tell, even a stopped clock is right twice a day. And what if for once he did something the proper way for a change?

"That is," she amended darkly, straightening, "if there is a proper way to do a thing like that."

"Huh," I said, thinking over what she'd told me as footsteps thudded up the back porch. Moments later Wade came in, kissed me on the ear, and went upstairs to change his clothes.

Behind him came Sam with the two dogs, Monday white-faced and arthritic beside Prill, a youngster by comparison. But at the moment they were both so invigorated from their walk, their names might as well have been Romp and Stomp.

"Sam, put them out in the ell until they calm down, please," I said, and he was quick to comply. Though we'd finished the chartering-a-plane talk, he knew I wasn't at all happy about it, and he wanted to appease me.

Last came Victor, uninvited and unexpected. But that man could smell shrimp casserole a mile away. "Hello," he said pleasantly, putting an extra bottle of wine on the table, then went on into the living room without offering even one critical remark.

Bella watched him go. "Is he mellowing?" she asked me. "Or is it my imagination?"

"Yeah, right," I scoffed, "and after that, Hannibal Lecter's going to become a vegetarian."

I'd have gone on but Sam called out from the hall closet to say he'd just broken the light switch in there and did I have any more of them so he could replace it?

That keep-Mom-in-a-good-mood program could operate to my advantage, I realized, if I figured out how to work it right. The trouble was, Sam didn't know how to fix a light switch.

Also, I didn't have any. So I ran down to the hardware store again and when I got back I had to turn off all the power in the house because I couldn't remember which circuit ran the closet wiring, and we did replace the thing.

Power off, old fixture out, wires onto new fixture–wrapped clockwise around the connection screws–and lastly, new fixture in. Not counting the hardware store trip it only took us about fifteen minutes, though afterwards Sam said he was glad he hadn't decided to become an electrician.

Too much nitpicking, he opined of my efforts to teach him how to avoid becoming an electrocuted person; he'd have assumed the circuit was dead once the breaker switch was pulled, instead of checking with the circuit-tester gadget I made such a religion of using.

But it was pleasant, doing it together. Then while I was putting the tools away Ellie arrived, along with her husband George Valentine carrying baby Lee, her high chair, and what I estimated was most of the other baby equipment in the world. Soon after that the oven timer went off, the baby woke up shedding clothing items and demanding to be entertained, and the dogs decided banishment to the spare room was boring, so could they dig a hole under the door?

The answer being yes they could, so I opened it to prevent this; next came dinner and all the hilarity that ensues when you combine babies, current and ex-husbands, shrimp casserole, and rowdy dogs, plus of course a pair of women like Ellie and me who are just trying to get a little food into our mouths, for Pete's sake.

"Got your deer yet?" George Valentine teased Victor from across the table. He knew that in Victor's opinion, hunting was right up there with standing on your porch spitting tobacco juice past the broken washing machine you kept by the front door, and if you were any good at it there was a broken lawn mower sitting out there, too.

" 'The unspeakable,' " Victor pronounced in reply, " 'in pursuit of the inedible.' "

But he smiled when he said it, and he had the good grace not to look surprised when George said he hadn't been talking about foxhunting, which was a different keg of fish.

"Hear there's poachers," George went on, turning to Wade. The Maine way: *poach-ahs*. "Over on Tall Island. Now, that's a bunch I'd like to chase around with some dogs and a bugle."

My father had slipped out the back door after shyly saying hello to the assembled company, carrying a covered dish wrapped in a towel that Bella had fixed up for him; sometimes he joined us for dinner, and sometimes he didn't.

George added to Victor, "Tall Island's a game preserve, no hunting at all. Long time ago it got made that way by local ordinance, since then everyone's just kind of agreed it should stay."

Wade nodded, digging into his dinner. "But it's the same every year. Always one or two can't play by the rules. Doesn't help that you can walk over there at low tide, either."

To Tall Island, he meant. When the tide went out, the inlet between the island and the mainland was a relatively smooth–though seriously slippery–stretch of sand and rocks. And since poachers of course didn't obey the "no hunting after sunset" rule, either–there was plenty of opportunity.

"Guys hunt without a license, or in protected places. Mostly with illegal equipment," Wade explained to Victor, whose dislike of hunting was rivaled only by his ignorance on the subject.

Victor reacted predictably. "What, like it's supposed to be a fair fight?"

But Wade's reply was serious. "To a degree, yes. There's not much sport in knocking the animals over with a bazooka. The idea is to bring the population down in a way that's not cruel to your quarry, while also providing a good experience for the hunter."

He ate a bite of casserole, washed it down with a swallow of the ale he preferred with dinner instead of wine.

"And I think you'll agree chasing a wounded deer through deep snow for half a day so you can finish it off isn't what most folks'd call a good time," he concluded.

George ducked, narrowly avoiding Leonora's thrown teething biscuit, then nodded agreement as he produced a replacement from his shirt pocket.

"Man, that's the truth," he said, teasing the baby's lower lip with the biscuit until she accepted it. Strapped into her high chair like an astronaut in a landing capsule, Lee uttered a few wet syllables of appreciation and began gnawing the morsel.

"These guys, though, they don't even bother to chase what they've wounded," said George. "They just let the poor thing..."

Time to change the subject, I thought, but Victor cut in before I had a chance to. "What kind of stuff aren't you allowed to use?" he asked.

Half listening to the answer, I regarded my nearly cleaned plate a little guiltily. What, I wondered, might Wanda Cathcart be having for dinner, and where? But other than that crystal ball out at the tenants' place, it seemed I had little way of finding out tonight.

Correction: no way. "...jacklighting," Sam was in the middle of telling his father. "That's flat-out illegal, blinding 'em with a bright light at night so they'll just stand still like they were hypnotized," he explained.

"Nothing but a handheld bow, no crossbows or anything like that," he went on after another forkful of his food; that shrimp casserole was fantastic. "You can't use a substance on the arrow tip to poison them, either."

"Or God forbid an explosive tip," Wade put in, making a face at an old hunting memory that I hoped he wouldn't share, and he didn't.

"Got to be a broadhead tip," George agreed. "And you've got a limit to how heavy a bow you can use. Not," he added, "that the heavier bow'll improve your accuracy any, anyway."

He drank some wine. "Pull it back, you're bobblin' around on account o' the draw's way too heavy, half the time all you end up with is your good old-fashioned *kertwang*."

"Wild shot," Wade translated for Victor. "Anyway, I'm sorry to hear that," he added to George, "about Tall Island. Any idea who's been doing it?"

George shook his head. "Kids, maybe. Reason they think it's bowhunters is, no one's heard shots. Also the warden was out there a week ago and he found a carcass. Sort of a mess, it was, had a really ugly kind of homemade arrow stuck in it that didn't want to come out."

At that, Ellie did change the subject, forcefully enough so that neither man could mistake her cue; hunting talk was one thing but we didn't need the gory details at the dinner table.

"Who wants more casserole?" she asked, and everyone did, and after that she skillfully drew Sam out on the topic of the Coast Guard course he was getting ready to take soon.

"It's the hundred-ton mate/masters with attached sail-and-towing certificate course," he informed us proudly, and went on to tell us all just exactly what that entailed.

Which was a lot, and involved some responsible tasks on boats that I'd have preferred not knowing about, much the same as I tried not to think too hard about Wade's job out on the water.

So while Sam described it I sat there recalling what he'd said earlier about Victor not feeling well, and tried keeping an eye on my ex-husband.

He was eating a little less than usual, I thought, and he'd passed on a second glass of wine–

We'd have omitted alcohol entirely but Sam wouldn't sit down with us if we did, insisting he had to remain sober in the real world, not some unrealistic be-careful-he's-a-reformed-boozer version of it.

–but otherwise Victor seemed his usual self. For instance, he caught me spying on him, his eyes meeting mine knowingly over the candle flame between us.

I thought he might say something about it, too, but by now it was time to clear the plates and he got up in a hurry instead, to avoid the kind of all-pals-together sort of labor he abhorred. And I'd have let the other husbands clean up as they offered, but Ellie and I wanted a couple of moments to ourselves.

Thus when we'd all had our coffee and the dessert had been served and eaten, Ellie and I met in the kitchen, where we fed the dogs, put Cat

Dancing's dish atop the refrigerator where she insisted on having it, then conferred together while we washed and dried the dishes.

"So," Ellie said when I had finished my report. "If Rickert and Eugene Dibble didn't know our house was being rented, they might've used it as a hiding place. Then once the tenants were in, Eugene might have had to sneak in, to retrieve the pills."

"Right," I said, admiring the way she attacked the stack of plates with a sudsy sponge. Like Bella Diamond, Ellie thought there wasn't much in the world that couldn't be improved by the application of enough hot soapy water, and often she was correct.

"But," she added, "now the drugs have been confiscated. So they can't be sold by anyone, can they?"

There was an angle I hadn't thought of. "And *that* means now that Dibble's dead, Mac Rickert–or someone–still owes someone else for the stash all by himself," I agreed.

"Wow," she said, rinsing a handful of silverware, "if that's true, he'd *better* stay out in the woods."

"Yeah. But why kill Dibble there in the house, I wonder, instead of some place where he wouldn't be found so soon? And then not even take the drugs with him?"

"*And* if Wanda saw Mac–then or earlier–why not take her right then? Why come back and run the risk of being caught all over again?"

"Beats me." I wiped the stovetop off with a wet paper towel. "Maybe he just didn't think of it then." When Bella came tomorrow, if that stove wasn't pristine she would fix me with what Sam had begun calling The Big Green Eyeball soon after she came to work for us.

Meanwhile Ellie's mind had begun running along a different track. "The other possibility, you know, is that this is all a fine theory. But that's all. Just a theory. You don't even know that girl you talked to–Luanne, her name was?–you don't even know if she was telling you the truth. And even if she was . . ."

She wrung the sponge, wiped the faucet with it. "Anyway, I thought we were just going to make a few calls," she continued. "Maybe check out the teenagers' usual hangout places."

Which I hadn't done, sending Sam instead and going right to Plan B myself. Because I was so sure already that Wanda wasn't in any of those places; that if she had been, some kid would have blabbed about it already.

That if she had been, I wouldn't be feeling this way about her.

"I'm just saying you seem intent on a worst-case scenario," Ellie went on. "Are you sure you haven't been jumping the gun?"

She shook her dishtowel out, folded it, and hung it on the rack. "Of course, if you hadn't we wouldn't know about Rickert at all. But even if he is involved, it could be he killed Dibble and Wanda *didn't* see it. Or," she finished, "anything else."

Spying a spot I'd missed, she licked her finger and rubbed a corner of the stovetop until the smudge was gone. "I mean, she is only fifteen, maybe with her head full of dreamy foolishness like any other kid that age. So maybe she did run off on her own just like Bob Arnold suggested."

"Yeah," I said reluctantly, hanging up my own towel. "You're right, I guess that's possible, too."

Even I'd thought so at first. Still I kept seeing Wanda's face: unrebellious, even passive except when she'd been coddling that tiny bat. She was dreamy all right, but in the short time I'd been with her I'd gotten the sense that her dreams weren't the bright-lights, big-city kind cherished by so many teenagers.

That instead they were childish, earnest, and unaffected. Like my own dreams a long time ago, in a past still so hideously well remembered it made me shiver, there in the snug, warm kitchen.

• • •

It was past ten-thirty when everyone left. Victor stuck around awhile to try promoting something better out of me than reluctant acceptance, which was where I'd settled on the plane-chartering business, while

Ellie and George gathered the baby's things. Meanwhile Sam finished his laundry before taking it and the rest of the leftover casserole in case he got hungry during the night, and headed for home, too.

"Oh, all right," I gave in finally as Victor went out the door, "have a good time, then, the both of you." I couldn't imagine why my blessing mattered so much to him, but it seemed to.

After they'd all gone and the dogs had been outside for the last time, I went upstairs to take a shower, pausing by the hall window looking out over Key Street on my way to get fresh towels from the linen closet.

The fog had come in, billowing off the water and drifting along the street, hanging in the skeletal branches of the trees like gray cotton batting. Within it the streetlights were hazy glowing blobs, eerily nebulous.

"Spooky, huh?" Wade said, coming up behind me and putting his arms around me.

I jumped about a foot. Then his arms tightened and I relaxed against him, muzzy from my final glass of wine and feeling safe for the moment from any goblins or ghouls that might be wandering outside.

But not, apparently, from things that go bump in the night. "Why, Wade," I said, turning to him. "I didn't know you cared."

His strong hands pressed into my waist. "Want me to demonstrate?" His voice rumbled in my ear. "Or maybe after the day you've had you'd just rather sleep."

At his touch I felt the rest of the tension go out of me. I'd missed Sam since he moved to his own place but there were advantages to knowing you were alone in the house.

"You do know how to persuade a person," I said into the side of Wade's neck. It smelled like shaving soap. "How about letting me take a shower first?"

He nodded assent. "What say I change the sheets and light some candles while you do?" he said, and let me go.

Whereupon I stood there gasping for a moment while he got out the clean sheets, a burst of faint lavender fragrance coming from the linen closet when he opened the door for them.

Smiling, he kissed me before he went away with them; I just leaned on the windowsill until my heart stopped racing. Which was how I happened to glimpse the barest suggestion of a shape in the shadows across the street.

A darkness against the larger dark, loitering there against a lamppost. Then came the pale flash of an upturned face.

Up toward my windows, the dark hollows of its eyes seeming to search for something. Or . . .

A car turned onto Key Street, its headlights making solid bars of the drifting fog. The lights strobed the place where I'd seen the shape, or thought I had.

I squinted, trying to make out what I'd glimpsed, the sidewalk and the streetlamp where the dark figure had seemed to lurk momentarily visible as the car went by.

Then the night was full of darkness and silence again, the fog so thick it seemed to press against the windowpane like a soft gray hand.

And there was no one in the street below.

• • •

No one at *all . . .*

Hours later I jerked from the clutches of a bad dream into full wide-awake mode, and to the sound of running water.

Torrentially running water. I was alone in the bed and the clock on the dresser said 3:27 A.M. in glowing red numerals.

Hastily pulling on a robe and slippers, I hurried downstairs only to hear another sound underlying the first. After an instant I recognized it as the *thrum-thrum* of a motor, and realized that it was coming from the cellar.

Water and a *pump* motor. Which could only mean . . .

"Wade?" I called down the cellar steps, the dogs pressing anxiously against me on either side.

"Everything's fine," he called back, but it wasn't.

"Step aside, girlie," my father said from behind me, rushing in the back door. Wearing rubber hip boots and a grim expression plus a pair of blue jeans and a flannel pajama shirt, he gripped a hammer in one hand and the biggest pipe wrench I'd ever seen in my life in the other.

Obviously Wade had called him. I'd never seen the wrench before, but from the size of it I thought it was the one you might grab for if you were on a submarine in an emergency.

And I hoped he knew how to use it, because from the sound of the water pouring in, any minute now a submarine was what we were going to need.

Pushing Prill and Monday aside, he hurried past me down the steps. "I got the tools," he told Wade.

"Dad?" I called after him, then nervously followed the sounds of splashing mingled with awful cursing to the third step from the bottom.

The second step was already under water. "Dad, what–?"

And then I saw them, way over in the corner where earlier in the day my father had been working on the foundation.

Only there wasn't much to work on anymore. An entire section of the old granite was missing as if exploded from the wall, leaving a ragged hole about the size of a refrigerator. And crossing the hole where a lot of the old stone used to be was the pipe he'd mentioned.

A *big* pipe, now obviously broken.

With water gushing out of it. I craned my neck so I could see to where the Bisley's lockbox was hidden in the base of a chimney at the other end of the cellar, behind a loose brick.

My emergency cash stash was back there, too, money I kept on hand against disasters. One of which we were certainly having; the rising water hadn't quite reached the height of the loose brick yet but that was the only positive detail I noticed.

"Was anyone planning to wake me?" I asked. "I mean, seeing as the house is apparently about to be floating away..."

That was when I spotted the firehose snaking out of the cellar window. "Under control," Wade gritted out, wielding the enormous pipe wrench my father handed him.

The cellar had French drains, like gutters running along the bottoms of the foundation walls, to carry any seeped-in water back outside. We had sump pumps, too, a pair of them set into the floor just in case.

But none of those devices had ever been meant to handle a flood like this. And anyway Wade had already shut the pumps down, I deduced from the way the fuse box door hung open, no doubt because their motors were (a) electric and (b) already submerged.

"Where's it coming from?" I asked, looking around. A couple of wooden pallets floated merrily near the furnace like makeshift life rafts; right about then I could cheerfully have gotten onto one and floated out to sea.

"Old reservoir," my father replied, busy helping Wade put the wrench on an ancient valve. I'd have helped, too, but from the expressions on their faces I was pretty sure one of them would clobber me with the wrench if I tried.

"Okay," Wade grunted through the gouts of water spurting from the pipe into his face. "See if you can break the..."

Whang! While Wade held the wrench in place my father hit its handle with the hammer, and I don't even want to think about what the impact must have felt like rattling up through their arms.

But the water slowed a little as the rusty old valve turned a fraction. The waterfall sound diminished, first to a trickling and then to a steady *plink-plink* as they got control of the pipe. Eventually the bottom cellar step became visible, then the second one from the bottom.

And so did an item I'd failed to notice earlier, owing to the fact that most of the water in the universe had been flowing into my house. "Just managed to muscle it out and move it before that thing went–"

Kablooie, my father's gesture communicated with perfect clarity when we had all gone back upstairs.

It was a chunk of the foundation, about two feet square and a foot deep. He and Wade had gotten it up the cellar steps; now it sat on the kitchen table; Bella, I thought, would have a fit.

"That old water pipe," he went on, "all that was holding it together anymore was the foundation structure. I took enough of that away, and–"

It seemed that at some time in the distant past new pipes had been put into Key Street and the old ones shut off. But they had clearly not been drained of the water they'd contained.

Until now. "The good news is..." my father began after a restorative gulp of coffee.

I looked around; the kitchen was in chaos, tools everywhere and the dogs prowling around and getting underfoot excitedly. Also a missing fifteen-year-old girl was on the island somewhere, in who knew what sort of ghastly difficulty. And I had a badly collapsed cellar wall, flood damage, and a hunk of the old house shedding mortar chunks onto the kitchen table.

But there was *good* news. I waited hopefully.

"...whatever's in that box didn't get wet," my father said, sounding pleased.

At the moment, unless there was a plane ticket to a resort on the French Riviera in the box, I didn't care about it.

"Wonderful," I replied. It was five in the morning and Wade was already in the shower; so much for a night's sleep. "Um, but listen, Dad, when you've finished your coffee maybe you could..."

"Scram" was the only possible final word to that sentence, and he got it.

"Y'know," he began, rinsing his cup before placing it in the sink–considering the condition of that kitchen it was a little like bailing on the *Titanic* but I thought it was a nice gesture–"I think I'll have another go with the sump pumps in case they're not as wrecked as I think they are. And then get to work chipping some more of the foundation off that box."

So he did, and a few minutes later Wade came downstairs and helped him wrestle the chunk of foundation into the ell, to the big workshop table there.

Hauling out the mop, I heard the mortar drill start up and figured that he was safely occupied for a while, or anyway long enough for me to get the kitchen cleaned up before Bella arrived. But shortly he returned.

"Miscalculated," he reported, holding the drill up to show me a few bits of stuff clinging to the end of the drill bit. "Box is bigger'n I thought."

He pointed. "See that there? Dark stuff's old leather, and the lighter, feathery stuff..."

It was obvious what it was. "Paper," I said, and he nodded.

"Back when this house was bein' built, somebody saw a chance to hide something. Bury it in the foundation, make that part of it super strong, there was a good chance it'd never see the light of day again."

I touched the end of the drill bit lightly. Ash-light shreds of yellowed old paper floated to the floor. Cat Dancing followed their progress with interest.

"Or anyway," he added, "that's what I'm startin' to think."

But the shreds weren't so small that you couldn't make out the ink on them, faded flecks in smooth, cursive little fishhook shapes that to me indicated handwriting.

And the leather meant...

"A book," I said, and my father nodded seriously.

"Someone buried it down there," he agreed. "Buried it there because they didn't want anyone ever to find it."

The question being... why?

Chapter 6

Later that morning I grabbed my toolbox and drove back out to Quoddy Village, leaving my father in charge of handling the cellar debacle. Through the open car window the air was fruity with the tang of rose hips, like the taste of a vitamin C drop.

Pictures of Wanda had been all over the TV news when I turned it on to check the weather report. Dibble's murder gave the story a sensational angle that I thought meant CNN coverage might not be far off, if she didn't show up soon.

And I didn't even want to think about the media circus *that* would be. So far I hadn't even been questioned by the state cops; Bob Arnold's vouching, I realized gratefully, had been effective.

But it was only a matter of time before they got around to me. And my being the daughter of an ex-fugitive they'd all heard of always put a certain speculative gleam in their eye, whether or not I deserved it.

So I wasn't looking forward to it, nor was I happy about the figure I'd seen lurking in the fog, on the street outside my place.

Or... hadn't seen. Because maybe Ellie was right. Maybe I was taking this whole thing too personally. Maybe my imagination had been revved, and I'd really seen nothing at all.

When I rounded the curve on Route 190, a woman came out of one of the houses by the road and set a jack-o'-lantern on the step. The thing had jagged teeth, triangle eyes, and a slit nose, all carved no doubt with an ordinary kitchen knife.

Harmless; amusing, even. But just like the shape I'd thought I'd glimpsed the night before, in the dark that pumpkin would be a frightener.

Thinking this, I pulled up in front of the Quoddy Village house. The small red bungalow appeared even more shabby and forlorn than the last time I'd visited, a couple of the shutters dangling and a clutter of small storm-tossed branches and other debris littering the front walk.

Also, it looked empty. Damn, the white van was gone again, even though I'd called in advance; these people were as hard to get face time with as the inhabitants of a space colony.

Then I looked for the boat, glancing across the road to the short, grass-covered bank bisected by a path leading to the stony beach. Now paved with dark mud, the path ran alongside a cluster of old pilings where the little craft should've been tied up.

And wasn't. Cursing a mental blue streak, I scrambled down to the rocky expanse, stretching fifty yards or so out into the cove at this hour of turning tide. Incoming waves were already transforming the exposed sand flats into a body of water again.

While I scanned for the boat, I pictured the cove in the recent storm, tons of water surging out toward the bay and the even more powerful currents racing there. Today the waves appeared innocent but their cheerful glitter was a malicious ruse; behind their smiles they were ready at a moment's notice to rush the ignorant or careless mariner into a wet grave.

No rowboat. Turning, I slipped on a slick rock and landed on my bottom in the chilly mud.

"Hey, are you all right?"

It was Greg Brand, coming down the grassy bank with his hand held out.

"Yeah," I grumped, struggling up to brush myself off.

His dark hair glinting in the sun, he wore a denim jacket over a white cable-knit sweater, navy corduroys, and new-looking white sneakers.

"Here, let me help you," he offered, but I ignored his hand, wiping at the cold grime and seaweed I was smeared with.

"Boat's gone," I groused. "Is Jenna out rowing again by any chance?"

An odd look passed across his angular features. "No, why?"

I got the impression that my mention of Jenna Durrell made him uncomfortable. *Good,* I thought, remembering his rudeness to me the night of the storm; whatever I could do to make him even more unhappy was fine with me at the moment.

He seemed to remember his behavior, too; apology replacing the unease on his face. "I'm sorry about the other evening, Jacobia. I was... upset. And I'm sorry about your boat, too, of course."

He gestured at the length of line dangling uselessly from an old pier's wooden support, all that remained of a wharf that was active here a hundred years before. "Was that where...?"

I nodded unhappily. The knot had been tied well enough when I'd fastened it onto the cleat on the boat's prow, under Sam's expert supervision.

"I guess maybe I should've come out the other night to check it myself," Greg added. "But with all that was going on..."

I shrugged, relenting; this wasn't his problem. "Not your job," I told him. "Probably it was already gone by then anyway. Jenna might not have known how to tie it."

Or that you were supposed to untie it from the tree, not the prow, I added with a final mental grump.

"Could be," he agreed. "And listen, not to be a tattletale but she's no genius with a pair of oars, either. I was watching her out there one day last week, it's a wonder she even got back without drowning."

"Landlubber, is she?" We climbed the grassy bank together, me still rubbing my muddy hands ineffectively on my pants legs.

"Yeah," he replied. "Way out of her element. You might want to mention to her what a life vest's for, if you do get the boat back. Not that I don't think you will, but..."

"Yeah, yeah," I told him as we reached the road between the beach and the house. At least the mud hadn't soaked right *through* my pants.

"Say," he said suddenly, "is that it way over there?"

I followed his gesture without optimism but sure enough it was, aground on the embankment below the causeway about a mile distant.

"Fabulous," I exhaled with glum sarcasm. "Now I'll have to drive out in Wade's truck and grab it, haul it up into the truck bed somehow," I said, and started away from him.

But he had another idea. "Why don't we just walk over there and row it back, the two of us? It's solidly aground, looks like, so it might take some muscle, but I can help you get it down to the water," he offered.

It was a decent suggestion and I might've accepted even if I didn't have the sense he was making it only because he wanted to talk to me. Maybe put over his own version of all that was going on, I suspected uncharitably, but not here at the house where one or more of the other tenants might show up any minute.

"Okay," I said, causing him to look confident and me to feel strongly that if I had anything to do with it, Gregory Brand was about to get more conversation than he'd bargained for.

Starting now. "So what's with the witch stuff?" I asked when we had set off. At least it was a good day for a walk, sunny and breezy with the water still twinkling under the clear sky. "I mean," I went on, "I wouldn't have figured you for a trainer in the occult arts. Or if you were, you'd have gone for a little higher level of student."

That got a laugh. See, when I wanted to I could behave well, too. "Long story," he said.

Yeah, no doubt. He had an even stride, faster than my usual but still easy to keep up with; once I'd gotten accustomed to it I just matched his steps and used him for a pace car.

"I'm actually here under a little bit of pretense," he went on. "As I guess maybe you've already figured."

Oh, no kidding, I thought, saying nothing. Leaving a great big silence for other people to fill works wonderfully well, I've found.

And this time was no exception. But what Greg Brand said next nearly made me trip over my own feet.

"I've known Gene Dibble for years," he admitted. "I saw you noticing my reaction when you mentioned his name. It was a shock."

Uh-huh. More silence on my part.

"Truth is, the two of us were crooks together back in Massachusetts," he went on. "Scam artists, I guess you'd have to call us. But I swear I didn't know he was coming to the house, or about the drugs," he added urgently. "And I didn't kill him."

"Oh," I said mildly. One foot in front of the other. "So that's what this is, the whole private seminar thing? A scam, you pretend to teach people how to . . . ?"

As if I hadn't already figured that out, too. "Access their inner earth-goddess," he confirmed, his voice mingling matter-of-fact honesty with contempt for his victims.

"A little Wicca, a pinch of mythology, New Age crystals, massage oils, and aromatherapy," he recited, "plus a whole lot of candles . . . Did you know there's a special candle you can burn if you want somebody dead?"

I did, actually. Back in the city there'd been a Santeria shop whose dusty windows, displaying a range of potions, powders, and magical charms, I'd stared into regularly for a time. Sam was almost two then and Victor was dating a cardiology nurse, coming home only to change his shirts and criticize my mothering skills.

"Kind of a big coincidence, though, you have to admit," I told Greg. "I mean Eugene Dibble being here, and now *you* being . . ."

He laughed once more, but without mirth. "Gene had mentioned the place a few times, talked about growing up here, in the old days when we were doing our thing together. I had no idea he'd come back here to live again, though," he insisted.

"So what, you just threw a dart at a map?" At least I knew now why Brand had decided to come clean to me.

If he was. But as things stood, no cop in the world was going to believe he hadn't killed Gene Dibble, his old partner in crime, and never mind that supposedly Greg had been in the van with the others when Dibble died.

Alibis, an old cop buddy of mine once told me, are made to be broken. To have even a hope of being thought truthful, Brand needed people on his side.

People like me. He shook his head dismally. "Like I said, I remembered Gene mentioning it. And I needed some really out-of-the-way place where we could..."

I stopped. "We? You mean somebody else is working this with you? Who?"

We'd reached Toll Bridge Road, a long curving lane with salt marsh on both sides. Here the incoming tide surged under the roadway through a series of large culverts, foaming as it came.

He frowned. "Hetty Bonham," he said reluctantly at last.

We started walking again. "She's hit hard times, I thought if I kept her around maybe I could–"

I made a rude noise. " 'Scuse me, Greg, but you don't strike me as exactly the philanthropist type. And Hetty..."

Well, not to put too fine a point on it, but Hetty was an over-the-hill, bleached-blonde harridan with grandiose delusions of youth.

"What's in it for you?" I demanded.

His pace didn't slow as we headed uphill toward the Quoddy Village parade grounds. Remnants of broken sidewalk showed where the Navy once mustered in full dress, row on row flanking the bright water that at the time might have hidden enemy periscopes.

"Hetty's my stepsister," Brand said reluctantly. "My dad married her mother."

Now the Navy was long gone–they'd had a hospital, stores, office and classroom facilities, the whole nine yards in addition to the housing, which was never meant to be permanent–but the area still attracted a blip of military interest now and then.

Just ahead on the left loomed the old factory building that had until recently made woolen blankets, for example, but was now an assembly site for chemical protection suits contracted for by the U.S. Army. "And my father was, shall we say, not opposed to having a young girl in the house," Greg said.

Putting a light, ironic gloss on it, but at his words I felt myself growing more alert on several levels. Did he know he was beginning to trespass on one of my personal danger zones?

Not consciously. I'd never revealed much to anyone about my childhood-from-hell, and if I had confided in someone it wouldn't have been Mr. Smoothie here. But a good scammer's instincts, I knew, were as sensitive as an insect's feelers.

"Dad thought I didn't understand, but I did. Even before it happened I knew he married Hetty's mom to get at Hetty," he said.

We reached Route 190. Across Passamaquoddy Bay the rolling hills of New Brunswick loomed greenish-brown in the foreground, fading to heather cloudlike shapes in the distance.

"Hell, I was a fourteen-year-old boy," he went on. "If there was anything like that going on within a mile, you bet I knew it was happening."

"And about this you did...?"

"Nothing," he replied quietly. "Dad sent me off to an elite boarding school the minute he twigged to the idea that I knew."

Having had an adolescent boy around the house myself, I thought Greg's account of his teenaged awareness of sexual matters sounded authentic. Not that I believed it, necessarily, because another thing my money days had taught me was that guys like Greg could make up plausible stories at a moment's notice, never mind with as much time as he'd had to think about it.

"But later," he went on, "when we were grown up, I hooked up with her again and tried to watch out for her a little. As much as I could. Hetty doesn't," he added with a wry smile, "always make it easy."

"So Hetty's just playing along, pretending to be one of your students of the occult?" I asked, and he nodded.

"Makes people relax a little more if they think they're not the only ones drinking the Kool-Aid," he agreed, and of course I didn't deck him right there on the gravel shoulder of Route 190.

But I wanted to. Then as we made our way along the side of the road the cab of an eighteen-wheeler blew by, spinning dust and sand; I blinked grit from my eyes.

Another truck roared past. "Let's get away from the road," I said, leading him down a trail between stands of long grass, whippy chokecherry saplings, and elderberry bushes. Here the road noise faded and the remaining few leaves were dusty crimson and purple, lending a pinkish glow to the light filtering in through silvery branches. Chickadees called sharply, fluttering from twig to twig in the underbrush, always just out of sight.

I steered the talk back to recent events. "And Marge Cathcart's the intended victim of your scam this time? How'd you pick her, a computer-dating thing?"

In my opinion, meeting up with some stranger you found on the Internet is equivalent to drawing a dotted line on your throat, with a little legend alongside it that reads "cut here."

But people do it all the time. "No, I advertised in a local shopping news," Greg replied matter-of-factly. "You get a lot of replies from those, and you can pick and choose better than if you have to do it by e-mail."

He pushed through a tangle of wild raspberry canes, keeping his hands high to avoid being scratched. "Marge," he added, "had both of the qualities I was looking for: gullible and rich."

At my expression he added, "Not filthy rich. Too much money, people tend to have professional advisors."

Correct; advisors like I'd been. If any of my clients had come in with a story about someone like Greg, I'd have popped the top on my industrial-sized spray can of Raid Financial-Parasite Killer.

"But her husband left her plenty comfortable enough when he died," Brand finished. "I figured I'd check her out some more at this seminar, see if she's marriage material. After all, Wanda's not going to be around home forever. Pretty soon she'll go off to school, or..."

He eyed me, I supposed to see how I was taking this; I kept my face carefully blank and my fists, both of which still wanted badly to pummel him, stuffed in my pockets.

"And if not marriage," he went on when I didn't explode, "then maybe just special friends. It's surprising how much money you can get out of someone like that once she really trusts you."

Not to me it wasn't. A new thought struck me. "How'd Jenna Durrell get involved?"

He made a rude noise. "I wish she weren't. *Especially* now, the nosy..."

Shorebirds patrolled the beach stones, their heads cocking this way and that as they scanned the crannies for tasty morsels at the edge of the advancing water.

"Because she's an ex-cop?" I asked as our feet hit sand. The outgoing tide had left parallel lines of foam, now dried to faint white tracery.

"No," he replied vehemently. "Because she's an ex-cop who's decided to become an *investigative reporter,* for God's sake, and she's got a little *notebook.*"

We stepped out to the rocks, gleaming wet now. "When she answered the ad I knew right away there was something wrong about her," he told me.

Too bad Marge hadn't known the same about him. Ahead, thick green ribbons of seaweed stretched, studded with the picked-over shells of crabs that the seabirds had made meals of.

"Stay out of the weeds," I advised him, stepping carefully through the slippery stuff onto a strip of glistening, pea-sized pebbles, then glancing back over my shoulder at him.

He just stood there studying the water. A few small islands were already in the process of being swallowed by the tide. "Wow, it really does rise fast, doesn't it?"

"Billions and billions of gallons," I intoned, thinking that what he'd revealed about Jenna solved one mystery, anyway. Join a group, receive secret knowledge, go on a mystical retreat... none of that fit the brisk, competent image I'd formed of her.

"You checked background on Jenna?" I asked.

"Yeah. Ex-cop, worked undercover, drug stuff and so on. When she started writing she put up a Web site with a bio."

He slipped, then caught himself before he could fall. "Even before she quit being a cop she had a few little things published and they were all exposés–crooked car repair, pyramid schemes, all stuff like that."

And he hadn't wanted to turn her away in case rejection made her feel even nosier, probably.

"So tell me," he finished, "if I'd worked at it, could I have gotten any more unlucky?"

Nope. "And you're letting me in on all this because . . . ?" I knew what I thought; I wanted to hear what he had to say about it.

"Because any minute now the cops are going to connect me and Eugene Dibble," Brand answered grimly. "It's only a matter of time, and when that happens . . ."

Right again. He knew as well as I did that dead guys and the live guys who used to be their crime colleagues go together like cookies and cream in the whodunnit department.

And as I'd suspected, he was telling me about it in hopes he could use me somehow. "You ever do any time together?" I asked. "You and Dibble?"

Pushed up onto a mound of seaweed by the last high water, the boat sat a couple of hundred feet away. I hoped the oars and life vests were still in her.

"Yeah." He clambered ahead of me toward the vessel. "Went up on fraud charges, did the bit in Springfield, Massachusetts. Six months."

Which meant that they could be linked in the computers as known associates. "Well, Greg, I'd have to say you've got yourself a serious problem."

It wasn't even high tide yet and the boat's keel was already beginning to float. We'd gotten here just in time.

And the vests and oars *were* still in her. "Here," I said, reaching in and tossing him the larger vest. "You tighten it by yanking on the straps across your..."

But he'd already pulled it on. "I've done a lot of this," he said assuredly, sliding the boat toward deeper water.

He swung a long leg over the side to put one foot amidships, then used both hands to steady the little vessel. "Hop in," he invited.

So I did, as he pushed smoothly off with the other leg and swung it in, too, all in one practiced motion and without scraping the boat's bottom. Next he chucked the oars into the oarlocks while I sat facing him in the bow; moments later we were away.

"I didn't mean to make you do all the work," I called as he hauled on the oars again.

"Don't worry about it," he responded. "Once we get out in the current it'll be a piece of cake. Sail us home, won't even have to... Whoa!"

Which was when those smiling waves showed their sharp teeth. At the center of the channel the water churned with the force of the tide pouring in full bore; he struggled for control, then got it and grinned happily.

"I used to do this all the time with an old lady in Rhode Island," he shouted over the wind. "Rich as sin. I was trying to get her to give me power of..."

Attorney, he meant to finish, but instead the boat's bow hit the current again a hair sooner than he'd expected and swerved whip-crackingly into it.

"Urk," I said, unnerved. The sudden change of course flung me half over the gunwale even though I was clinging to it with both hands, struggling to stay upright.

"Hang on!" Brand called out unnecessarily, spray hurling into his face as he pulled hard first on one oar and then on the other. Then as water slammed the side of the boat lurchingly, "Lean!" he shouted. "Lean the other way!"

The bow flew up; behind Brand's desperately rowing figure the transom fell low and to the left, dipping suddenly under the green water. I threw my weight to the right, feeling air time and the conflicting forces of tide and current melding murderously around me.

My only grip on the boat was through my hands, still fastened to the rail in the clench of imminent death. The water rose greenly toward me, smelling of whatever is kept way down at the very bottom in Davy Jones's locker; they'll have to cut my hands off this boat when they find me, I thought.

If they ever did. If our bodies didn't get tangled in all the seaweed and just hang there, feasted upon by marine life until our skeletons fell apart and drifted bone by bone to the rocks below....

The boat fell suddenly as if dropped from the sky, its flat bottom slapping the water with a *smack!* My butt slammed the hard wooden seat with similar force as we finished coming around, the jolt hurtling up through my spine. Then aligning itself with the powerful current once more, the boat shot forward, nearly tumbling me back out over the bow again.

But not quite. The boat righted, settled itself.

"Hah!" Brand shouted out exultantly, his dark hair plastered to his forehead by the spray and his eyes alight.

"Oh, that was a close one!" he laughed, lifting the oars.

Which was when I understood why he was a con man. Like most of them, he was hooked on risk-taking behaviors. This being a condition with which I, having survived and thrived in the money business, was also reasonably familiar. "Yeah," I gasped when I could breathe again. "Too close."

But after listening to his story I'd gotten the feeling that this time, Greg Brand had grabbed a little more gusto than he could comfortably handle. And when we got back to the cove and pulled the boat up to high ground where the tide couldn't reach it, I said so.

"You should call the state cops, tell them what you told me, and then cooperate in any way possible," I advised seriously.

The answering look on his face was that of a kid being urged to try broccoli just one more time. It was almost enough to make me feel sorry for him.

Almost. "I know it's not an attractive prospect," I conceded. "But d'you really want *them* to have to come to *you*?"

We walked up toward the rental house. "Yeah, I guess you're right," he replied discouragedly. "I just thought..."

Sure; he just thought that he was going to become my new best friend and then I'd be able to put in a good word for him with Bob Arnold or even with the state guys, me being a local and all. But like they say, my mother didn't raise any stupid kids.

Actually, she didn't raise any kids at all. She died before she could, but that's another story.

"Where are they all, anyway?" I asked Greg, meaning the other tenants. The house still radiated emptiness and the white van hadn't returned.

"Out searching for Wanda." His tone conveyed how useless he thought this was, and how little he cared. But even as he spoke the white van pulled into the driveway, and the three women of the ill-fated group–Jenna Durrell, Hetty Bonham, and Marge Cathcart–got out.

Wanda wasn't with them. Marge looked devastated, pale and shaky as if all the blood had been let out of her; it occurred to me that if this went on much longer she would need a doctor.

"Have you heard something, have you found her?" she babbled as soon as she saw me.

I shot Greg Brand a glare that should've shriveled him in his tracks; bottom line, this was all his fault. But he didn't seem to notice. "No," I told Marge gently. "Not yet."

Her hair was as messy as a tight, graying permanent wave can ever be, her housedress-and-cardigan costume hung disheveled from her slumped shoulders, and her eyes were red with weeping.

"And since it's been thirty-six hours or so now," I began, "I think you ought to–"

"We talked to the state cops again when we were in town," Jenna put in briskly. "They were at the Eastport police station."

Heavying out on Bob Arnold, probably; I imagined the chief's delight at the visit.

"I told Marge it was about time we should check in with them again," Jenna went on. "But there was no news about Wanda. That's how we got delayed," she added, glancing at her wristwatch. "Sorry."

"That's okay," I said. "You're here now. I'm going to do a couple of the repairs you asked for the other night, but I also want to see Wanda's room. And," I told Marge, "I've got a few questions for you."

In response she nodded despairingly at me, waited while I got the toolbox, then tottered beside me up the front walk and into the house.

• • •

Inside, Marge excused herself for a moment. I took the opportunity to corner Jenna, who was in the kitchen making coffee.

"So have you done any research on the rest of them?" I asked her, hefting the toolbox onto the counter. "I mean besides Gregory Brand?"

She shot a knowing look at me. "So he made me for a snoop, huh?"

"Before you even got here." The faucet dripped steadily; opening the toolbox, I hoped this job wouldn't require the washer I'd already used at Luanne Moretti's.

"Figures," Jenna said darkly. "Clever little shit, our Mr. Brand." She pulled the kitchen's swinging door closed.

Even with the electricity back on, the little house was as gloomy and chilly as ever, made even less inviting by the clutter of loose-leaf folders and cheaply reproduced booklets all over every flat surface.

Your Hidden Powers, one cover read; *Behold Your Magic,* read another. I glanced around for the one called *Stick Your Finger Down Your Throat,* but couldn't find it.

"I guess the housework doesn't get done by magic, either," I observed as the coffeemaker began burbling.

Neatened up, the place was at least a shelter. But now with dishes in the sink, emptied food packages overflowing the trash, and dirty cups littering the counters, it was becoming a hovel.

I moved some of the dishes aside, turned the water off under the sink, and started on the repair.

"Marge was in a hurry to get going this morning," Jenna explained, but not with a lot of concern. "And I'm sorry but I'm not doing maid duty for this bunch."

She took the last two clean cups from the cabinet, offered me one. I shook my head, busy with the faucet handle screws. At least they weren't rusted.

"You didn't answer my question," I pointed out. Another day, another faucet, but it is a rule of old-house fix-up that no two jobs are ever quite the same. Even if they seem that way at the start, they won't be when you finish.

For instance, this time *both* handles were leaking. Jenna poured coffee for herself. "Did I check up on all of them? Yeah, sure I did," she said. Then, "Have you seen the paper yet?"

She pushed the morning's issue of the *Bangor Daily News* across the counter at me. *Missing Girl Search Continues,* read one headline. *Downeast Death Investigated,* read another.

"It says they got a .38 slug out of Dibble's head," Jenna said, waving at the second story. "But that they won't be able to do much with it."

I turned inquiringly to her. "It's not like on TV, you know," she explained, "where the coroner gets a pristine bullet out with a forceps, ten minutes later they know the gun and who it's registered to."

I did know, actually. In the operating room, Victor had evicted lots of bullets from the unfortunate skulls in which they'd been lodged. Half the time he'd had to dig them out in pieces; many of the others were so badly misshapen someone might as well have taken a hammer to them.

"Anyway, Hetty's a piece of work, too," Jenna continued. "Plenty of convictions, for fraud, mostly. What d'you want to bet they were really Greg's idea but he let her carry the load?"

I nodded, pushing the paper away. The headline story about the missing girl said a group of local mothers were putting flyers together for store windows and bulletin boards, and that an Amber Alert had been issued.

But there was nothing else in there I didn't already know. I fished around in the packet of faucet washers; two of them fit, but one of the screws I'd removed was stripped. I searched the toolbox, hoping there was a matching one in it.

"Any drug problems, either one of them?" I asked Jenna.

"Not that I could find out, which means probably not."

She drank some coffee. "Hetty was in California for a while, acting in movies. X-rated ones, Greg's listed as the producer. Which I figure must mean the bankroll."

I glanced queryingly at her. "He's this black-sheep kind of guy," she explained, "rich family. In real estate development out West."

So much for good old Greg looking out for his abuse-scarred stepsister. Or whatever she really was; I'd had a feeling there was more to that story, too. Then a puzzle piece clicked into place in my head, just as the toolbox yielded up a pair of possibles in the faucet-screw department.

I held the screws up alongside the stripped one. "*That* Brand family, huh?" The smaller screw looked better for the job. "Interesting. I hadn't made the connection."

But now I did. In the old days when I'd navigated big money the way Greg Brand had just piloted my rowboat through wild water, Brands International's head money guy was in the news for raiding the Brand family trust funds, with special emphasis on some that were really just overgrown piggy banks.

But Brand kids got lawyers pretty much the way other kids got driver's licenses, the minute they turned sixteen. The lawyers let it be known that the kids didn't want to own ranch land in Utah or silver mines in Colorado; they wanted the cash.

Got it, too, via some tactics that would've done their old man proud if the fallout from the scandal–it turned out that the trust-fund raider wasn't exactly working alone–hadn't ended up giving him the stroke that killed him.

Talk about your basic evil empire. "To be a black sheep in the Brand family," I remarked, "you'd need to be Jack the Ripper at least. Anything less, they'd figure it's just business as usual."

I dropped the screw in, tightened it; so far, so fine. "Don't you want to know," Jenna asked, "why the rich kid turned into a rip-off artist?"

What the heck, she'd done all that research work. "Sure."

"Greg and old man Brand had a falling-out. Join the business or get cut off. It's all been written about, anyone can find it," she added. "I guess Greg didn't like wearing a three-piece suit, or something."

Yeah, or something. Then a different thought hit me. "Listen, Jenna, about the boat."

As I explained what had happened she bit her lip, looking embarrassed. "I'm so sorry, I had no idea that rope wasn't–"

I cut her off. "No, that's okay, the line was my problem. I got it back, anyway."

"You did?" Relief brightened her face. "Oh, that's–"

"But I need you to be sure you wear the life vest if you take it out again, okay? Because really, the water is very . . ."

That much Greg Brand had been right about. Jenna was already nodding agreement.

"You're right," she admitted. "I should've worn it. And you know, I think I won't be taking your boat out anymore anyway. They've got some rentals down at Quoddy Marine, I saw when we were in town. I might just try paddling around in the boat basin. Get my sea legs," she added a little shamefacedly.

"That's a fine plan," I said, remembering Greg's comment about her seamanship. Besides, I liked the idea of her being on someone else's conscience if she went overboard.

Turning the water on again, I discovered my screw choice had been correct. *One down, one to go;* I closed the toolbox, turned my attention reluctantly to the electrical problem.

The first step in fixing it was going into the crawl space under the house, to the fuse box. That meant hauling the toolbox and a flashlight through a trapdoor and then down a ladder, over a dirt floor to the far wall where the fuse box hung, while trying not to crack my skull open—there was hardly any headroom down there—*and* not running into anything in the near darkness.

Just as I put a foot through the trapdoor in the back hall, however, Marge reappeared. She'd combed her hair and pressed a cold cloth to her face; dents from the washcloth's nubs had left shallow troughs in the reddened skin of her eyelids.

And she'd put on a different cardigan; seeing me, she straightened her shoulders under it.

"Come on, then," she said. She led me to Wanda's room and stepped aside to wave me ahead of her.

In the doorway, embarrassment made me pause. Scant daylight filtering through a pair of too-small windows revealed where the fake-wood paneling and scarred wallboard met up with the uneven floors and cheap, poorly installed orange shag carpet.

"What a dump," I said, stricken. Ellie and I had meant to tear it all out, but now as I noted the new water stains on the ceiling—oh, goody, a roof leak—it hit me that maybe we ought to have the house torn down instead.

"I'm ashamed that we rented this place to you," I blurted. The bed had only one thin blanket; I wondered if Wanda had been cold. The linens and furniture had come with the house, and though we'd done our best to clean the place, it was still awfully shabby and depressing.

"Anything different about it?" I asked her. Suddenly the crawl space looked positively attractive; all I wanted was to flee this grim little chamber. And Marge's presence was about as energizing as a dose of poison gas.

"And Wanda's things, are any missing?"

She frowned. "She had a little backpack that I don't see anywhere. And she used to read by flashlight, I'd see it glowing in here at night but I don't see it now."

The only light was a bare bulb hanging from the center of the ceiling, controlled by a switch near the door.

"And . . . boots," Marge murmured, her forehead wrinkling. "She had a pair of hiking boots but they're not here. And her jacket's gone."

"But not her pills."

"What?" Marge seemed startled for a moment, as if she'd been thinking about something else. A wince of pain crossed her features fleetingly, then vanished. "Yes, her diabetes pills. Here." She produced a small orange bottle from her cardigan pocket.

"How critical is it that she take these?" I squinted at the writing on the label. Sulfa-gluca-something-or-other was the chemical name for whatever had been prescribed for Wanda, to be taken twice a day.

Marge bit her lip worriedly. "Very important. It's a new drug, not insulin like most kids with the disease have to take."

"So she's not collapsed somewhere in a diabetic coma?" I didn't know much about that kind of problem–Victor's harangues, back when we were married, stuck strictly to surgery when they weren't focused on my child-rearing deficiencies–but I did know untreated diabetes could be fatal.

And although it was harsh to ask under the circumstances, I needed to know. "Talk to me, Marge. Is this a medical emergency on top of everything else?"

She shook her head. "I don't think so. Not yet. Her form of diabetes isn't the usual kind kids get. Most youngsters end up on insulin just about right away." Wistful affection smoothed her features. "Trust Wanda not to do things the usual way. Under normal conditions her body makes enough insulin to get along, as long as she eats right and takes the pill every morning and night."

The smile vanished. "But this isn't..."

Right, these weren't normal conditions. This time of year it got cold out at night just as soon as it got dark. And as I'd wondered before, who knew what–or even if–Wanda was eating?

"You have more of these?" I asked Marge, and when she said she did I dropped the bottle into my own pocket. "In case I run across her I can give her one of them right away," I said.

"Yes," she replied gratefully. "That would be–"

There was nothing to be grateful for yet. "The bottom line," I interrupted, "is that Wanda could have left on her own and not brought her pills along. The jacket and boots argue that way, too, and so does the missing backpack. But I'm still not so sure that she did."

Marge went on looking relieved until my point penetrated. Then her face crumpled once more. "You... you mean you think someone might have *taken* Wanda?"

"I'm wondering about it," I admitted. "Where was Wanda that morning, on the day of the storm? Jenna said she thought she was with you, Hetty, and Greg Brand, out in the van somewhere."

Marge put it together. "When that man was shot in the house, you mean. It... it could have happened while we were out."

She took a shuddery breath. "But Wanda *wasn't* with us. She wanted to stay home and make a nest for that little bat. She was here, alone in her room..."

Which reminded me, where was the bat? I didn't see it, or a nest for it either. "Did you tell the police that?"

She shook her head, then persisted anxiously, "I never even realized... she never... you mean she might've *seen*... ?"

"It's not certain," I said firmly, feeling a pang of guilt for adding to her worries. "Could she have gone home? I mean, back to–"

"No. I called the neighbors, they checked. And the parents of her friends. She does have friends," Marge added wistfully.

"Of course she does," I said, taking pity on her. "And if someone had grabbed her they wouldn't have been very likely to wait around for her to put a traveling kit together, would they?"

Or one for the bat. "No. No, I suppose they wouldn't," Marge agreed.

So there we were. Some things argued one way, some another. "Marge, how *do* you and Wanda communicate? Because if she doesn't speak or write..."

I tried to think about a life without words, stopped trying as Marge answered almost cheerfully again.

"Oh, she has receptive language. That means she understands what you say," she added at my blank look. "And she's very expressive when she wants to be. With her hands, her eyes...she gets her message across."

As she had tried to the night of the storm, possibly? Again I saw Wanda gazing imploringly at me, recalled my decision to ignore the strange little girl with the bat peeping tranquilly from between her fingers.

But at the time, she'd had her mother there with her; she hadn't been my responsibility, I reminded myself with an effort as I left the girl's room.

Marge followed; turning back, I saw yet another repair job. All by itself the closet door had drifted open. Like the other doors in the place, it needed rehanging to make it level: *hammer, chisel, new wood screws*...

"I just can't picture her taking off alone," said Marge. "In a storm, when it's so awfully dark out–where would she even go?"

I had no idea. But by then I was only half listening anyway, because the closet had a shelf and on the shelf lay a baglike thing made of soft, shiny fabric, too small for a laundry bag but with the same kind of drawstring at the top.

Seeing it, I knew suddenly that Wanda hadn't been cold, and I knew why. She'd had a sleeping bag; probably she'd used it for a blanket. The thing on the shelf was its carry sack.

She'd taken the sleeping bag, then, but maybe she'd been in too much of a hurry to stuff the bag in its sack, even though it would have been much easier to transport that way.

More runaway evidence? I thought of mentioning it to Marge, decided not to. It would only confuse her more.

Just as it was doing to me. "Has Wanda ever done anything unpredictable before? Or . . . maybe the two of you had an argument that night that I didn't know about?"

I was grasping at straws. But if she'd gone on her own there was a reason. Marge shook her head slowly. "She resisted taking her pill. But no more than usual. And she's never run away."

Her posture straightened in defense of her daughter even as another wince of discomfort pinched her face. "She's perfectly intelligent. Just because she doesn't speak . . . we've been to a lot of specialists but no one's been able to tell me why. She's unusual, yes. But not disturbed, not poorly adjusted, or . . ."

Her voice broke. "It's my fault she was here. Such a fool I was, I believed that awful Mr. Brand's lies. Jenna told me about him while we were out. I . . . I believed he was going to *help* her!"

"Now, now," I said, mentally scolding myself for what I'd been thinking about her earlier, that she'd been a fool to come here. It wasn't so unusual to do desperate things when you were trying to help your child.

I'd done plenty of them. "Try to stay positive," I added.

As I said this Hetty emerged from the other bedroom, where she'd obviously been listening to us. In addition to the bungalow's many other flaws, the walls were polite fictions in the privacy department.

"Come on, honey," Hetty crooned, guiding Marge toward the

kitchen. "Let's have coffee, you'll feel better. You don't want Wanda to see you like this when she comes home, do you?"

Which was exactly the right thing to say, and it made me feel bad about my earlier opinion of Hetty, too.

"I know, we'll sit down and do your horoscope," Hetty went on as the two women moved away. "At bad times like this we always can find our way with the stars to guide us."

Too bad the stars couldn't do anything about that fuse box. But if I didn't check it I'd just have to do it later, so I grudgingly hauled the toolbox down the ladder to the crawl space.

It was like going into a grave: smelling of damp earth and pitch dark until I stepped off the ladder and had a hand free for a flashlight. The yellowish beam didn't stop hanging cobwebs from exploring my face with their shudder-producing tendrils.

Still, I made it to the far wall, opened the fuse box, and soon discovered the reason why Hetty Bonham's hair dryer, Greg Brand's shaver, and Jenna Durrell's electric toothbrush–not to mention the overhead light and the pair of fluorescents on either side of the bathroom mirror–had suddenly stopped working.

Blown fuse. And of course none of them had come down to try correcting the problem, which was annoying, too. But at least I could repair it without much trouble.

Lined up atop the fuse box was a row of fresh fuses in the sizes the various circuits required. Choosing the correct one was a simple matter of matching the blown fuse's color with its similarly color-coded replacement.

In other words, wham-bam. I changed the fuse and dropped the old one in my pocket, and when I was done I aimed the flashlight up into the wiring above the fuse box, just checking to make sure everything looked shipshape.

Which was when the huge spider dropped directly into my hair and skittered across my face. "Bleargggh!" I shrieked, or something very like it, and dropped the flashlight to free my hands for wild rubbing, brushing, and swatting motions while my legs did the little hopping dance my nervous system threw in for good measure.

Gradually I stopped, alert for the tickle of spidery feet. When that didn't happen, I groped very cautiously on the dirt floor for the flashlight, found it, and switched it back on–amazingly it hadn't broken–moving the beam over the earth to search for the offending creature.

Relieved, I saw no sign of it. But on the floor under the fuse box I spotted a small white object.

Spider egg, I thought with another reflexive shudder; squinting harder, though, I saw that in fact it wasn't one. Spider eggs are round, and they don't have a line scored across them to make them easier to divide into halves.

I picked the thing up between my fingers, examined it by flashlight though by now I already knew what it must be; there had been a recent article on rural drug abuse in one of the news magazines Wade and I subscribed to, with pictures.

Some of the photographs had been taken in Eastport, others in a pharmaceutical laboratory.

What I'd found was an oxycontin tablet.

• • •

When I left a little while later, Hetty Bonham followed me to my car. "There's something you should hear," she told me. "About the dead guy, Eugene Dibble. You know much about him?"

I stopped with my hand on the car door. "Yep. Rabble-rousing self-styled fundamentalist preacher, not of the goodness-in-his-heart variety," I recited.

"He talked as if fire and brimstone were his personal weapons systems," I went on. "Liked to hang out with a lot of other losers and get them all fired up against somebody, too. Why, what else should I know?" The oxycontin tab was in my toolbox.

"That he was married before," Hetty said, her voice hardening. "Before his wife here in Eastport, I mean. First one divorced him after he was convicted of abusing her young daughter."

She eyed me, gauging my reaction to this, then went on. "His step-daughter. Girl of about fifteen, I heard about it later from Greg. Dibble got three years, all but six months suspended. So I guess he had some pretty good reasons for wanting people around here to keep focused on the bad stuff other folks did. That way he was more sure of keeping the spotlight off himself."

"I guess so," I said slowly, stunned by this news. "Anyone else know about this?"

Hetty shook her head. In daylight the little lines around her eyes were cruelly visible. "Around here? Not from me. I'll tell you what, though," she declared, throwing her blonde head back angrily.

"One," she ticked off on a long, crimson-tipped finger, "if I'd ever faced him with a gun in my hand I'd have shot the son of a bitch myself. Six months, my ass. And two, I've been waiting for Wanda to come back on her own. Because of the jacket and backpack and the sleeping bag, I really thought she would."

So she'd noticed what I had: that the missing items spelled runaway. Just . . . not quite straightforwardly enough.

"But it's starting to seem like she isn't going to," Hetty went on. "And that's not the kind of thing I signed up for, some poor little girl in trouble. It's why I figured you'd better know about Gene Dibble, too."

She straightened determinedly. "So when I go back in that house I'm telling Greg to call your police chief, tell him everything."

"Right," I said, "that's just what he should do."

"Because Gene Dibble was a damned child molester and I don't care what anyone says, those guys never change. What they do is find other creeps to hang out with, share their *enthusiasms*."

"And if someone *took* Wanda—" I was thinking aloud.

"That's right," she replied tightly. I thought about what Greg Brand had told me about Hetty; if it was true, she had her own good reasons for hating guys like Dibble.

"Because if some *other* bad-guy creep took Wanda, why else would he be hanging around to even know about her, other than that he was here with Gene?" she demanded.

Again it was what I'd thought, but now the theory had taken on a stomach-turning twist. Hetty stared across the wide cove as if reading her next words off the water.

"While they were here they *saw* her," she said flatly, her opinion once more mirroring my own.

"Think Greg had anything to do with it?" I asked. Might that account for that pill being in the cellar? Maybe he'd hidden them down there, dropped one somehow.

"You mean do I think Greg knew the drugs were here? Or brought them himself?" She shrugged expressively. "I doubt it. It's not something Greg would do, let someone else complicate his own scene like that."

By, she meant, ending up dead. I leaned against the car.

"But," she went on, "I can picture what else might've happened. One guy wants to take Wanda. The other doesn't. Partner says screw you, I'll take the drugs *and* the girl. Shoots Eugene..."

I put a hand up. "But then *doesn't* take her?"

"He worries someone might've heard the gunfire, books out of here without anything." She brushed off my objection.

Hetty was turning out to be a far more detailed thinker than I'd given her credit for. I completed the scenario. "Comes back later but by then the drugs are gone, confiscated by the cops."

Except for that one tablet, of course.

"But Wanda's still here," she pointed out. "His consolation prize."

All of which was still only speculation, but it intensified my darkest worry. I drove home discouraged, filled with a sharp new foreboding about the possible whereabouts of Wanda Cathcart.

And about her possible condition.

Chapter 7

Life in my old house has a habit of going on in my absence whether I like it or not, and when I got home that day my first reaction to its progress was *negatron,* as Sam would've put it.

I'd stopped at Bob Arnold's office but he wasn't there and I didn't want to leave the pill without talking to him. So I went on up Key Street until I noticed that an enormous metal Dumpster had been deposited in my front yard.

I'd ordered it thinking a Dumpster would make it easier to perform step two of the porch-rebuilding project; i.e., disposing of the debris. But due to the press of recent events, I hadn't yet completed step one: turning the porch into debris in the first place. That was why half an hour later I was out there swinging the sledgehammer.

Or it was part of the reason. The other part was that if I didn't take a break from thinking about Wanda, my head was going to explode. It should've made me feel better to know that she probably wouldn't die of a medical problem before she got found. But it didn't, and I didn't know what that oxycontin tablet meant, either.

Nothing good, though. So I'd thrown myself into physical work, hoping it might help calm the emotional stuff down. But this plan turned out to have its drawbacks, too; when the hammer hit a porch board, the nails were meant to loosen and the board was supposed to rise up so I could pull it free with the end of the crowbar.

Only the plan didn't account for two facts: (a) the hammer was very heavy, and (b) the nails were the solidest parts of the old porch. Thus each time the sledgehammer connected with a board, my feet came off the ground.

It was a classic example of too much weight at one end (the whole porch) and not enough (me) at the other. I did manage to chip off a few more small rotten bits but they weren't enough to fill up that Dumpster.

Not by a long shot. Soon I was standing there wondering if maybe I could just hire a construction crane from the marine terminal and get it to deposit the old porch into the receptacle whole, which was where I'd gotten in the project when my father drove up in his battered pickup truck.

"Set yourself a task, I see," he observed, sticking one big hand into an overall pocket and strolling over to me. His other hand held a heavy-duty drill; more foundation work, I realized. I'd dreaded even going down to look in the cellar.

So I hadn't. "Yeah." I swung the hammer again. The impact vibrated up my spine and made my eyeballs bobble around as if I were a cartoon character, while the board I'd hit moved upward about a sixteenth of an inch.

"I don't know, though. This is taking forever. I might," I admitted reluctantly, "have bitten off more than I can chew."

He eyed the project. "Maybe. But maybe not."

Inside the entryway lay the tools I'd gathered up at the end of my last work session. My father examined them, first picking his way up the ruins of the porch. It was safer with the rotten bits broken off; at least now you could *see* where your foot was going to go through.

He came out carrying a pry bar. "Dad, you'll never be able to–"

"Just watch." With that, he smacked the top of the board with the sledgehammer. The board flattened back down onto the support it was nailed to.

But the nailhead stayed *up* a little, because he hadn't *hit* the nail. He'd hit the *board.* So now there was about a sixteenth-of-an-inch gap there, between the nail and the wood.

Not much. Just enough so he could slip the crowbar's claw tip under the nailhead.

"Oh," I breathed, beginning to get the idea.

But not yet the whole idea. Next he inserted the sharply curved, pronged end of the pry bar under the nail. Then he leaned hard on it, using the bar's curve as a fulcrum so the pronged end pulled the nail upward.

Creaking loudly, the old nail slid almost all the way out of the board, freeing the board from the porch structure.

Whereupon he handed the pry bar to me. "There you are. Go thou and do likewise."

The whole project had been transformed. Now I only needed to hit each board twice; once from below, once on top. "Yes," I said, eager to get to work on it again.

But he wasn't finished with me. "You lookin' around for that little girl that's gone missing?"

Wade had told him, I supposed. I got the feeling they talked me over more than I'd have liked knowing about, every so often.

"Yes," I said again, "but I'm not having very much luck with that either."

He nodded sympathetically. "Girl's about the age you were when you went," he commented.

When I took off from the aunts and uncles who were raising me, he meant; my mom's folks. At the time, I hadn't seen my dad in thirteen years.

They'd told me that he was dead. I sat on what remained of the steps and after a moment he sat down beside me. "Different situation, though," I said.

He laughed a little bitterly. With his long gray ponytail and a red bandanna sticking out of his overalls pocket, he still resembled a nice old jeans-wearing, long-haired ex-hippie-type fellow left over from the sixties, not a care in the world.

Which he wasn't. "You never know," he said. "I mean, about situations. I guess you must've thought yours was the worst."

"Mmm." That spurred my own bitter laughter but I kept it inside. He didn't know what the worst was; no one did, and even now that we were on comfortable terms I had no intention of telling him.

Or maybe because we were. "That's all in the past," I said, deliberately letting him off the hook again.

All alone in Manhattan at age fifteen, I'd had ridiculously good luck: decent waitressing jobs, streetwise pals who hadn't hustled me or worse. Eventually I got into school, married Victor, had Sam, and started making some serious money as a financial professional.

All of which led me in a roundabout way to Eastport. Then, just when I'd decided my father really must be dead, he'd showed up again, no longer a fugitive but still on the run in his heart.

"I don't know, though," I said. "I mean whether or not we–Ellie and I, that is–can possibly find Wanda Cathcart."

Changing the subject. He caught it, shot me a look. You couldn't put too much over on a guy who'd survived thirty years on the wrong side of a wanted poster. "You don't think she's maybe with some of the town kids?"

"Sam's been asking them. Checking in their places, too, this morning." He'd phoned just as I got home to tell me so: no luck.

"But you know kids," I went on, repeating the rest of what Sam had told me. "They might hide one of their own. But not somebody none of them has any loyalty to. And especially not an odd duck like Wanda."

He nodded, picking apart a scrap of rotten porch board with his work-hardened fingers. "Sure. Give her up in a heartbeat. Do a favor for the cops, then maybe get off easier sometime when one of them gets in a little bit of trouble."

"Exactly. If they had her, they'd have told on her by now."

As I'd been thinking pretty much from the get-go, but never mind. Across the yard, bluejays called echoingly to one another in the treetops.

"And I doubt I'll get to talk to this Mac Rickert guy who might be involved in the drugs they found in the house, either. He's supposed to be pretty elusive." Assuming he even had anything to do with Wanda's disappearance.

My dad got up stiffly. On autumn days like this one you could tell his old bones were starting to creak.

"So," I sighed, "maybe it's all a waste of time. Maybe I should quit. Because if Sam can't find Wanda and the ladies putting up posters can't find her and the *cops* can't find her, I don't see how *we* are going to..."

I stopped. He was smiling again but the look in his eyes was sad. Sometimes I thought he actually knew my whole story without needing to be told.

Knew too that no matter what I said now, I wasn't quitting on Wanda. The way he–or so I'd believed for years–had quit on me. He took up the pry bar again.

"Thing is," he said, "you haven't got the weight to knock that porch board off with the sledgehammer."

His turn to change the subject. I watched while he banged another board up, smacked it down again, and pulled the nail out.

Again the board came free easily. "That's what tools are all about," he said. "Add mechanical advantage to your brute force, get the right angle on a thing, multiply the weight you do have."

It occurred to me that by being here so often and working on my old house, my father was getting the right angle on me. Adding, as he would have put it, some mechanical advantage.

Which he must have felt he needed. And the truth was, now that the novelty of having him around had passed, I still wasn't so sure he didn't.

"It's all physics," he concluded. "Which is just a fancy way of talking about how the world works. Figure that out, it'll lead you, when you're stuck, to maybe a better tool."

How the world works. My mouth felt dry suddenly; despite my chat with Marge I didn't have the faintest idea how Wanda's world worked.

Maybe I should find out. "So," I said, my mind already percolating with the possibilities of this notion, "what're you going to do about the old box from the foundation, and the book you think is inside it?"

His smile grew wolfish. You could still see in his blue eyes and in the contours of his age-lined face the amused confidence that must've been one of the first things to attract my mother.

"Why, I'm going to get the book *out* of the box, of course."

He winked. "Physics," he repeated, and with that he hefted the drill and strode off jauntily toward the back door, the one leading to the kitchen. It was the entrance he always used to carry his tools inside.

I wondered if just possibly it could be because Bella was there. "Thanks," I called after him. And then, "Hey, Dad?"

I don't know what I wanted to say to him. *I love you,* maybe. Or possibly just *Be careful. Don't hurt yourself with that drill.*

But as it turned out I didn't say anything because he didn't pause, only waved without turning back, having used up I supposed his supply of family intimacy for one morning.

Such as it was. But that was okay; I was under no illusions about it. I mean about the fact–regrettable but still perfectly obvious to both of us–that I'd used mine up, too.

• • •

Soon after Bella Diamond came to work for us I noticed there were places in my old house she wouldn't go.

The third floor, for instance, where in a tiny room that I imagined had once belonged to a live-in servant the unmistakable fragrance of perfume had a habit of materializing. Nor would she visit the cellar in which a shallow pit showed the spot where a coal furnace had once stood, behind that the low unframed door to the coal bin yawning dark as a tunnel entrance.

Once I thought I glimpsed a pale green light glowing deep in that coal bin. At the sight of it I'd abandoned my errand and hurried back up to the kitchen, not venturing to the cellar again until days later when the orbital sander I was using tripped a circuit breaker and I had to creep down to reset it.

And then there was the cold spot lurking unnervingly on the front stairs, second step from the top. I wouldn't have minded so much except that every time I reached it–on my way downstairs, never going up–the same thought always popped unbidden into my head: *Here's where he pushed her.*

And I was reminded of all that when I went in later and found Bella and Ellie in the kitchen with an enormous kettle, one I knew Bella must have sent Ellie to the cellar to get.

"Rappie pie," Ellie said by way of explaining the kettle.

I'd pried most of the porch boards off and loaded them into the Dumpster. My shoulders ached and my fingers were stiff from gripping the pry bar, but the job was moving along again.

"Beg pardon?" I paused in the act of pouring coffee.

Rappie pie was an old traditional downeast Maine recipe, as delicious as it was laborious. Just for starters, the first line of the recipe read: *Boil two chickens and a peck of potatoes, then squeeze the water out of the potatoes with a cheesecloth.*

"You mean buy some, right?" I asked, looking back and forth between Ellie and Bella Diamond. "Someone's made a lot of it for a fund-raiser or something?"

Bella stood at the stove. With her henna hair skinned back into its usual ponytail, shirtsleeves pushed up, and her green eyes bugging in a combination of thyroid trouble, determination, and way more energy than your average highballing freight locomotive, she was boiling potatoes in the kettle.

Lots of potatoes. “Have a doughnut,” Ellie said, distracting me with the bag of them she’d brought with her. But not so much that I couldn’t see what *she* was doing: writing a grocery list.

“Ellie, please don’t tell me you’re going to…”

Good simple food, carefully created and consumed with great pleasure, was one of the things I’d learned to love most since moving here to Maine; farewell, nouvelle cuisine.

But rappie pie was an exception in the “simple” department. If you put it on a TV cooking show, its preparation would take up all the episodes in a season. I looked over Ellie’s shoulder.

Chickens, the list read. *Fresh green beans, mushrooms, lard.*

“For the piecrust,” she explained when my eyebrows went up at this last item. “Rappie pie needs a homemade piecrust.”

I bit into a doughnut. Ellie got up before dawn to make them for George and his pals to eat in the truck while they were on their way to work.

This to me sounded a lot like getting up and digging to China with my bare hands, but Ellie enjoyed it. Also, the minute I tasted the moist, buttermilk-and-molasses-flavored inside of this delicious morsel, I felt its energy flood my brain.

Just as she’d intended. While I chewed, Bella put a lid on the potatoes, transferred a load of laundry from the washer to the dryer, and refreshed the dogs’ water bowl.

“Get ’em here, get ’em all eating and drinking, and *get ’em talking,*” she advised, wiping down all the cabinet fronts, the kitchen counter, and the inside of the oven in what Sam would have called one swell foop if he were here.

Which he wasn’t; I wondered if he was with Victor again. But then what Bella had said sank in.

“Get *who* eating and drinking?” I demanded, taking another doughnut; the things were addictive.

"Because I'll tell you this much," Bella added, "there's a lot more to them people than meets the eye."

Then I got it; she meant the tenants. She and Ellie had been having a little discussion about them, apparently.

I closed the doughnut bag resolutely. "Huh, that's a thought." It went with my idea of trying to find out more about Wanda, too; I'd been wondering how I might manage that. "But d'you think they'd even come?"

Ellie finished her list. "Are you kidding? After what you told me they fed you the other night?"

I'd described the meal to her, with dismayed emphasis on the freeze-dried-potatoes part of the menu.

"You could be right," I said. "Once I tell them the kind of dinner we're having..."

Ellie continued: "*And* I've been thinking a little more about your theory, too, and I've come up with a possible way to get in touch with Mac Rickert. Because maybe we don't know where he is, but he's got a brother. One we *do* know how to find."

"He does?" I said stupidly. And then, "We do?"

So far today I'd rattled my own skeleton with an enormous sledgehammer, nearly drowned in a rowboat, and been the unwilling recipient of an old water main's suddenly released contents.

Not to mention that spider, and I hadn't even had lunch yet unless you counted the doughnuts. "An accessible brother? But why didn't... why isn't someone already...?" I'm not sure but at this point there's a good chance I began waving my arms ineffectually. "...out talking to *him*?"

"Because nobody's searching for Wanda but us anymore," Ellie replied simply.

Hearing this, I thought yearningly of the cold water under that rowboat. Probably it was quiet down there, too.

"Bob Arnold called a little while ago while you were out front working on the porch," Ellie went on. "Based on their talk this morning with

Marge, the state cops have decided that Wanda is a runaway, not a crime victim."

Oh, phooey. "Because she took stuff with her. A sleeping bag, her backpack..."

The decision would lower the intensity of the hunt for the girl. And now when Marge went to them with the story about Wanda possibly being there during the shooting, the police would think it was just to get them fired up about looking for her again.

Ellie nodded, her eyes on the kitchen clock. It was time to pick up Leonora from day care.

"Sooner or later I'm sure the state boys *will* visit Joey–that's his name, Joey Rickert–and talk to him about where his brother Mac might be, just on the strength of those drugs," Ellie said. "Combined, I mean, with Mac's reputation."

Which they probably knew about, even though I hadn't. But sooner or later might not be soon enough for Wanda.

Ellie moved toward the door. "I've got to go now, but I'll do the shopping and call the tenants to invite them for tonight. If," she added, "it's okay with you."

"Fine," I said tiredly; after all, I had to eat sometime. I could call Sam and have him bring Victor, as well. That way maybe I'd get a little advance warning if Victor decided to buy Sam an airplane instead of only chartering one.

"So where's this Joey guy live?" I asked. Might as well get that over with, too.

"In the boat basin," Ellie replied; she'd known I would jump on the idea. "You know the boat, it's an old cabin cruiser with a rocking chair on the foredeck and the Jolly Roger draped over the side?"

At this I felt my heart sink abruptly, which was what just about everyone in Eastport hoped would happen to the boat in question.

"You're kidding," I said, knowing she wasn't.

"Nope. I'd go but I'm already late for..."

She waved her satchel, stuffed full of baby equipment and clothes. I hadn't even had a chance to tell her yet about the oxycontin tablet. "So congratulations, Jacobia," she said, "you're about to make your maiden visit to..."

Uh-huh. To the ugliest, most notorious little bucket of rust in the harbor. I didn't know her owner personally but I knew of him, and everyone in town knew the boat's name. It was scrawled on her stern in a whimsical mix of capitals and lowercase black letters: *GhOulIE gUrl.*

And I just hoped she wasn't going to take me on the voyage of the damned.

• • •

Twenty minutes later I faced Bob Arnold across his desk. "Yeah, it's an oxie, all right," he confirmed, dropping the pill I'd found into a plastic bag and then into a desk drawer. We were in his office in the old Frontier Bank building, just one door down from the Peavy Library.

On my way I'd stopped in there to grab up another fact for the 1823 game, and come up with a nice one from an old Eastport City Directory they turned out to have on microfilm.

Now I finished explaining to Bob how I'd found the pill, and where. "Which could mean one of the tenants brought the drugs, hid them in the crawl space, and maybe dropped one when..."

But I didn't know when. "Whenever," I finished inadequately.

"*Or* whoever else hid 'em in the house, *if* that's where they were hidden, could've dropped it," he answered at once. "Dibble, for instance, could've gone down there, retrieved 'em, then got shot on his way out."

No arguing with that. "Hear anything about Wanda?" Bob asked.

I repeated the story Greg Brand had told me. "But nothing else," I added.

No sense rattling on about the Rickerts either, not yet. Because any theory, notion, or wild supposition I might be entertaining always had a way of sounding silly when surrounded by Bob's gray file drawers, his sputtering police-band radio, and his sheaf of wanted posters in their hanging clipboard.

But then he surprised me. "The state guys're looking for a local fella, name of Rickert. Druggie type, they think he might know something about the pills."

"That so?" I said evenly. "I've never met him. Interesting, though. And that reminds me: How come the state police haven't wanted to talk to *me* yet?"

He hitched his belt up. "They will. You're on their list, you and Ellie. Just not very high on it. That all you wanted to tell me, then? What you found in the cellar?"

The Greg Brand info hadn't impressed him much, or anyway not enough for him to speculate about it with me.

"Yeah, that's it," I agreed. "How's your fellow doing? The one with the kids?" My own problems, after all, weren't the only ones anyone had to worry about.

He grimaced. "Okay so far. Long as I keep my nose clean, keep checkin' off the chores on my list."

From this I gathered that even though the state guys didn't want him directly involved in their investigation, they were still keeping him hopping with a variety of associated errands.

And he didn't like it. "Not gettin' yourself in any trouble, are you?" he asked, glancing at me sternly. "Asked you to have a look for the girl, remember, not go off half-cocked, get yourself into something you don't have the policing skills to handle the situation."

I wasn't convinced. Bob knew Ellie and me, knew too that half-cocked was pretty much our standard operating procedure precisely *because* we lacked policing skills. *Follow your nose* was the advice we went by; it was the only method we knew.

So he'd understood what he was getting. But he couldn't very well tell us to go out and court trouble, could he? Meanwhile just having that oxycontin out of my possession made me feel a lot better. In fact, it made me feel almost as if I weren't in any situation at all.

"I'll get the pill to the state boys, tell 'em where you got it," he added. "And I'll pass it along about Brand. He's comin' in?"

I nodded.

"But right now..." His voice trailed off as I went out the door with him and he locked it behind us.

I got the picture; more scut work. His squad car was idling at the curb. "Take care," I called as he got in, but he'd slammed the door already and I didn't think he'd heard me.

After he pulled away I stood on the steps a moment taking in the wide blue expanse of the bay, the marine smells of salt and creosote, and the sound of a bell buoy clanging somewhere. Across the street the flower shop's windows were full of autumn-themed arrangements, strawflowers and pompon chrysanthemums.

Then I began thinking once more about what I might say to Joey Rickert. But bribing and threatening were the only two strategies I could come up with, and anyway, as I passed the old brick storefronts on my way down Water Street, I kept getting distracted.

Wadsworth's Hardware store had a set of fine wood chisels in its window; sharp at the business ends and featuring scrimshaw bone handles, they'd fit nicely in my toolbox and were just what I needed for those doors at the rental property. Unfortunately, as I was standing there admiring them I also caught sight of my own reflection in the glass: lean face, short dark hair, straight nose, regulation mouth.

Nothing special, though I didn't break mirrors. On the other hand, my clothes all looked as if they'd come out of a trash bin: faded jeans, a too-big gray sweatshirt with paint smears on it, a navy cardigan. Pure ragamuffin, in other words.

The old city directory had informed me that in 1823 a dressmaker named Annie Hadley had kept a millinery shop upstairs from Wadsworth's present spot, and as I spared a last yearning thought for the chisels, I could almost hear her begging me to come in for a fitting.

On the other hand, I'd also learned from the directory that she'd specialized in the kind of black dresses meant for women in mourning, fastened up to the chin with tiny black jet buttons. . . .

And now I really was procrastinating; the *GhOulIE gUrl* awaited. So I continued on down toward the harbor, pausing only to inspect the Moran Building's windows, where silk scarves hand-stenciled with the shapes of ginkgo leaves spread like treasures of some *Arabian Nights*–inspired seraglio.

This place too had been transformed since the 1800s, its upper floors once home to a tariff collector on one side and the mahogany-paneled, Belgian-carpeted consulting chambers of a local surgeon on the other.

Everything in Eastport had been something else, it seemed, a long time ago. Ellie said there'd been not one but two secret societies in the room over the old drugstore, then a bookbinder's shop. The most recent had been part of a post–Civil War plot for an invasion of Canada, ten thousand men strong at its height in Eastport and surrounding areas alone.

But the earlier group was even more curious. Its members were rumored to have odd symbols branded into their palms, to greet one another with strange foreign-sounding syllables, and to practice a ritual of peering into a looking glass in order to predict the future.

As far as I knew, no record existed of what they might have seen, but as I passed the fish pier, where seagulls made perches of the wooden pilings and the tugboats resembled a pair of massive bathtub toys, I decided that if it really was the future they saw then it mustn't have made them happy.

Because after shipbuilding went downhill, Eastport hit hard times. No longer could you buy a cigar, a grand piano, or French wallpaper in the shops on Water Street. Nor, I supposed, did the mysterious handshakes survive, though Ellie said the old men in town spoke of the secret society as recently as her father's era.

Meanwhile the closer I got to the boat basin, the more the *GhOulIE gUrl* visit felt about as alluring as one of those dark visions glimpsed in the secret society's mirror. But the store windows up and down the street also featured computer-scanned photographs of Wanda Cathcart, on paper flyers stuck to the insides of the glass with cellophane tape.

MISSING, the flyers trumpeted in big black capital letters. So I strode on past the small white cottage housing Eastport's biweekly newspaper, the *Quoddy Tides*. At the moment, the office overlooking the harbor was busy getting out the new issue, people inside visible through the windows squaring up freshly printed stacks.

Next came Rosie's Hot Dog Stand and the cobbled launch ramp leading down to the water, and finally the brand-new Coast Guard building: big, white, and red-roofed except where the seagulls had already begun their job of anointing it.

After which there was nowhere to go but down the metal gang to the floating docks; egad.

The gang was steeply angled, the docks swaying to the subtle movements of the tide and waves. Which at the moment weren't so subtle at all, especially not when the Coast Guard's big orange Zodiac boat zipped swiftly into her mooring, sending a surge of fresh instability in my direction.

It wasn't the first time I'd ventured onto the metal ramp, its surface dimpled with bumps that were supposed to make keeping your footing easier. Ellie's big, broad-beamed open boat bobbed only a couple of docks distant; she'd coaxed me onto it regularly over the previous summer, trying to get me comfortable.

But it hadn't worked. Making my way down the ramp in baby steps, both hands on the cables that substituted inadequately for railings on either side, I envied again my friend's easy skill at all things watery. Wade said Ellie was the best amateur boater he'd seen, safe as houses and with the kind of deep, bred-in-the-bone instinct for sea and weather that turned a good mariner into an excellent one.

Unlike myself. "Yeesh!" I said, stepping off the ramp, and grabbed onto a dock piling.

It turned out to be a good move, since standing there with my arms wrapped around it gave me a chance to size up the *GhOulIE gUrl* at close range, while the Zodiac's wake subsided.

As the turbulence calmed I inhaled the mingled aromas of boat exhaust, salt water, and fish, all floating on a breeze so freshly sweet you could've bottled and sold it.

By contrast, the stench emanating from the *GhOulIE gUrl* was of trash and unrinsed beer bottles. Even the sea breeze didn't really dissipate it, just churned it around a little.

"Hello?" I called. "Is anyone down there?"

A face appeared in the hatchway. Eyes squinted at me painfully in the afternoon brilliance. "Yeah. Whadeya want?"

Unshaven, shaggy hair uncombed, little scrim of dried spit in the corner of his mouth. I'd woken him up.

"My name is Jacobia Tiptree, I want information, and if you're Joey Rickert I'm willing to pay for it," I said before he could vanish belowdecks again.

Bingo. "I'm Joey," he allowed grudgingly. "Jesus, what time is it?"

"Never mind that," I said, stepping aboard without bothering to ask permission. He eyed me in annoyance. But he didn't push me overboard. Instead, he shielded his eyes with one hand to scan the dock area cautiously.

I gathered there might be people Joey Rickert didn't want to run into, ones who might be waiting for him to stick his head recklessly up into the light of day.

Something, anyway, was making him behave so carefully. He waved toward the fetid little hole in the water that he lived in. "Awright," he conceded reluctantly. "You c'n come on down."

The cabin area was as filthy and unpleasant as I'd expected: pizza boxes in the galley, girly magazines on the floor, a pile of clothing heaped in a doorless storage locker.

"You need to use the head, it's over there," he offered in an oddly courteous gesture, flicking his wrist at a tiny wooden door with a crescent moon painted on it.

Not on your life. "Thanks. But all I came for is to find out whether you've–"

He stuck out his hand. "The money," he said flatly.

Yeah, I'd figured him right. I pulled out a twenty and his fingers clamped onto it so hard, I nearly lost my own.

"Heard from your brother lately?"

Joey squinted past me as if he feared I'd brought someone with me. But seeing no one in the bright square of hatchway light, he answered succinctly.

"No. And if that's all you want, that's the easiest twenty I ever made." He grinned, revealing teeth like smashed piano keys.

Not much time for dental appointments in Joey's busy life. But the grin was short-lived as, spying something on the floor half hidden by a pair of grayish underpants, I kicked the garment aside and plucked it up.

It was a pink plastic barrette. "Hey, Joey. What's this?"

His lower lip pooched out sullenly. "Gimme that."

I stuffed it into my jeans pocket, praying that Joey was as ineffective at injuring others as he obviously was in the rest of his existence.

But there was no sense pushing my luck, so I switched to a more conciliatory approach, even though the barrette made me feel like just clobbering him and getting it over with.

"Joey, your brother is in trouble and I think I can get him out of it. But we've got to move fast."

Jeez, I sounded like a TV cop show. But how else could I instill a sense of urgency in him?

Maybe a cattle prod would do it. Joey slumped down on the shaky metal step stool that was the cabin's only seating, other than the berth he used for a bed. "Mac's not in trouble," he said.

Oh, for Pete's sake. "Yeah, and you're not an idiot."

I'm not proud of what happened next; there's no excuse for it. But with that damned pink barrette burning in my pocket like a hot coal, I kicked the stool out from under him, then stood over him waving another twenty right in his beer-bloated kisser.

"Hey, what'd you do that for?" he whined injuredly.

I was two-for-two in the character-assessment department so far; the little jerk *still* didn't have the gumption to get mad at me.

"To get your attention," I told him. "Do what I say, you can have this and four more and Mac can pay off whoever it is he owes for the drug stash the cops confiscated after they found Dibble's body out at my rental house."

All pure improvisation; between paying Luanne *and* Joey Rickert, I was draining a lot of twenties from my cash stash. It would be worth it, though, if it got Mac Rickert into a position where someone could drop a net over him.

Because maybe he had Wanda. But at my words Joey's whiskery face creased with the same animal cunning that a rat's does, after it smells cheese.

"What about Dibble?" he demanded.

"If Mac shot him, he's on his own about that. But at least he won't also be on the run from whoever fronted them the pills in the first place. All I want..."

I pulled the barrette from my pocket, waved it at him. "All I want is the girl."

My working theory now being that Mac shot Dibble, Wanda witnessed the murder, and Rickert saw her witnessing it. And he couldn't have that, so later he came back and took her, using the storm for cover. Kept her here on Joey's boat, maybe, till the weather cleared.

In which theory there were many holes, such as how did Mac know Wanda hadn't *already* revealed what she'd seen? And–since in fact she hadn't–*why* hadn't she?

Furthermore I'd never seen Wanda actually wearing the hair clip, just one sort of like it, but it bolstered my suspicion that she–or some other young girl, and how likely was *that?*–had been aboard the *GhOulIE gUrl* recently.

Joey got up off the floor. "You're crazy. I got girls here all the time, one must've dropped that hair thing."

Yes, I was sure the young ladies were lining up to be his guests on this floating garbage pail. Also, as he got to his feet Joey was thinking so hard, his eyes were practically crossed; he didn't like it that I'd found the barrette, and why would that be?

"Joey, I'm sorry about what I did just now. I lost my temper. And from all I know, Mac's not even a bad guy."

Well, except for the part about the hole in Dibble's head.

"Probably he doesn't even *want* the girl," I said.

Or anyway I sure hoped that he didn't. Hetty Bonham's idea that maybe Dibble's partner in the drug deal was a child molester still weighed heavily on me, too.

But it wasn't a notion I was about to float for Mac's brother. That *would* probably get me tossed overboard.

No, let's just keep it a clean, cash-on-the-barrelhead swap. "So I'll trade. The girl for whatever he owes on the drugs."

Which was when Joey Rickert dropped the mild-mannered scumbucket act and *sprang* at me. "Yeah?" His hot, sour breath gusted into my face. "What if I've got a better idea?"

For a boozy little lowlife he was surprisingly strong, and he hadn't forgiven me for kicking him off that stool. His hand fastened around mine, pried my fingers open as he slammed me hard backwards into the bulkhead.

My head smacked a locker and it fell open, showering canned goods down onto my skull, as his grimy fingers closed around the barrette. Then he shoved me toward the hatchway.

"G'wan, get outta here! You don't know nothin' an' you ain't got nothin,' so why'ntcha just get lost, huh? I don't need your aggravation and my brother don't need it, neither. Ya got that?"

I stumbled out into the fresh air and daylight still holding the other twenty-dollar bill, until a hand stretched past me and plucked it away.

I turned, indignant. His face confronted me defiantly.

"Price of admission," he snarled. "You come back here, I'll take it outta your hide."

To which there was really not much that I could say. My head felt as if someone had been dropping canned goods onto it and I was pretty sure my thumb had been sprained.

I did manage a parting shot, though. "Tell Mac I was here," I said once I'd gotten safely back up onto the dock. "Maybe he's got more brains than you. Like I said, I'm willing to give him the money he needs in return for the girl, unharmed. No cops, no questions."

Joey snorted derisively, forty bucks ahead and with his sad, hungover notion of pride intact.

"Sure," he sniggered, bouncing unsteadily on the balls of his feet like some punch-drunk prizefighter, goofy with triumph. "How 'bout instead I tell him an' everyone else you paid me forty just to let you come down here with me?" he taunted.

Yeah, how about that? I thought tiredly. Not many people in Eastport would be willing to believe it; Joey was just too awful.

Still, there were some. And on top of the story about drugs in the Quoddy Village house–not to mention a dead body–as grist for the gossip mill I'd just raised my own standing another couple of notches.

"Tell him, Joey," I urged, turning away.

But as I made my bruised, unsteady way back up the gangway I had little hope that he would.

• • •

"Because I was stupid, that's why," I told Wade soon after I got home.

He frowned down at my cut forehead, gently dabbed some more antiseptic onto it as Monday watched alertly, whining a little; Prill the Doberman, that supposedly ferocious breed, had already left the room and hustled downstairs, unable to stand the sight.

"Ouch!" I winced, tears springing to my eyes. But they were more from embarrassment than pain.

I'd managed to slink past Bella Diamond and my father in the kitchen, then crept upstairs to the bathroom to try cleaning up the mess Joey Rickert had made of me. But Wade had been in the bedroom getting a clean shirt, and when he saw me the jig was up.

"I should never have gone there alone, and I shouldn't have antagonized him, should've known a jerk like him can't stand–"

"–a woman getting over on him," Wade said soothingly, his fingers kind as he applied a square of gauze and adhesive tape.

I examined his face in the bathroom mirror. "You don't sound very angry," I ventured.

At me, I meant. Because it had been dumb. Joey could've had a knife and the bottled-up rage to use it.

Without warning a sob rose into my throat; I forced it back. "Wade, what if Mac Rickert's really got that girl somewhere right now and he's just gearing himself up to..."

"Hey, hey," Wade murmured, trying to comfort me.

But it was no good. All the fears Wanda Cathcart's situation had reawakened in me were boiling to the surface.

Including the ones I wouldn't reveal. In particular Hetty Bonham's words kept haunting me, triggering old memories. *They find other creeps like themselves... his consolation prize...*

Wade hugged me hard, then pushed me away from him, seizing my shoulders so he could look into my eyes.

"Jake," he said helplessly.

He didn't know what was wrong or how to fix it and that was terrible for him. I could see it in his face.

Because he was always on my side, no matter what. "Jake, if you wanted me to, I'd go down and smack the living daylights out of Joey. In fact I've got half a mind to do it anyway," he said.

Monday shoved herself between us consolingly as I dragged in a wet sniffle, trying to get control of myself. Going to pieces never helped anything.

Never had. "No, I don't want you to get your hands dirty. I'm not really hurt. And anyway, I started it. He could have me arrested for assaulting him, for heaven's sake. I just feel like an idiot, that's all."

He kissed the top of my head. "Yeah, well. I know how it is when your subconscious gets hold of a problem."

I felt myself go still in his arms. "Missing kid, right away you think of Sam, how he used to disappear for days at a time in the city. Makes you feel the same way as then, I guess," Wade said.

"You're right," I agreed. "That must've been it."

I should have told him the truth right then, of course. But it is a character flaw of mine that I'd rather be burned alive than pitied, especially by someone I care about.

Wade didn't seem to notice anything amiss. "Just don't put yourself in that position anymore," he added.

I couldn't believe he was taking this so well. "Okay. And the head feels much better, thank you."

He let go of me. "Smacking Joey wouldn't make him more talkative, anyhow. He's as loyal as a terrier to his big brother Mac, always has been."

Of course Wade knew Mac; Joey, too. Like Ellie and George, Wade had lived here in Eastport all his life.

"Not that Joey's loyalty is worth much, but there's always the chance he will tell Mac what you said," Wade continued as we went downstairs together.

In the kitchen Bella ignored us, zipping busily from stove to refrigerator and out into the dining room. Peering in there, I saw the table set with the good china and silver, and the last of the autumn snapdragons from the garden arranged in a centerpiece.

Fresh birch logs lay on the hearth, too, and new candles set into the chandelier promised the kind of light that always makes everyone lovely.

"Oh," I said, my aching head momentarily forgotten.

"Yeah, huh?" said Wade, catching Bella's eye appreciatively as she hurried on to some fresh task.

"So anyway, don't give up yet on maybe Joey helping you out on this thing," he said when she had gone.

Bella bustled back in, stopped in front of me, and wordlessly put a big glass of seltzer and ice with a slice of lime into my hand. She really was a very good housekeeper.

"*But,*" Wade added when she'd gone, "from what you're telling me, you don't *know* the barrette belonged to Wanda and you *also* don't know that Dibble and Rickert *were* partners in drugs or any other scheme, either. Something else could be going on."

Something, his tone implied, that didn't necessarily merit my going off the deep end.

It was what Ellie had tactfully implied the night before, too; that maybe I was getting too preoccupied by all this. And that she didn't understand why, which she liked even less.

Wade took my glass and had a sip from it, then handed it back to me.

"Something else entirely," he said.

• • •

There were still a couple of hours left before our guests arrived, so when I'd finished my seltzer I went out to bash at the porch some more. Every jolt of the hammer sent a throbbing surge of pain through my head, but I needed to hit something.

And the porch didn't hit back, unlike some other obstacles I'd hurled myself at lately, though even with my dad's new method it still resisted very stubbornly my ongoing efforts to dismantle it. Hauling on yet another of the old boards, I reflected how shaky a structure could seem until you tried knocking it down.

Or how solid, until you stepped in the wrong place and your foot went right through.

Like me. I swung the hammer viciously in full view of the street, not caring who saw me making a fool of myself. And as it turned out, that was just what the job needed; soon only the side supports remained, so soft they broke off when I pulled on them.

Then they were gone, too. I was muscling the last one up over the side of the half-filled Dumpster when Ellie came out with an aluminum lawn chair in one hand and the baby in her other arm.

"Hi," she said, and sat down on the chair with the baby in her lap.

The baby wore a red long-sleeved tee, a navy jumper with an American flag embroidered on the bodice, and tiny little sneakers in blue denim over red socks with red-white-and-blue cuff trim.

"Hi, yourself," I replied, wiping hastily at my face with my sleeve.

Ellie gave no sign of having seen that I'd been weeping as I worked. But after a minute she pulled some tissues from her smock pocket and held them out to me.

"Blow," she commanded.

I obeyed. "Thanks."

She didn't ask what was the matter, either; Ellie rarely did. As a result people told her things they'd never dreamed of telling.

But not this time. She just sat silently again as I finished cleaning up the remnants of porch.

There wasn't much left; a few wood scraps, some brick chips from an earlier time when the porch had apparently been held up by masonry, and a heap of newly exposed leaf mold, thick and darkly ancient.

"Okay," I said finally, dusting my hands together. But just then the baby laughed, waved her arms around, and began wiggling as if trying to escape.

"Leonora," Ellie admonished the infant smilingly, "what are you going on about?"

Which was when I too spied the tiny yellow gleam that had attracted the baby's attention, shining from between the layers of leaf mold. I picked it up as Ellie came over to peer at it with me.

"Wah!" Leonora said, reaching out. It was an old gold coin, just one edge of it eye-catchingly bright. Rubbing grime from it, I exposed the number 1823.

The year the house was built. "Oh my gosh," Ellie breathed when I showed it to her. "That's weird."

"Yeah. Someone dropped it here. Or put it here."

A long time ago. "What's that?" Ellie pointed at the coin's back. The front showed a man's head: George IV, probably, the king of England at the time.

"I'm not sure. A man and a sea monster?"

Then the answer popped into my head; I'd had a client once who collected old coins. "Saint George and the dragon," I said.

Across the lawn, late-afternoon sunlight caught in droplets from the storm still clinging to the grass blades, creating tiny mirrors. Ellie hoisted the baby over onto her other hip.

"How'd it get here?" she wondered. "Maybe a worker dropped it or something when they were building the house?"

"I don't know," I said doubtfully. "This was a lot of money back then."

The coin-collecting client had known a lot, and even then I'd had what's called in the money business a head for the stuff. So facts about cash stuck with me.

"Maybe about ten dollars," I said. "And that was at a time when a good dinner cost about a nickel, a night in an inn maybe a dime. Two thousand or so in today's money."

"Wow. That's a lot to lose." The baby put her head back and yodeled cheerfully, singing to the sky.

"If it was lost. If it wasn't put there on purpose," I said. "Sometimes the old builders did that sometimes, left something of value inside a wall or under a floor. Like a kind of good-luck charm for the house."

Or an X-marks-the-spot. I didn't know why the idea occurred to me so strongly, but it did.

"I guess it means that even long-gone things can be found again," said Ellie.

"People, maybe, too," I agreed.

Or so I hoped. I dropped the thing into my pocket, felt it weighing there, and wondered whether the old piece of gold might also help restore my peace of mind.

But I didn't expect this. With few exceptions I'd given up on magic a long time ago, or it had given up on me.

Same difference.

Chapter 8

"Old Horeb Cathcart," Ellie's husband George Valentine said that night at the dinner table, "was a water witch."

He'd learned while being introduced to Marge Cathcart that she had family connections in the area. Now he was enlarging upon the topic while she and the other Quoddy Village tenants met rappie pie.

With, I thought, varying degrees of pleasure. "Though I've noticed it ain't takin' no magical mumbo jumbo to get some of 'em to eat it," Bella Diamond observed from her post in the kitchen, on the other side of the butler's pantry pass-through.

"Now, Bella," I said, trying not to smile, "keep your voice down." I handed her some plates. "Seconds on these, please?"

She rolled her eyes at me. "I'll bring 'em in. Need to fill up Dr. Tiptree's glass, anyway. You want another bottle out?"

"Yes," I said, momentarily worried. Victor's appetite, ordinarily so dependable, was picky again tonight. But unlike the last time he'd been here, he was drinking more than usual.

"Horeb could find water by holding a branch out, seeing how it felt to him in his hands. When the branch bent down, he would say 'Dig here,'" George continued as I sat down again.

"Oh, come on," Greg Brand reacted skeptically. "That's just old wives' tales."

Bella's glance at him was deceptively mild as she put filled plates in front of Wade and Jenna Durrell and placed a new bottle of wine on the table. Chicken and potatoes baked with gravy in a pie pastry, green beans, and rolls plus spiced cranberry sauce and a relish dish had hit the spot with those two, anyway.

But Victor poured another glass of wine immediately, having pushed his plate away. I looked a question at him but he only smiled dismissively, then reached to pat Monday, who blinked up at him in surprise at the gesture.

"Wives' tales or no, people would find water," George said. He ate some chicken and potato. "And water wasn't all Horeb Cathcart found, either. Back when I was a little boy he went out to try to find a missing child. For hours people'd searched all over the island till at last someone thought to ask Horeb."

"And?" Marge Cathcart asked breathlessly. The story of a lost child must have flown like an arrow to her heart; I was surprised she had been willing to sit down at a table with Greg Brand at all.

"He cut a willow switch," George said, and drank some wine. "Put his hands on it, followed that twitching tip out to the edge of the kid's parents' yard, into the brush and trees."

Noticing that Victor had begun petting Monday, Prill leaned in on his other side. I braced for the explosion of fuss-budgetry to erupt from Victor.

It didn't. "Then what happened?" Ellie wanted to know.

George picked his cap up from where he'd set it by his plate and turned it thoughtfully in his hands. "Horeb followed that switch through the underbrush till it led him to an old well they'd all forgotten about. And when he looked down—"

"Oh, come on," Greg Brand interrupted. "You're just trying to put one over on–"

"When he looked down," George repeated, "there was a little boy clinging onto a tree root, bawling his head off, only nobody had heard him. You *couldn't* have heard him, 'less you stuck your head over the edge, leaned way down in there."

At this, even Wade paused with his fork halfway to his mouth. It seemed he hadn't heard this story before either.

"And the way I know it's true," George said into the silence at the table, "is that the little boy was me."

"George," Ellie said. "You never told me that."

He shrugged. "*Quoddy Tides* has an old photo of me hangin' on that root while the men lowered a line. Had a time gettin' me to grab it. But when I got more hungry than I was scairt, I did."

Victor got up, taking care not to step on any dogs. "Quite a story," he remarked, patting George on the shoulder genially. "Glad you made it out of the well." Then, offering his apologies all around, he excused himself.

I went to the door with him. "Are you all right?"

He hadn't even wanted any of the quince jam, though I'd offered him some. Now his eyes were bright; with wine, I thought. And one of them was bloodshot.

"Got something in it," he explained the redness. "I'm going to go home, wash it out. I've got an early morning tomorrow, too, so I should call it a night."

His words weren't exactly slurred but they weren't crisply enunciated, either. "You're not driving, are you?" I asked.

I stepped onto the back porch with him as Sam pulled up in the street out front in Victor's car, tapped the horn gently.

"He's taking me," Victor said. "Thanks for dinner." Pulling me nearer he planted a swift, chaste kiss on my forehead.

Throughout my whole history with Victor I might as well have expected a thank-you from one of those dogs. I wanted to ask what was going on, but he hustled down the steps and out to the car.

"You're welcome," I said into the night as it disappeared around the corner.

When I returned to the table Jenna Durrell was telling Wade about her adventures in boat rental; it seemed her struggles with rowboat navigation had been nothing compared to the hard time she was having learning to run even a small outboard engine.

But she was cheerful enough about it. Meanwhile Greg Brand gave the rest of the table the benefit of his knowledge regarding, it seemed, just about everything; at the moment he was pontificating about food.

"...peasant cookery," he pronounced condescendingly, a lofty wave of his left hand indicating the rappie pie.

He took another greedy bite of it, continuing as he chewed. "It's a bowdlerized version of the higher-class form of the dish, altered to include whatever game meat happens to be available to the working folk."

"Bowdler," George pronounced appreciatively. "That's some kind of a hat, isn't it?"

His own was an old black gimme-cap with the words *Guptill's Excavating* embroidered on it in orange script.

Greg didn't answer, rolling his eyes–I guessed that at the high-class meals he was used to, this constituted good manners–while beside him Jenna went on working on her second helping.

"Go on," she told Hetty Bonham. "Your diet won't fail on one night of decent food."

But Hetty remained hesitant. With her blonde hair teased in glamor-queen style and her nails polished tomato red, she wore so much eye makeup along with her fake lashes it was a wonder she could even see her food, much less notice its likely calorie content.

"I suppose," she allowed doubtfully, forking up a green bean and eating it, then favoring the rest of us with a big smile as if this were a photo op.

"I remember rappie pie," Marge Cathcart remarked sadly. She wasn't eating much, either.

"My great-aunt used to make it for Sunday dinner when we visited her. She was from New Brunswick, just over the Canadian border from here," she explained.

George finished his buttered roll and looked for another; I handed him the basket of them. After a day out fixing whatever had gotten broken in the storm–a fallen gutter, a split tree, or a strip of shingles peeled from the slant of an old roof–he was hungry enough to eat the gold off the rim of his plate.

"So you must have heard the stories about Horeb," he said.

"He was my husband's grandfather," Marge agreed. "I never met him but the family said he did even more than find water and lost kids. He was," she said, scorching Greg Brand with a look that dared him to disagree, "a talker to animals."

"I did hear one time that he had a tame fox," Ellie put in. "But I don't know if it was true. I was little when he died."

"Brought him rabbits." George nodded. "I know it for a fact. Fox hunted for him, he was so old an' poor by then he couldn't get meat no other way."

George cast a sideways eye-flicker at Greg, whom he had not forgiven for the comment about low-class food. "He used to give my folks some of the rabbits when he had more'n he could use. But like I say, he was an old man by then."

He ate part of his roll. "Last time I saw Horeb he was out at Ship's Point, sittin' way out there on the high rock, all by himself."

He took a final sip of his wine. "Anyway he was alone if you don't count the lynx by his side, and what I was pretty sure was an osprey perched on his arm like one o' them trained birds, what do you call 'em?"

"Falcons," Wade supplied quietly. There was a long moment of silence around the table as a sudden vivid picture popped into my head, not of old Horeb Cathcart the talker-to-animals, but of his great-granddaughter Wanda.

With that bat. Somehow the memory gave me hope, and when I looked across the table at Marge I could tell she was thinking something similar: Wanda was a strange child, and maybe in some way none of us could imagine, her strangeness would help her.

But then Greg was talking again. "Sorry, but I can't swallow that nonsense," he said. "Turning some old codger into a myth is all you're doing, and–"

George interrupted him smartly. "Come on, Greg, aren't you a magic teacher? Got these here folks to pay up for your expensive seminar, teach 'em to harness their powers and so on?"

He gave the word "powers" just enough of a twist so we all knew what he thought of Greg and his seminar. Then, without waiting for an answer:

"Tell the truth, I think I've probably got some magic powers myself." He eyed Greg up and down, not disguising the fact that he didn't like the other man even a little bit.

"Bet I could make you disappear," he said flatly. "You and your hocus-pocus."

Greg didn't answer, having perhaps become aware of the sudden atmosphere in the room: not Greg Brand–friendly. Instead he got up and excused himself curtly, leaving before I could follow him to the door with even a sham apology.

"George," Ellie admonished. "That wasn't very nice of you."

"Ayuh," he concurred. "Guess the peasants are rowdy tonight. Good dinner, though, even if it weren't quite up to Mr. Brand's highfalutin tastes."

And that was George, so laid-back and mellow you could get the impression it was safe to patronize him. It wasn't a mistake you'd be likely to make a second time, however.

He got up. "Come on, Wade, let's help Bella with the dishes, pay our way for all this fine grub. We can have dessert later and watch some of the football game while we eat it."

It was a suggestion Wade liked, freeing him as it did from Hetty, who'd begun trying to flirt. So this time I decided to let the fellows do kitchen duty, just as they wished. And when they'd gone, Hetty instantly found a new topic: Greg Brand himself.

"Poor Greg," she commented acidly. "He's not himself tonight. Guess he's upset about Eugene Dibble. And about Wanda of course," she added to Marge.

She was drunk, I suddenly realized. "Why would he be upset about Gene Dibble?" I asked innocently.

Because it was one thing for Greg to confide in me about his old partnership with the local ne'er-do-well, but I had a feeling Hetty's slant on it could be something else entirely.

She smiled slyly around the table. "I've known Greg a while, and I *happen* to know they were friends a long time ago."

She refilled her wineglass, drank it down. "Those two were thick as thieves then," she declared, clearly pleased to have an audience. "They ran a con on women Greg met, a lonely-hearts scam, in Massachusetts. They targeted women who didn't have husbands or boyfriends but who *did* own houses."

Tactfully Ellie poured a little more wine into her own glass and a lot more into Hetty's. "How did that work?" she asked.

"Greg got a lady's confidence, took her out, romanced her. Then he introduced her to Gene and *he* sold her... oh, vinyl siding. Driveway resurfacing. New windows, a roof." Hetty swallowed more wine, looking smug. "Any kind of crap that Greg could convince her she needed, and that Gene could get a down payment on–I mean a *really* hefty one–before starting the job."

Up until this point Jenna had been paying a lot of attention to her plate. But now she looked up.

"And then he wouldn't do it," she said harshly. "Or if she had a lot of money and they could keep running the con on her for a while, it would get done but shoddily."

She aimed her fork at Hetty. "Substandard materials, lousy workmanship–by the end the house was a wreck and she'd've run through all her money, every cent they could get out of her. She might even lose her home."

"How'd you find that out?" Hetty asked, blinking owlishly, but Jenna didn't get to answer. Instead, Marge Cathcart seized her own wineglass suddenly and flung it.

"You *knew*? How *could* you?" she shrieked. The glass missed Hetty and shattered against the fireplace mantel. "Because we're plain people it's all right to take advantage of us? *Fool* us? And now my daughter's gone because of *you*!" A sob escaped her. "Oh, how could I have been so *stupid*. . . ."

Jenna studied her hands; apparently when she'd clued Marge in to Greg's real nature, she hadn't added any information about Hetty. When her head came up again I raised an eyebrow at her.

"Give me a break," the ex-cop said in reply. "You saw Hetty giving Marge the mother-hen treatment out at the house. What was I supposed to do, take that away from her, too?"

She had a point. Poor Marge was pretty clearly at the very edge of a breakdown; it wouldn't take much more to push her over. I wasn't sure I'd have told her about yet another betrayal either.

And I certainly wasn't going to press her now for more details about Wanda; so much for the main point of this evening.

Even Hetty appeared taken aback by Marge's reaction, but of course didn't blame herself. "If Greg wasn't such a wimp we could at least get out of here," she said. "And go home."

"Marge." Ellie spoke sharply past me at the weeping woman. "This wasn't your fault. You were only trying to do the right thing."

"What do you mean?" I asked Hetty, intrigued. "What's stopping you?"

"The police investigators asked Greg to stick around a few days," she explained. "Greg's afraid if he doesn't cooperate they'll take it wrong. So he agreed to."

"Anyone talking fraud?" I asked. Eugene Dibble's murder wasn't the only problem on Greg's plate, I reminded myself.

Hetty shook her head. "Somebody would have to press charges for that."

And at the moment of course it was the last thing on Marge's mind; she just wanted her daughter back.

"I don't know," Hetty finished, "what's going to happen. I just want to get out of here, that's all."

Across the table Ellie went on trying to console Marge. "And it sounds to me as if Greg Brand's a very accomplished liar," she said. "He's fooled more sophisticated people than you, people who should have known better."

"That's right," Jenna put in flatly.

"Oh, how would *you* know?" Marge wailed wretchedly, but at the expression on Jenna's face she broke off her retort.

"Because," Jenna answered slowly, "I know another very smart woman that it happened to. In Massachusetts on Nantucket Island."

She bit her lip, then went on. "Like Hetty just said, he had a routine of conning lonely women who'd never in their lives had to deal with anything so mundane as maintenance problems.

"I was thirteen and my dad had been dead a year when Greg Brand broke my mother's heart, cleaned out her bank accounts, and ruined her. *And* me," she added. "Part of the money was meant to be my college fund, that my dad left for me."

"But then why hasn't Greg recognized you?" Ellie asked.

Jenna made a face. "Why should he? He barely ever saw me. He made it very clear to my mother when he married her," she added, "that he didn't like kids."

She took a deep breath. "Oh, I could live in the house, eat their food, sleep in a bed. But he wasn't to know I was there. It was a condition of their agreement, and my mother . . . well. She was terribly lonely."

Brief silence until Marge broke it. "Jenna, it's kind of you to see it that way."

Wry laugh from Jenna. "Yeah, maybe. Whatever. Anyway, for a couple of years I made sure I was out of the house in the morning before he got up. Didn't come back until they were both in bed."

Twirling the stem of her empty glass, she concluded, "Like a thief in the night until finally I left for good. He took off, too, eventually. Turned out he didn't like sick people either, and by then my mother was dying and all the money was gone."

She looked up. "And that was the end of that."

• • •

"So there was a reason why Jenna decided to investigate Greg Brand for her latest writing project," I told Ellie later in the kitchen.

"Sure. Why make a target of some other crook when you can track the one who victimized you and your mother?" Ellie agreed, depositing a dustpanful of Marge's wineglass pieces into the trash.

"And by coming clean to everyone now, Jenna might've thought she could get Marge and maybe even Hetty to open up to her," she added. "Maybe give her even more ammunition against Brand."

"Yep. Scam's over. No point sticking with her cover story anymore."

Greg had taken the van, so Wade had driven Jenna, Hetty, and Marge back to Quoddy Village, Marge at first insisting she wouldn't be able to stay there. Instead she'd take a room at the Motel East, she said, so she wouldn't have to tolerate Greg and Hetty. But in the end she'd decided that if Wanda returned, it would almost surely be to the Quoddy Village house. And she wanted to be there when it happened.

Tiredly I poured what was left of the last bottle of wine into jelly glasses for Ellie and me. "The baby okay?"

"Mm-hmm." She sank into a kitchen chair. "Asleep on a blanket on the floor. George is on the couch."

She pantomimed a snore. Between the workday George had put in and the amount of wine he'd drunk, it was a good bet he'd be there until she shook him awake.

"You know, though..." she began unhappily.

"Yeah," I agreed. "It didn't exactly come out in an organized way, did it? But there was a lot of information in what those women said. And none of it makes things any easier."

Ellie sipped wine, grimaced, then dumped the rest down the sink. She'd never been much of a drinker.

"Jenna must hate Greg. It's why she wanted to take him down publicly, detail his scams for everyone to read," she mused aloud.

"Assuming that's all she's really doing." After seeing Jenna's face while she told her story, I wasn't so sure.

"Crucifying him in print might be satisfying," I said, "but maybe not quite bloody enough."

Ellie got out the milk, waved the carton inquiringly at me, then poured two glasses and sat again.

"What if Jenna wanted to get Greg into even more trouble than she could by writing about him?" I mused. "Kill Gene Dibble, then somehow manage to put the blame on Greg? If Greg hadn't decided to do it himself, she could've worked it so *she* was the one who told the cops about the connection between Greg and Dibble."

"It would sound bad for Greg, that he'd lied about whether or not he knew the victim," Ellie agreed. "But then why not tell the cops right away? Instead, Jenna kept her mouth shut."

She thought a moment. "And what about Hetty Bonham? She's obviously not crazy about Greg either."

"Still mad at him, maybe, for not rescuing her out of that situation with Greg's father. If *that's* even true," I added.

"I don't know," Ellie replied doubtfully. "He seems to be the one with the money, and she strikes me as smart enough not to cut her nose off to spite her face."

I drank some milk as Wade came in from where he'd been buttoning down his workshop for the night. He bent to kiss me, then headed upstairs.

"And then there's Marge," I said when he'd gone. "But I can't think what her motive would be. She wouldn't have involved Wanda deliberately. And I can't see her firing a gun, or even knowing how to use one, can you?"

With a shop full of firearms attached to my house and a husband who'd made a point of getting me at least competent with guns, I sometimes forgot that not everyone enjoyed similar opportunities for high-caliber enrichment.

But Marge was the kind of person who'd probably cringe at pulling the trigger on a cap pistol. "Unless she found out Greg was putting one over on her sooner than we think, *and* she's a lot more vengeful than she seems..."

"No," Ellie said firmly. "Too complicated. For one thing, you're right about Wanda. Marge wouldn't endanger her. And the person she'd have had a motive to shoot is Greg, not Gene Dibble."

She finished her milk. "But the big problem is the timing. Greg could've wanted to kill Dibble, too. We don't *know* he wasn't aware Dibble lived here. But they're all each other's alibi."

"Except for Jenna, and she was out in the boat," I said. "Which if she *hadn't* been, the boat wouldn't have gotten lost, and..."

And then I wouldn't have nearly drowned in it. "Wanda was the only one we know of in the house when it happened. Ellie, you don't suppose she..."

But before I could finish this thought Sam came in with the dogs. "Mom," he began worriedly, releasing them.

Ellie got up. "I've got to go," she said. "Or start. It'll take half an hour just to get George awake and up off the couch."

She hesitated, and from her face I could tell there was more she wanted to say to me. Something like *Hey, take it easy, okay?*

Or *Don't do anything stupid.* Because she hadn't forgotten me weeping and bashing at those porch boards.

But she wouldn't mention it in front of Sam. "What'd you do with the old gold piece?" she asked instead.

"Got it right here." Changing my clothes for dinner, I'd transferred it into my skirt pocket.

"Cool," Sam said when I produced it. But he still sounded worried.

"Hang onto it," Ellie advised me a little while later on her way out the door with George and Leonora. "Maybe it's lucky."

Which was what I thought: a golden amulet, arriving as if by magic. But as I waited for their car to depart before I shut the yard lights off, I shivered and decided it might just be fool's gold.

• • •

About an hour later the phone rang. I grabbed the receiver at the first hint of a jangle, before it could wake Wade.

It was just after midnight. "Hello?"

I'd been sitting alone in the dining room staring at the red embers in the fireplace, thinking about what Sam told me after Ellie went home. And waiting, because if that telephone *was* going to ring, it could do it tonight.

"I hear you want a deal," a man's deep voice said.

I said nothing. This wasn't about me talking.

"I've got the girl," the voice taunted. "How come you didn't tell the cops about the barrette? And never mind," he added, "how I know you didn't."

So Wade had been right about Joey. "Good question," I said.

But I had the answer ready. I'd examined my conscience from here to hell and back about it.

"Would it make it any easier for anyone to find you if they knew about the barrette?" I asked.

Bitter laugh. "No."

As I'd thought. And Joey wouldn't tell the police any more than he'd told me. But if I could *find out* more...

My hand closed on the gold piece with its raised relief of Saint George. Touching it pinged a memory but for love or money I couldn't quite think of what.

Too tired, and too damned terrified all of a sudden.

That I would screw this up. "Rickert? You there?"

Silence.

"Rickert?" Had he hung up?

"Yeah."

Sure he was there. I'd played my hole card by offering money and money always brings the vermin out of the woodwork.

"I'm here," he went on calmly. Like there was no urgency in any of this, and maybe there wasn't. Wanda could already be dead. He could've dropped her by the side of a road somewhere.

Or maybe he'd never had her; you could buy pink barrettes in Wal-Mart. Some other woman might have ventured unwisely onto Joey Rickert's boat, just as Joey had insisted.

Dropped it there in her rush to get back off again, perhaps. But the rest of what I'd imagined could still be true. Nervously, I filled the silence.

"I meant what I told your brother. You need money and all I want is the girl back unharmed."

While I spoke, my rising anxiety was creating the sensation of an out-of-body experience, as if my physical self had simply dissolved and the rest of me hung there, floating in thin air.

Only my fingertips on the old gold piece felt real. "Well, it's not quite that simple," Rickert said.

"Why not?"

The words rushed out of me despite my resolve to seem calm. "Because if you don't tell anyone, and I don't tell anyone..."

"Shut up," he cut in mildly. "I need her pills."

So he had her alive. *Thank you,* I breathed silently.

Or maybe that was just what he wanted me to think. "How did you know she needs pills? Did she tell you? Is she all right?"

Brief silence. Then: "You want to do this or not?"

My turn to pause. I had cash in the house. But...

Sure, why not meet in the middle of the night with a drug dealer who was also possibly a kidnapper and maybe even a murderer?

Not to mention what else he might be. And it was *that* thought that made my decision for me.

"Of course I do," I answered. "Where do you want to do it?" I could wake up Wade, get him to go with me....

"Tell anyone or bring anyone and I'll kill her," Rickert said, as if reading my thought. "I mean it."

"I understand," I replied, thinking *Damn,* and waiting for him to tell me where he wanted me to meet him.

Instead... *click!*

He'd hung up.

I stared at the phone, wanting to reach through it and drag Mac Rickert back. He was *playing* with me, the son of a bitch–

But then in the silence of the big old house at night I heard footsteps on the back porch. Next came the unmistakable faint creak of the mailbox being opened.

The dogs didn't even wake up. I dashed for the porch but by the time I got there no one was around, only the fog drifting ghostly in the street under a silent streetlight.

A foghorn moaned in the distance. A skunk scuttled across the driveway, its white stripe waving like a danger flag.

Tucked into the mailbox was a sheet of lined notebook paper.

A map.

• • •

...risk-taking behavior...

A year or so later somebody built a house at the end of Toll Bridge Road, but that night the gravel turnaround overlooking the water was silent and deserted.

Leading downhill was a track made of broken chunks of old pavement interspersed with clumps of grass. Once this had been the only way to the mainland, via a wooden bridge and before that a ferry; now the causeway curved a couple of miles to the west, beyond a wide stretch of forest and another rocky beach.

In short, I was alone, in the middle of the woods and almost in the water. *One o'clock,* the scrawl on the hand-drawn map read.

I aimed my flashlight hesitantly ahead. It was twenty to one now. I'd figured I'd better arrive a little early, get the lay of the land if I could and at least not be taken by surprise.

Halfway down the grassy track the tip of my shoe caught on a chunk of the old pavement, sending me staggering. Once I managed to get my balance back, I thought I heard something to my left, in a thick stand of blackberry bushes backed by maple saplings.

Lit from below, the bare branches of the trees reflected my flashlight eerily as if reaching out. But nothing was there and after a moment my heart stopped thundering and I went on more carefully. A sprained ankle wasn't going to advance my cause any.

Nothing will. The thought came unbidden; I brushed it away.

Nothing can change what happened to you.

But I didn't expect it to, did I? Even I wasn't that much of an idiot. Once I'd thought this, the voice in my head fell silent.

I knew how foolhardy it was coming out here alone, too. But I couldn't risk telling anyone; someone who might follow, meaning only to help. Someone whose presence might provoke Rickert into making good on his threat.

Or so I told myself, taking another step. Ahead wooden pilings loomed, remnants of the old bridge, now leaning crazily one way and the other like a clump of giant mushrooms growing from a single center.

I shone the flashlight among them in case someone was hiding there, but no one was. Then I stepped down onto the beach.

Stones and shells crunched under my feet. Across the water a single house stood silent under a bright white yard light, the fog turning the glow into a wavering nimbus. Beyond the trees to my right, the causeway hummed occasionally in the distance with the passage of a middle-of-the-night car or truck.

Otherwise nothing. The air smelled of iodine, sharply medicinal, and the fog lay like a cold cloth on my hot forehead.

I breathed it in, wishing I could spread it on my heart. *A girl alone...*

I'd never told anyone the real reason why I ran away from my mother's folks, who'd taken me in when she died. The closest I'd gotten was entertaining Ellie with stories about my hound-dog boy cousins, who'd chased me around the packed-earth yard and among the outbuildings of the old farm as if I were a little rabbit.

What I didn't say was that sometimes they caught me.

So I shouldn't have come, and I should have woken Wade, and I should have told someone where I was going; elementary. But it might have meant explaining, and that I couldn't do; I'd tried, but the words always refused to come out of my mouth.

So instead in one pocket I had the gold piece and in the other I had a .22 pistol, courtesy of Wade's gun collection. The Bisley was too big to handle fast enough out here in the dark, and the .22 was plenty.

My foot slipped on a wet rock. Flailing, I struggled to keep my balance but the other foot hit a mess of seaweed, slick and treacherous as glare ice.

Oh, this is going to hurt, I thought on the way down.

But I never landed. Strong hands caught me easily. Relieved not to be bashing my brains out on a boulder, I didn't even struggle until one of the arms tightened around my waist.

Then a hand pressed something to my face.

The sweet smell of chloroform rushed into my lungs, filled my chest. Across the water, the fog-shrouded light shriveled to a pinpoint, racing away into a dark tunnel, dragging me along.

Until the darkness swallowed me whole.

Chapter 9

I **woke up groggy, nauseated, and with a headache so bad that** it felt as if my skull had been run over by a truck.

Cold, too; under a rough blanket I was shivering helplessly. Also, I was apparently on a boat: cold spray, rolling waves...

Groaning, I let my head loll over the rail and gave up just about everything I'd ever eaten in my life. After that my stomach felt better but my head felt worse. My teeth kept chattering, and the jackhammer effect this produced in my skull was nothing short of excruciating.

At the far end of the boat a man operated an outboard motor, its sound a low grumble barely audible in the rush of wind and water. I lay sprawled in the bow feeling the wooden seat dig into the back of my neck. Straight overhead, the clouds were breaking apart enough to let the stars shine through.

Lots of stars, which meant we were far from any artificial lights. And Eastport was full of them, so where the hell...?

I sat up, squinting through eyes that felt bruised and swollen. The blanket had begun helping a little, and now that my stomach had nothing in it the cold fresh air was scouring some of the nauseated feeling away, too.

I spotted the lights of Campobello Island laid out in a long broken line, and in the other direction the dock lights over the tugboats tied up at the fish pier in Eastport. Soon after that, my chloroform-insulted brain came up with three facts:

(1) We were motoring, without any lights of our own, in an open boat in the middle of Passamaquoddy Bay, (2) the guy in the stern with a hand on the tiller was almost certainly Mac Rickert, and (3) the thing in his other hand was my gun.

"Bastard," I muttered. Mac didn't react. Instead he dug into a satchel, then leaned amidships to hand a small tin pillbox and a glass bottle to me.

That was when I noticed he was wearing a life vest. And that I wasn't. "Wash 'em down," he advised cryptically.

Squinting, I saw he'd given me a tin of aspirin tablets and a pint of Wild Turkey. I gathered he thought these would dull the side effects of the anesthesia he'd administered. I thought bonking him with one of the oars lying by my feet would make me feel even better, but there was that basic life-jacket mismatch to consider: him, yes.

Me, no. And if I went over the side while trying to clobber him I would certainly drown. So I sat where I was and fumbled the tin open, chewing two aspirin before slugging down a mouthful out of the whiskey bottle. When the stuff hit my stomach and stayed there, I took another swallow and put the bottle between my feet.

Now if I could only get the gun. One in the kneecap should do it....

"Don't try," Rickert said as if reading my mind. On his feet were a pair of wading boots, the kind hunters wear when they're out in a marsh hunting ducks. The boots' tops were rolled down, I noticed irrelevantly.

"Bottled courage won't make up for the weight advantage I've got on you," he said.

Unfortunately, he was correct; physics again. "What do you want with me? I thought we were just going to talk."

"We are. I didn't know if you were smart enough to go along with my instructions about not bringing anyone, that's all. So I snatched you up quick in case someone was about to join you."

Dumb enough was more like it, I thought, ashamed all at once of my own stupidity. What the hell had been the matter with me? Now I was going to end up missing, too, just like...

"Where's Wanda?" I demanded. "What've you done with–"

"Don't worry about her. You've got bigger problems."

A sudden rush of fright nearly swamped me. What was *this* all about, now, and why hadn't I seen it coming?

But I knew. I'd wanted to be a heroine, save the day all by myself. That way I wouldn't have to tell anyone what was really going on with me; simple as that.

"So I guess it was you out on the street the other night. Under my window." My tongue felt thick; chloroform was a disgusting drug, and where had he gotten it, anyway?

Then I remembered: he was a drug dealer. He could probably get his hands on plutonium if he wanted some.

He nodded. "Luanne got in touch, said you'd been over at her place asking about me."

Of course. She'd lied about not being in contact with him.

"Figured I'd have a peek. Nice house you've got," he said.

Oh, spare me the small talk.

"Luanne was afraid I'd be mad at her for mentioning me," he added. "Had herself an attack of nerves. She thinks I'm dangerous, I guess. Real outlaw type."

"Great. Thanks for sharing that. And you got me out here to tell me about it because..."

Hey, even bullies must need to unburden themselves once in a while, I thought bitterly. Lighten the old psychic load. He aimed the boat toward Eastport, waved at one of the few houses with its lights still on in the village.

"I know the woman who lives there," he remarked, seemingly apropos of nothing.

And as if I cared. In the darkness he negotiated the tide and currents expertly, keeping us heading at a slight angle into the waves to minimize choppiness.

"Sold me half her oxycontin scrip last week. Now she's up with bone pain, I suppose," he went on.

You are a shit, I thought but didn't say. Once in a while a patient of Victor's got bone pain from a tumor.

"Why would she do that? Sell her pain medicine when . . . ?"

When she knows that very soon she will need it herself.

It was another thing I'd learned from Victor. When the time came for painkillers, he'd give you enough to fell a horse if you needed it, and if it wiped out your breathing and blood pressure, well–well, let's just say no one had ever objected to the medication regimens he prescribed.

"What do you care, anyway?" Rickert wanted to know suddenly.

"My son's a recovering addict," I replied. "So I've got my opinions."

No answer from Rickert. Then all at once the reality of my situation washed over me and with it another wave of chloroform-muddled terror.

"My ex-husband just found out he has an inoperable brain tumor," I blurted.

Then I upchucked again, the booze and aspirin coming up in a sour rush as if my gut was trying to unload this new knowledge as well. It was what Sam had told me, that when they'd gotten back to Victor's after the dinner party Victor had asked him to come inside, and then he had told Sam.

"I don't know why I told you that," I said.

Sam said Victor had seemed calm and sort of consoling about it when he told Sam. When he got back outside, though, he could see his father through the kitchen window, at the table with his face in his hands.

"Sorry to hear it," Rickert said finally, not sounding concerned. "Anyway, the woman I was telling you about, who sold me the pills. Reason she did it is, her daughter's going to a big dance at the high school next week. Needs a dress."

He lit a cigarette, cupping the match in his hands so it lit his face for an instant. "And of course there's no money in that house," he went on, flipping the match away.

"She asked around, finally got in touch with me, bound and determined she was going to sell those pills."

He leaned forward, took the whiskey bottle and drank from it. "I didn't buy 'em, somebody else would. And I didn't bargain her down on the price, either."

"Yeah, you're a real Robin Hood. And your brother Joey, he's your faithful sidekick, I guess."

But right away I could tell this was the wrong thing to say. His face hardened as his hand tightened on the engine's throttle.

Too late I remembered that Rickert wasn't a loser like Gene Dibble. Stories of how he was only helping out poor widows aside, he was the genuine article, a guy who would hurt you if he had to.

Or maybe even if he only wanted to. The notion didn't scare me the way it probably should have, though. In fact, now that my nausea had partly cleared and my head had stopped hammering like the piston on a well-digger's drill, I was feeling better all the time.

Not about Victor, of course. But about Rickert. The reason being that back in the city when I was a hotshot money manager, I'd dealt with bad guys who by comparison made Mac Rickert look about as dangerous as Howdy Doody.

And he was *hesitating*. If he'd wanted to kill me he could've already done it. Gotten away with it, too. Also his body language was all wrong for somebody who was about to commit mayhem.

In my checkered past, I'd seen people who were about to do things, really bad things that were going to end with other people being stuffed lifeless into car trunks, for instance.

And their preparation was always the same. They stood or sat up straight, squaring their shoulders and formalizing themselves bodily for the event. On some level it felt important to them, almost religious. Even if they'd done it before, when the moment came to actually go out and do it, they took it seriously.

As my eyes went on adjusting to the darkness on the water, I saw that Rickert sat sort of hunched over, his head cocked to the side. He was frowning inquisitively at me as if wondering whether or not he could trust me.

Which told me that, like me, he was caught in the middle of something he didn't understand. And that he didn't quite know what to do about it. So I decided to try easing him back to the crux of the problem.

"All I care about is Wanda," I said.

He lit another cigarette, flicked the match away. In the momentary glow his face was dark, bearded, with bushy eyebrows and a shaggy mane of dark hair under a knitted cap.

"What do you want, Mac? When I talked to Joey I said I'd pay you for her return, assuming she is unharmed. Have you got me out here to make the deal, or is there something else on your agenda that we need to get out into the open?"

Risky, cutting to the chase that way. But I had to believe that if I offered him some kind of a solution, he might go for it.

More silence. Then: "Tell your buddy Bob Arnold to wait," he uttered abruptly. "Couple days, no longer."

I blinked in surprise. "Wait for . . . ?"

He dragged hard on the cigarette, tossed it away. It hit the water with a little hiss. "There's something I need to finish. When it's done I'm going to turn myself in." Saying this, he flashed a surprisingly white grin. "Scout's honor," he said.

As soon as the words were out of his mouth I remembered: Saint George. The saint on the coin was shown seated astride a white horse, like a knight in his shining armor. And Saint George was the patron saint of...

At the same moment, too, I saw clearly the gun in Rickert's hand.

...Boy Scouts. As for the gun...

The safety was on. Which meant either (a) he wasn't familiar with the weapon, which I didn't believe for a minute–

Around here, guys like Mac started handling guns about the time they put down their baby bottles and blankies–

–or (b) he didn't intend to shoot me. This thought, however, might have encouraged me into feeling just a little too confident. "So what exactly do you want me to do besides play messenger?" I asked.

Because if that was all it was, he could have written Bob Arnold a note. Stuck it under the wiper of the squad car maybe, or had his brother Joey do it.

"And," I pressed on, even more unwisely, "why should I believe you haven't killed Wanda already? She must've been a witness to Dibble's shooting, that must be why you kidnapped her in the first place, right?"

I took a breath. "So why shouldn't I just run screaming to Bob Arnold the minute you put me ashore, when there's still time for him to get out and catch up with you?"

But my confidence evaporated when in the silence following my remarks he lit another cigarette and by match-gleam I got a glimpse of his eyes.

"I didn't kidnap her," he said coldly.

Not Boy Scoutish. Also, he didn't *have* to put me ashore. He could shove me overboard and then the only messages I'd be sending would be in the bubbles escaping from my lungs.

"Right, sure you didn't. But what else do you *want* from me?" I backpedaled, feeling that I'd better reestablish the notion that I might be useful. And this time he answered my question bluntly.

"I've already got it."

Then it hit me: Wanda's pills. Which–I checked my pockets–he'd already taken, along with the gun.

"Killed Dibble with one just like this," he remarked. As he spoke he leveled it at me, thumbed the safety off.

He'd wanted the pills, that was all. The diabetes medicine; he needed it to keep his teenage captive alive.

"You son of a *bitch*." I heard the words burst from me, felt myself hurtling at him, my fingernails aiming for his eyes.

And for a glorious instant I had him at a disadvantage; what I was doing was suicide, so it was the last thing he could have expected. With my weight pushing him back on the engine mount, I kneed him hard.

"Christ," he grated out, and dropped the .22.

I scrabbled for the weapon, but where was it? In the dark I couldn't find it, and now the water began to make trouble, as well, rolling the little vessel treacherously.

Rickert's hand flopped ineffectually, searching for the tiller to bring us around. A wave hit, knocking me sideways, and when I fell my head smacked the rail with a sick *clunk!*

The gun, where was the gun... *There.* But as I reached for it, his right boot came up, grazing my chin. I landed in the bow, my shoulder first smacking the wooden seat and then sliding halfway under it. I was stunned with pain and as helpless suddenly as a turtle on its back.

The boat swayed, then settled as with one hand Mac seized the tiller, his other hand reaching down to secure the weapon and aim it at me again. Gunning the engine, he raced us away from the open water, where now that the stars were out there was a chance we might be visible from shore.

If someone happened to be scanning in our direction, that is. And if they'd alerted the Coast Guard on account of us having no running lights, maybe being in distress.

But even at this distance I could see the Guard's big orange Zodiac boat, empty and motionless. No cavalry was riding to my rescue. Then the lights of town vanished as we hurtled around the south end of the island, past the cargo docks at Prince's Cove.

I could have jumped overboard. The trouble was, I couldn't swim to shore. Not in this water, so frigid that a person without a special dive suit would die in twenty minutes, even if they were wearing a life preserver.

Because the challenge wasn't keeping your head above water; it was getting your body out of it before all the vital systems chilled so low that they shut off entirely.

Rickert throttled down. The only sound was the engine wetly grumbling in neutral, the only light a distant, diffuse glow from the runway beacons at the airfield, half a mile distant.

He picked up an oar. For a moment I thought he meant to haul engine and row in, that the rocks here were too numerous for the boat to land under power. But then he spoke.

"I meant what I said. They have to wait. I need a few days. Or maybe just one."

Sour bile rose in my throat; I averted my mind's eye from an all-too-clear picture of what he might want to finish.

"Leave her alone," I whispered.

Ignoring me, he stood. If I'd tried it, I'd have capsized the boat immediately. But this guy moved as surely as if he were on shore.

"Out," he ordered, gripping the oar. *That* got my attention. We were still a hundred yards from land.

Then he hit me with the oar. Not hard, but the flat part smacked the side of my head convincingly. If he'd done it with the edge it would've taken the top of my skull off.

Woozy with pain and fear, I clambered up. "Listen," I began, "we can talk about this–"

Everything seemed to have ratcheted way down into super-slow motion; the waves, my heart. Rickert swung the oar again. This time the flat blade connected with my shoulder the way a bat hits a ball, lifting me and carrying me over the rail.

The last thing I saw was his face watching impassively as I splashed down. Then came the sudden roar of the outboard as he motored away.

Leaving me in the icy water, kicking and flailing.

• • •

Drowning. The shock to your system is indescribable and the first thing you do is begin gasping, uncontrollably and in a way that makes you panic.

But panic spells doom; you must think, and eventually the gasping will pass. Sinking, I kicked hard. That sent me up again, my face breaking the surface just long enough to drag in a breath. And then...

My arm hit something solid. Instinctively, I went after it, and it bounced away, floating. Once more I sank, then somehow found the thing again, whatever it was, clawed at it knowing it would be only a clot of seaweed and no help to me, but unable to stop myself.

Another hopeless grab, punctuated by a throatful of salt water. Gagging and weeping, I felt my hand brush the seaweed clump and somehow fasten upon it.

Only it wasn't seaweed. It was Mac Rickert's life jacket.

With the last burst of non-drowning purposefulness I could muster, I shoved an arm into it. That gave me enough hope to get my other arm into the other side, and my head through.

Next I took a ragged breath, immensely grateful merely to be inhaling air instead of water, and after that I assessed my situation.

Verdict: still terrible. But not quite *as* terrible. *In with the good air and out with the bad* made a lovely mantra, under the circumstances. Grimly I forced my iced legs to start kicking and my hands to begin paddling.

But time was running out. My hands were little more than numb clubs. Soon I would be so chilled that my mental processes would quit working, too.

Although you could argue they'd stopped functioning usefully a whole lot earlier, like way back when I'd decided to meet Mac Rickert out here at all....

But that was a scolding I could give myself later, if there was one. For now I kept kicking, paddling, and breathing, nearing a stony shore whose cruel battering I would soon be enduring.

If I was lucky. Which by now I'd decided I was. After all, I *could* have gone into the water with a bullet in my head.

But I hadn't. And *that* meant...

My foot brushed a rock. A slippery, unhelpful, murderously treacherous rock. My shoe skidded on it, hurling me face-forward into the cold brine; sputtering and coughing I struggled back up, my eyes burning and my hands stinging and bleeding.

I could feel warmth streaming from them. And... I could feel the *bottom.* Jagged, uneven, littered with granite edges so sharp they were practically serrated...

Sobbing with relief, I scrambled on hands and knees, never mind the pain. I was ice cold, bruised, bloody, humiliated, and madder than hell; half at myself for getting into this mess, and half at Rickert for shoving me overboard, leaving me for dead.

But I wasn't in deep water anymore, and that was something.

Everything. Crawling up onto Deep Cove Road, I searched the darkness, spotted a window glowing yellow about a quarter-mile distant.

Struggling up, I began trudging toward the light.

• • •

The people in the house were very kind. They didn't dither or demand to know what I'd been doing out there in the first place. The only real trouble I had was in getting them to take me home instead of to the hospital.

Especially since my teeth were chattering so hard I could barely speak, which was the first thing Wade noticed.

And that I was soaking wet. "Jesus," he said when I turned on the light and woke him, and he got a look at me.

As he swung his legs out of bed I was already stripping my clothes off, my icy fingers struggling. He ripped my shirt down the front and pulled it from me, muscling me toward the shower.

"Okay," he kept saying when he got me under the warm water. It felt scalding hot. "Okay, now, you're going to be okay."

I couldn't stand up by myself, so he lowered me to a sitting position and got the rest of my clothes off. By then I was shuddering uncontrollably, unable to speak.

But later I did, dressed in warm flannel and wrapped in blankets, a mug of hot milk laced with brandy cupped in my hands, sitting up in bed.

"Alone," Wade said grimly when I'd finished. "Without telling anyone."

It was four in the morning. "Jacobia, you know there's not a thing you can do or ever will want to do, that I'll ever tell you not to. But this..."

I nodded wretchedly in reply. The superficial shivering had ended; now the shudders were slower and more painful, seeming to come from the insides of my bones.

Also, my nose was running. Wade took the mug from my hands and replaced it with tissues, then caught sight of my hands.

"Let's see," he said sternly.

Reluctantly, I held them out. They were a mess, with long, water-bleached skin flaps that if they were any deeper would have required stitches to close. As it was, they just stung like hell.

Wade looked silently at them for a moment. Then he sat on the edge of the bed and put his arm around me.

"You poor kid," he said as I began weeping again, hating myself but not able to stop. By now anyone else would've been shouting at me, I knew.

Wade just sat there until I was finished. "I'm so sorry," I whispered. "I thought if I found out what he wanted..."

It still didn't make sense unless you knew what sent me out there, and maybe not then either. Anyone else would have told me what an idiot I'd been.

But Wade heard the silences between the words. And didn't press me. Instead he concentrated on Mac.

"He drugged you, held a gun on you–"

Wade's gun. We hadn't even gotten yet to the part about Mac still having it. Or that I'd taken it without asking.

Or about Victor. "... hit you and forced you overboard."

He stood up, turning away. Probably so I couldn't see his face; under most conditions Wade was the gentlest of men.

But this wasn't most conditions. "Yeah," I said. "It was pretty pitiful, actually."

I drank some more hot milk. My heart wasn't palpitating anymore, another symptom I hadn't mentioned to Wade.

When he turned back his face appeared carved out of stone. "Well, then," he said. "I guess there's no choice. I'm just going to have to go out and find the son of a bitch and kill him."

The gentlest of men, but at that moment he wasn't kidding. And in downeast Maine, he didn't have to be; guys vanished here. Not often; years might go by before a sort of unofficial court of last resort passed down an unspoken verdict.

But over the decades this remote part of the world had disposed of enough proudly unreformable wife-beaters, predatory child molesters, and other innocent-victim-creating monsters to form a precedent: if you were bad enough, and the justice system didn't get you, sooner or later someone else would.

"Wade, if I hadn't been so dumb he'd never have had a chance to do anything to me."

Wade said nothing.

"Also if he has got Wanda and something happens to him, we might never find her," I went on.

Wade studied his hands.

"I'm sorry I didn't tell you where I was going, or bring you along," I added. "It was foolish of me and I won't take that kind of risk again."

He was listening.

"But don't let what's happened make you do something foolish, too," I pleaded.

His hands relaxed.

"When you walk into a buzz saw," I said, "if you get cut, you don't blame the saw."

Reluctantly, Wade nodded. He hadn't put away the idea of punishing Mac Rickert, but there wasn't going to be any vigilante justice dispensed tonight.

"Okay," he said. "But don't do this to me again, Jake."

His face was gray and exhausted. "I mean it. Don't make me wonder where you are every minute, what's happening to you. Because I can't take it."

I nodded. Part of me argued silently that if I'd been a guy we wouldn't be having this conversation. But the other part–the sensible part–knew that getting hijacked by your own obsession was a gender-neutral form of stupidity.

"All right, then," he said finally. "You'll be okay alone here for a minute?"

And when I said I would be, he padded downstairs; I lay there listening to my husband moving quietly around the big old house.

Appliances off, check; door locked, check. Dogs in their beds sound asleep and Cat Dancing atop the refrigerator, double check.

Later, safe in the darkness with him, I noticed every one of the differences between this and the cold water I'd struggled in. I was aware too of him lying there awake beside me.

"Jacobia," he said after a while.

The word made a warm burst of breath on my neck. Every inch of his skin where it pressed on mine radiated like fire.

"You can tell me. Whatever it is, if you ever want to, you can."

"I know," I said. But the truth was that I still couldn't. Instead I turned into his arms, heedless of the pain in my shoulder and hands, heedless of everything but having been returned to the land of the living.

He kissed me very carefully but with wonderful effectiveness considering the night's circumstances.

Or any circumstances, actually.

He was an effective man.

Chapter 10

Ellie arrived at my house the next morning at a quarter to seven; Wade had already called her.

"He says you need your head screwed back on straight," she told me frankly. "But he didn't say why."

I was out in the front yard gazing at the place where the old porch had stood. Around dawn I'd wakened to the rumble of enormous gears grinding; looking out, I'd been treated to the sight of a big truck backing from the street onto the lawn.

"So?" Ellie went on, squinting at me with a cup of coffee in her hand. Sam had already come by to take the dogs out. "You look awful, by the way," she added.

Yeah, no doubt. Now the Dumpster I'd filled was gone, along with the pieces of the old porch I'd demolished; time marches on and all that, but at such moments I always felt sorrowful, as if its parade route led over my heart.

"Well," I began. Also, time's marching always left a trail of destruction for me to clean up. Unhappily I noted the trenches that the garbage truck's wide tires had dug into the lawn.

Topsoil, grass seed... But not until after the porch was rebuilt. The lumber still lay under the blue tarp, ready for me to begin measuring, sawing, and hammering.

Instead I felt like crawling under the tarp myself. "I did a kind of a careless thing," I admitted.

Right. Stepping off a twenty-story building could be called careless, too. Oh, I felt like the world's worst fool.

Ellie wore a cream knit turtleneck, denim coveralls with red hearts appliquéd to the bodice and pockets, and tan suede clogs. For her it was a remarkably color-coordinated getup except for the orange and green ribbon she'd braided into her red hair.

"Anyway, you're coming with me," she said, not waiting for me to explain any more. "I've got our day all planned."

She didn't mention my hands, I noticed, though they were a disaster, too. Apparently Wade's conversation with her had been quite detailed; yet another wave of humiliation washed over me.

In the kitchen I hesitated; down in the cellar my father was getting ready to plug the broken water pipe for good. With him was Toby Sullivan, head of Eastport's public works department. And when I stepped out the back door to see what else might be involved, I saw that Toby had brought along–*shudder*–a backhoe.

"But Ellie..." How could I leave when they were planning to assault my home with a digging machine?

"You're coming if I have to put you in a sack and drag you," Ellie repeated firmly.

Just then Sam and Victor arrived, apparently in hopes that I would fix breakfast. Fortunately Bella chose that moment to show up too, though, and so did Ellie's husband George.

"Thought I'd keep an eye on the proceedings," he said. Which meant he would supervise the pipe work, thank goodness.

"And what about you?" I turned to Sam, whose day was supposed to be spent at the boat school. What I really wanted was to get Victor alone for a minute, but he avoided eye contact.

"I'm hangin' out with Dad," Sam said. "What with him taking off tomorrow and all. He just told me he's going."

"Seminar," Victor explained. His eyes still didn't meet mine. Cat Dancing watched him skeptically.

Me too. "In Denver, on surgical techniques," he added. "One of their presenters canceled, they asked me to fill in. Couple of days. A week, tops."

Uh-huh. *We'll talk more later,* I telegraphed to Victor, who this morning seemed fine. Sam must've misunderstood his father last night, I thought, annoyed.

Still, it all left me at liberty just as Ellie had hoped, so that half an hour after dropping the baby off at day care–George intended to spend the afternoon with Lee, I'd been informed–we were on our way out of town.

"Wow," was all Ellie said at first when I'd told her what had happened. "So he's really got her. Have you told Bob Arnold?"

No lecture; *thank you,* I thought at her. "Tried," I said. "Wade said there wasn't much point waking him up in the middle of the night. So this morning I left a message for him but he hasn't called back."

In Eastport, if Bob wasn't at a phone, your call got routed to a county dispatcher, which wouldn't be helpful either. "Wade said he'd keep trying," I added. "But hell, what I did was so nuts I'd be surprised if Bob even believes me."

Along Route 190 the bronze needles of the hackmatack trees glowed against the hard blue sky, while in the old orchards along the road leafless apple trees drooped, still heavy with fruit.

"Anyway, what good'll it do talking to Bob?" I went on in frustration. "The state cops are already looking for Rickert and I don't know where he is. What more *do* I know, other than that he is really capable of murder?"

Ellie took the long curve past the airfield and shot uphill toward the

Quoddy Village turnoff. There a girl walked backwards along the shoulder, her thumb stuck out. Wearing a black jacket, heeled boots, and a miniskirt, she jerked her hand down when we got close enough for her to see our faces.

And realize that we weren't potential customers. "That was Luanne Moretti," I said as we went by, craning my neck around.

A pickup slowed and pulled over to let Luanne in.

Ellie watched in the rearview mirror. "Mm-hmm. I've seen her out here a few times before. I'd be scared to just get in a car with some guy, wouldn't you?"

The pickup pulled back onto the road. "Yeah. Probably she is, too. But I guess everybody's got expenses to cover."

Ellie slowed for the speed trap at Pleasant Point, the cop behind the wheel of the parked squad car gazing motionless from behind his dark glasses. A couple of minutes later she stopped at the corner of Route 1 to wait for a log truck, then turned left.

"Anyway, I guess I could also call the state cops," I went on, "but if I do it's going to come out why I was out there with Rickert and then *Bob's* going to be in trouble. Which if I thought it would help, that would be one thing. But..."

"But it doesn't give them any better places to look than they had before." Ellie finished my sentence. "I'm not so sure your little adventure last night was completely useless, though," she said, pressing the accelerator again.

We began by heading for Machias, the next town to our south. But soon she turned onto a side road, narrow blacktop winding along a river where mallards floated among the cattails.

"Oh, yeah?" I retorted, swallowing hard. With Ellie at the wheel, we might as well have been at the Indy 500. "Name me one helpful thing I learned," I demanded as she steered expertly through a trio of hilly S-turns. Between her speed and a lingering chloroform hangover, the curves set my bruised head spinning.

"That maybe he's not a murderer." She noticed my discomfort, popped open the glove box. Inside lay a pint bottle of Scotch.

Meanwhile she went on driving very fast. I couldn't decide whether to stare at the bottle or at the truck headed suddenly at us, straddling the yellow line as it rounded the next curve.

"Ellie!" I exhaled as her left hand hit the horn, her right hand downshifted, and her feet did a complicated maneuver on the clutch, brake pedal, and accelerator.

"Hang on," she advised. Instants later we had bumped through a ditch luckily cushioned by barberry and bittersweet and were back on the road, Ellie flipping a middle finger out the window.

Thoughtfully, I opened the pint bottle and took a swallow, considered putting it back in the glove box, then tucked it between my knees instead.

"As I was saying," Ellie said as we zoomed onto an uphill straightaway, "it strikes me that this life jacket you fastened onto was just a little too convenient."

Surrounded on both sides now by stone wall–fenced pastures, the road just went on climbing. "What do you mean?" I demanded. "I told you, if it *hadn't* been there, I'd have . . ."

Then I stopped as the road crested the hilltop. Ahead and below spread hundreds of square miles of trees, lakes, and hills, the blueberry barrens wine-colored with the autumn leaves of the fruit bushes and the farthest mountaintops already snow-covered.

"Oh," I finished in a small voice. "You think . . ."

She slowed between a dairy farm whose barbed-wire-and-cedar-post enclosures featured salt licks the size of concrete blocks, and an auto graveyard whose sign promised *Good Used Partz!*

"I mean the last time you saw that life jacket, Mac Rickert was wearing it." We started downhill. "And if he'd wanted to kill you . . ."

We passed a Grange hall, its front porch decorated with dry corn sheaves, a wreath of mountain ash berries and hydrangea blossoms, and a poster: *Jack-o'-Lantern Carving Party To-nite.*

"Right," I said. "By that time he had my gun. One shot, even if anyone heard it and decided to investigate–"

"Which is pretty unlikely, right there," Ellie put in.

"–he'd be long gone by the time they got out there. And if I *hadn't* found the life preserver..."

"He could've come back to rescue you himself," Ellie agreed. "You were likely too busy not drowning to notice how far away he actually went."

True. And it put a whole new spin on the matter, didn't it? Having a near-death experience, that is, then finding out it was not much more than a fistfight followed by a cold bath.

That Mac Rickert might never have meant to harm me at all. "Hey, where're we going, anyway?" I asked.

Ellie had turned onto a tiny dirt lane; now she followed it between a double row of massive cedar trees to a gravel parking area and stopped the car.

I looked around. A hand-carved sign read *Elderberry Cottage* but there was no dwelling visible, just a curving white pebbled path leading off into what would have been a forest if it weren't so well groomed, not a fallen branch or rotten stump in sight.

Through the trees, water sparkled distantly as I got out of the car into a silence so complete that it made my ears ring. The air smelled richly of crushed apples, damp leaves, and the smoke of a hickory wood fire burning slowly somewhere nearby.

"Ellie, what are we doing here?" I asked as a little black spaniel danced welcomingly out of the woods toward us. "I really don't have time for..."

I wanted to call Bob again myself and confess the whole hideously embarrassing story of my escapade, plus the information it had yielded. Such as it was, but at least it might change the state cops' mind about Wanda being a crime victim.

Even if it wouldn't help find her. "Etta," Ellie greeted the spaniel familiarly, smoothing its ears, and in response the dog danced joyously around some more.

And then to me: "Lunch," she pronounced, though I saw no food unless you counted the acorns under the trees. "Trust me, lunch is *good* for screwing heads back on," she declared.

I could agree with that, though I still didn't see where we were going to get any. Also, it was too early for lunch.

Etta pranced in delighted circles around my feet. "And while we eat it I'm going to explain a few things to you," Ellie told me.

She took the Scotch bottle from my hand, put it back into the glove compartment. "But first I have activities planned."

She guided me onto the pebbled path with the black dog still gamboling around us. I must've glanced back rather wistfully at the bottle.

"Don't worry," she finished confidently. "Where we're going, you're not going to need *that*."

• • •

Ellie was right; I didn't need the Scotch. Instead I had the mineral baths, a mud soak, an herbal wrap, and special eyelid-soothing gauze pads soaked in something cool and puckery-feeling, as if all of my puffy skin cells were being shrunk into positions they'd last held when I was about eighteen.

And there was more: a pedicure. I'd never had one before. Plus acupuncture, which I wasn't sure I wanted until the pain in my shoulder suddenly gathered itself and fled, flapping its dark wings before magically exiting the top of my head.

After that, bliss. A little over three hours later, dressed in my own clothes, which had been washed, dried, and–oh, best of all, *ironed*–I sank into a cushioned wicker chair at a table in one of Elderberry Cottage's three small private dining rooms.

"Better?" Ellie inquired, beaming. She'd had a facial and a vitamin-enriched hair wash.

"Are you kidding?" I asked, sipping mineral water. "My whole body has been *replaced*."

By, I might add, a newer model, one with features the old body never dreamed of possessing. A mind, for instance, that was running on all its cylinders.

Ellie smiled. In addition to all the other ministrations that had been applied to me, I'd had a massage so therapeutic it was as if my joints and major muscle groups had been disassembled and put together again, in vastly improved ways.

After that my hands were anointed with herbal oils, wrapped in cloth light and slippery as silk, and placed in a mysterious sandalwood box with a switch on it that, when turned on, emitted a warmish hum so deeply soothing I'd wanted to stick my head in there.

"But Ellie, who's paying for all this?" In the cottage's large main room youngish women in flowered smocks took appointments on the phone, showed clients to the dressing rooms, and generally behaved charmingly while displaying skin so perfect it might have been scrubbed with soft brushes.

Which around here maybe it had. As lovely aromas floated from an unseen kitchen I sipped my cold wine, savoring the fruity wallop. "Because," I added guiltily, "it must cost a..."

Fortune. And of course I'd be paying for it; who else? No way I would let Ellie cover it.

Another thump of guilt hit me, and not only about the money. "Ellie, what am I doing here? There's a kid out there somewhere and Mac Rickert's got her."

She eyed me across the table. "Okay. I understand that. But which is better? Trying to do anything about it the way you felt before, or now? Or anyway, after we eat," she added as a woman in a white apron arrived bearing plates of food.

On mine was a toasted whole wheat roll stuffed with chicken salad, avocado slices, and lettuce. Beside it were potato wedges crispy with broiled butter, coleslaw redolent of buttermilk and celery seed plus fresh dill weed, and a chunk of goat cheese with olive oil glistening iridescently on it, stuck on a toothpick.

I regarded it all for a moment. "Now," I decided, answering Ellie's question and addressing the feast with an energy that I would've thought impossible a few hours earlier.

"Wade's paying," Ellie said later as we were eating dessert: chocolate mousse, real whipped cream, and a candied violet on top.

"He said was there anything I could do in a few hours that would really take care of you, and I said yes but it was kind of expensive, and he said go for it," she went on.

I sipped my coffee: Jamaican Blue Mountain.

"He also said we'd better find Wanda Cathcart before you got sick over it," she added. "Or really got hurt."

Implicit in this comment was Ellie's awareness that I hadn't called *her* last night, either.

That I'd gone out alone. "So," I asked lightly, changing the subject, "what else have you been doing while I've been having my chassis waxed?"

Because did I mention? Leg waxing. From knee to ankle I was as smooth as a baby's behind, and it felt *fabulous.*

Ellie pulled out a sheaf of notes. "Thinking," she answered briskly. "And writing it down."

"About how I blew it." Another sobering wash of shame flooded me.

She looked up, surprised. "What are you talking about? I meant what I said before. You really did elicit an amazing amount of information, Jacobia. And you accomplished something else very important, as well."

News to me, but with that we got up. Outside, sunlight slanted through the trees in that poignant, October-afternoon way that meant evening would be here before we knew it.

"First of all," Ellie said as she put the car in gear and headed us back to the road again, "you got Wanda's pills to her."

I'd expected to go home but she turned in the other direction, past a small lakeside park with picnic tables, a wooden dock that had already been pulled out of the water for winter, and a boat-launch area.

"So that's one worry taken care of," she said. "And we know two more important things, too, on account of you."

Oh, goody. "What?" I asked, feeling that at this point it was probably a fine idea to let her summarize them; I didn't have a clue.

"First, that he didn't mean to kill you. He *tossed* that life jacket at you, he must have. You were just too busy to notice."

"Then why did he dump me in the water in the first place?"

"To be sure of getting away," she replied simply. "Because if he just let you off on shore, you might get to a house with a phone and call the Coast Guard."

Instead, by the time I'd made it to the house, it was already too late.

• • •

We came to a fork in the road; she chose the right-hand turn, passing a small white church with a bell-tower steeple and a neatly mowed graveyard out back. About a quarter of a mile down the road a small sign said *Passage East Gallery.*

Seeing it, Ellie nodded minutely to herself, then dropped the bombshell. "*And* he didn't kill Gene Dibble," she finished. "Despite what he said."

We turned between a pair of enormous copper beech trees, their trunks swooping gracefully up to form an entry to a pine-needle-carpeted parking area surrounded by evergreens.

She turned to me. "And how do we know this?" she inquired in a bright, professorial manner.

Got me. I felt my face screwing up in a way that should've had a dunce cap on top of it, whereupon she patiently supplied the information herself.

"The gun, Jacobia. Think about the gun that killed Dibble."

"It was a .38," I said. "The medical examiner..."

Then I stopped. Not a .22 like Wade's. "But Rickert said–"

"Exactly," Ellie responded, pleased.

Ahead spread a grassy field lined on one side by a bed of daylilies, groomed and mulched for the coming winter. A small log house with a screen porch stood at the end of the lily bed, its narrow brick walkway laid out neatly in the jack-on-jack pattern.

"Mac was lying about killing Dibble, Jake. I don't know why, maybe he just wanted you to think he's dangerous. An ego thing, you know?" She thought a moment. "Or . . . maybe he wants to take all the suspicion off somebody else, someone we don't know about yet?"

We got out. I still didn't know what we were doing here. A crow's harsh call sounded once somewhere very nearby.

"What we do know is, he admitted to doing murder but if he doesn't know what kind of gun it was—"

"Then he didn't," I finished for her as she led me along the path. "But if he didn't kill Dibble, then Wanda couldn't have *seen* him do it, could she? So why take her?"

But I thought I knew the answer to that. *Because he wanted to, that's why. Because he'd seen her and* wanted *her.*

A wisp of smoke curled prettily from the granite chimney and now I could see the things artfully arranged inside the porch.

"Don't know," Ellie replied. "And neither do you," she added emphatically. "But I've been thinking about *where* he might've taken her, too," she finished.

She opened the screen door to where the gentle warmth of a woodstove radiated a welcome; it was only two-thirty but the afternoon's gathering clouds added to the chilly gloom, the last leaves in the maples flaming redly against the fading sky.

"And?" I demanded, but Ellie was already examining the lovely objects in the screen porch: bentwood chairs and matching footstools with crazy-quilt cushions in jewel tones, bunches of dried flowers poignant with the sense of summer gone by, and a birdhouse made to resemble an old-fashioned general store, with tiny shingles and real glass panes in its miniature double-hung windows.

"And I'll tell you all about it when we're done here," Ellie decreed firmly. "Go on into the main room."

I obeyed, wondering a little impatiently about what further restorative measures she could have arranged. Whatever they were, they surely couldn't hold a candle to what I'd already enjoyed or make me feel more fully repaired.

Or so I thought.

• • •

An hour later, equipped with several pairs of new earrings apiece and feeling the pleasant sensation of well-being that can only be produced by really good retail therapy, we did go home.

"The thing is this," Ellie picked up the conversation again as we drove. "Mac's probably got the girl off-island. Because now we know he's moving around by boat."

So the roadblock on the causeway wouldn't have bothered him. But if that was true Wanda could be anywhere; there were a thousand places Mac could reach with that little boat of his.

"Still," Ellie added encouragingly, "that doesn't widen the territory as much as you might think. Because it's deer season, remember?"

Speeding down the hill we'd climbed earlier was a good deal more exciting than going up, especially as Ellie seemed to think I needed a thrill ride on top of everything else.

"Ellie," I began when she didn't put the brakes on. But she was already talking again.

"Deer season means people in the woods. And he wouldn't want that. He wants privacy. So where would *you* go?"

I thought a minute, long enough for my heart to climb back down out of my throat as we reached the foot of the hill. Then:

"Tall Island," I said, remembering. "It's a preserve, no hunting at all, not even bowhunting. George said there are poachers, but..."

She nodded, turning left onto Route 1 toward home. "Uh-huh. Tall Island's so wild, and pretty big, too, so a fellow like Mac wouldn't have too much trouble avoiding a few poachers."

She thought a moment. "In fact, poachers would probably want to avoid him. Worried he might be a game warden hunting for *them.* And Tall Island's a difficult water access."

I hadn't known that part. And after what I'd been through, I wasn't interested in any water access at all. But what Ellie said next made sense as well.

"He could've gotten Wanda to Joey's boat when the storm was so bad." She shot past two cars and an eighteen-wheeler with what felt to me like suicidal glee.

But in a born-and-bred downeast Maine native, that was normal driving. "It's a few miles from Quoddy Village," she admitted, "but they could have walked it."

I hadn't wanted to. But then, I hadn't been fleeing a murder scene with a young girl in tow, one I wanted to hide *pronto.*

"Once the weather settled the next day, he just waited until dark, got her into his own boat, and took her . . . well, wherever he took her," Ellie continued.

She slowed for the long curve of the Route 190 turnoff, then whizzed down it. "And he *was* wearing high boots turned down low, like you said. Correct? You're sure?"

Leave it to her to pick up on a tiny point of description. But fashion details weren't tops on my list of interests at the moment. "Yes, but what difference does that–"

"It means I'm right," she said decisively. "It's somewhere he has to wade ashore, like Tall Island. The way the rocks are there, from a boat you can't get onto the beach without waders."

The boots, she meant. "And what do you want to bet Joey's ferrying supplies to him?"

She wasn't just quick on the uptake *and* detail-oriented. She was brilliant. "So if we followed Joey . . ."

"Yep." She accelerated onto the causeway. "Betcha we'd find Mac. But there's one other thing we need to think about, too."

I was following her line of thought more easily now, due to the fact that I felt like a new woman. Eight hours earlier I wouldn't have been able to follow a four-lane highway, and if I'd tried I would've gotten flattened on it.

But where her thinking led wasn't a comfortable location at all. Because as she'd realized, if Mac Rickert hadn't shot Eugene Dibble then somebody else had.

And if Rickert hadn't kidnapped Wanda–if instead she'd gone with him even semi-willingly, as he'd implied–then one possible reason was that Wanda knew the identity of Gene Dibble's murderer.

And that it wasn't Mac. "If Wanda saw who did it..." I began.

"And she realized whoever it was *knew* she knew..." Ellie put in.

"Maybe *that's* why she ran," I finished.

Maybe. But one thing was for sure: Before we got Wanda out of a fire, we needed to be sure we weren't dropping her right back into a frying pan, instead.

That is, right back into the grasp of a killer.

• • •

Autumn dusk was gathering and the other cars had their headlights on when Ellie dropped me off in front of my house.

In the front yard the backhoe stood idle and the trucks of the town men and water company workers had departed. But a trench six feet deep flanked by two big piles of fresh dirt stood open like a grave from the pavement all the way to my foundation.

A tarp nailed to the clapboards said the old stones had also been breached. Translation: They'd had to dig into the cellar to reach the water pipe.

Phooey. On the other hand apparently George Valentine hadn't thought supervising the pipe project *and* caring for Leonora was enough work for him, so he'd started on the porch steps. As a result the risers for the steps were installed, nailed to a pair of six-by-sixes that he'd fastened to the house with railroad spikes.

Or anyway they resembled railroad spikes. George had gotten out the circular saw, too, and cut the step treads as well as planks for the larger porch area. Now the whole yard smelled of newly cut, fresh-milled lumber, and the wood itself glowed under the porch light.

Pleased, I went inside. No one around, but a note from Bella said the dogs had been walked and all three animals fed.

Better and better: alone, choreless, and fully energized by the pampering I'd received. It went a long way toward balancing the hope and terror I felt at the thought of what Ellie and I had outlined for the evening.

We'd finalized our plan while driving the rest of the way into town. And right now there was really only a single tool that could express how I felt about it: a nail gun.

There was a message from Bob Arnold on my answering machine: Call him. But when I tried I got the canned spiel again, telling me to hang on for the dispatcher or dial 911; otherwise, he'd get back to callers when he could.

Which at this point I wasn't even sure I wanted him to. So I hung up and got the nail gun from the third-floor workroom, where I'd used it on scrap lumber just to practice operating the thing.

In fact it was the only way I'd ever used a nail gun, since if you don't plant your feet very solidly and brace yourself when you fire it, your next try will be from a seated position; also, the noise it makes is... impressive.

But I didn't want to think too hard about what Ellie had talked me into doing, and anyway I had to occupy the rest of the afternoon somehow. Thus I grabbed the gun and some packets of nails—you load it like an automatic weapon, with clips full of nails, not individual ones—and I got the hearing protectors and safety glasses, too, and took them all out to the front porch.

Then, pulling on the earmufflike hearing protectors and goggle-ish safety glasses, I got to work. *Bang!* The nail gun shot a nail into the first step tread while not quite knocking me backwards with its kick; encouraged, I continued nailing the treads onto the structure until the job was done.

By that time it was nearly dark, all the lights on in the houses around me. Through the bare branches of the trees, the moon came up over the water, deep fiery orange like a bubble of lava on the dark horizon.

My shoulder felt like hot lava, too, my earlier massage now only a pleasant memory. But as I got up with my back aching and the *bang!* of the nail gun echoing distantly in my head despite the hearing protectors, I felt a pleasure that had nothing to do with getting the porch project advanced, or running the nail gun with halfway decent competence, either.

It was the nail gun itself that had attracted me, with its hair-trigger firing mechanism, explosion of power, and bulletlike steel projectile. Because every time I thought of Wanda Cathcart, all I really wanted to do was shoot everything in sight.

• • •

"Okay," I told Ellie later that evening, "we bring her to my place, and we don't tell anyone we've got her except Marge."

Ellie nodded grimly. "If she's there. *And* if we can get her away."

We were in Ellie's car on the dock watching Joey Rickert's boat, the *GhOulIE gUrl.* From what I could see, the vessel hadn't gotten cleaner or more shipshape in the brief time since I'd been on it last.

More importantly, however, Joey wasn't on it. Just as we'd hoped, we'd watched him leave on foot, followed him the few blocks to the grocery store–at a safe distance so he wouldn't realize he was being shadowed–then returned to the dock to wait.

Another attack of nerves hit me. "But what if we're wrong? Maybe we *should* just tell Bob Arnold we think they're on Tall Island. Or call the state cops."

"And let them plus maybe the Coast Guard make some kind of half-assed assault landing?" Ellie asked in reply. "Somewhere Mac might be able to see them coming, maybe even start shooting?"

This didn't assuage my fears about our own expedition one bit. "Okay," I gave in, "but I've got to tell you this whole thing is driving me–"

"I know. Crazy," Ellie said, and there was a silence between us.

Then, "Jake, do you remember before the baby was born when I insisted on having that special ultrasound exam in Portland? And you drove me all the way there and back without asking why?"

I remembered, all right. Wild winds, thunder and lightning, and sheets of driving rain.

"Yes, but..."

She stared out the windshield. "I was too scared to say why I wanted it, even to George. If I said it, it might come true. That the baby had a problem, a birth defect or something, and no one was telling me."

I turned to her, surprised. "Ellie, that's–"

"I know. Unreasonable. But you didn't say that, then. You drove me. And then you waited around all afternoon and brought me back."

Another silence. Then: "Wade home?" she asked.

"Getting there about now." The tug was at the dock already; it took

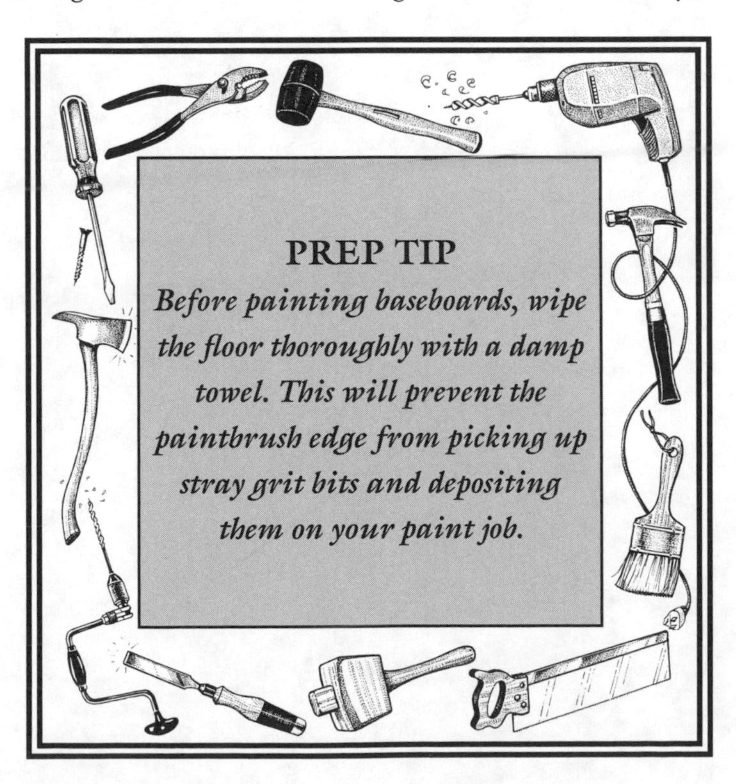

around an hour for his paperwork, and Wade was as regular as the tide in his habits.

The tide also being a crucial–no, indispensable–part of *our* plan. "He should be walking in the door any minute," I said.

Walking in, reading the note I'd left.

The detailed, very specific note. Ellie sat up straight.

"There's Joey now," she said.

Chapter 11

We sank down in our seats like a couple of spies. But Joey Rickert didn't even look in our direction. He was too busy managing the sacks of groceries he was carrying back from the market.

"Our timing was right, anyway," I said as he made his way down the gang to the *GhOulIE gUrl.*

We hadn't known for sure he'd be getting supplies tonight. But if he was helping Mac Rickert hide out with Wanda, he'd have to do it sometime.

And it would have to be after dark. "Lucky for us," Ellie said. "Hey," she added, her tone turning alarmed, "he's getting ready to go out right away. We'd better–"

Hurry. He'd gone below with the bags but now he reappeared to cast off his lines. Instants later he was on the bridge of the unpleasant vessel, its diesel inboard grumbling to fume-billowing life.

Ellie put the car in gear, waiting only until the foam of his wake cleared the mooring at the entrance to the harbor and his running lights passed the tugboats.

Then she U-turned hastily toward the street. "He's heading south," she said. "Toward Tall Island, like we thought. And if we make it fast I think we can still–"

There was only one way to get onto the island by land: wait until low tide and walk over. But once the tide came back in, you couldn't return; not until the *next* low tide.

Suddenly she slammed the brakes on so hard I got a chance to notice how well the seat belt worked. Also I noticed Wade standing in front of the car with his hands raised.

"Room for one more?" He opened the passenger door. I climbed out and then into the tiny backseat while he climbed in front.

"Got your note," he said.

"Yeah, huh?" I replied, inadequately.

I don't know what I'd thought might happen, only that I had promised to let him know what I was up to. Now I half expected an argument of some kind.

But I didn't get one. Wade addressed me again, a gleam in his eye as we hurtled out Route 190.

"Sounds like fun," he commented mildly, and sat back for the ride.

A *wild* ride. The cop at the Pleasant Point speed trap must have been home eating his dinner, because we made it through at speeds very nearly approaching liftoff without getting pinched.

Ten minutes later we were pulling to the end of a dirt road in darkness so thick it was like being wrapped in black velvet.

"Where...?" I began, then shut up as a set of running lights appeared on the water.

"We're a hundred yards south of Tall Island," Wade said quietly; sound travels well on water, especially when everything else around you is silent.

Even over the boat's engine, Joey might hear us if we weren't careful. Or Mac might, which could turn out a lot worse.

"See there?" Wade pointed at a paler section of darkness. "That's the sandbar. It'll be there another hour or so. After that–"

His arms made swimming motions. I squinted around for Ellie, couldn't spot her. "Wade, are you sure you want to..."

Do this, I meant to finish. But I couldn't because before I got the words out of my mouth, he was kissing me on it.

"Oh," I said softly when he was done.

"When I tell you I'm on your side, what I actually mean is, *I'm on your side,*" he said. "Now skedaddle."

So I did, scrambling over the wet stones, mindful that in just a couple of hours the water here would be ten feet deep.

But what I witnessed soon after I got to the shore of Tall Island made the tide seem a small thing, indeed.

• • •

"Over here," Ellie whispered urgently as I struggled through the vines and thorny branches that made Tall Island an obstacle course at night.

We were at the edge of a clearing. At the shoreline twenty-five yards away, two figures carried bags ashore, not speaking. But they weren't nearly as interesting as the smaller figure crouched by a little fire, concealed from view on the water side by a dense thicket.

"It's Wanda," I uttered, jumping up.

"Wait." Wade drew me back. One of the men slogged out to the *GhOulIE gUrl* and climbed aboard, returning moments later with his arms full again. Meanwhile the figure by the fire held her hands out to warm them.

Another wave of protective fear surged through me, worse than before. "If he wants her alive, that could be worse than if he'd wanted to kill her," I managed through the sudden lump in my throat. "The *bastard...*"

"Jake, I've never heard a word from anyone about Joey *or* Mac Rickert liking little girls," Wade said evenly, understanding what I implied.

The two men approached the fire, lighting cigarettes and dropping the last of the supplies in a heap near a small tent that was pitched nearby, with a bedroll in it.

A nice tent, not just some saggy little A-frame, and the bedroll was a good-quality item, too, with the unmistakable loft of high-fill goose-down. Room enough for one in it.

Or two, if what I still feared was true. "You never do hear," I said bitterly. "No one hears a thing, and afterwards . . ."

A sob caught me by surprise. I tried swallowing it, fearing I might burst into tears; it caught painfully in my chest.

But it went down. "Afterwards people say they never dreamed he could do a thing like that," I said. "When it's . . . when it's too *late*."

The sob burst out with my final words, raw with all the pain and bitterness I'd been hiding. But not anymore; in the silence that followed, what I'd said hung in the air like an evil mist that once released can never be captured again, and it was clear that I knew just exactly what I was talking about.

And now they knew, too. "Jake," Wade said softly, but I just shook my head.

"I'm fine, okay? We can talk about it later." But I didn't want to. What I wanted was to walk into the water until it came up over my head.

And keep walking. "I'm going down there," Ellie whispered at last. "I want to hear what they're saying."

Then she was gone, slipping along the edge of the clearing until we couldn't see her anymore. Once she'd vanished, Wade still stood there, silent, as misery flooded through me.

"Wade," I began, "I'm sorry I never . . ."

Told you. He turned suddenly.

"You're sorry?" he demanded brusquely. "*You're* sorry?"

One long step and he was beside me, his arms wrapped around me. "Don't ever say that." He spoke into my ear. "Don't you ever apologize. And don't feel you have to talk about it, you hear? Or not talk about it."

His embrace was ferocious. "You stick with me, and whatever happens we're in it together, Jake. The two of us no matter what. Got that? *Do* you?"

"Got it," I whispered, nodding against his shoulder, tears running down my cheeks. But then I looked up at him, and at the sight of his face smiling gently down at me I had to smile, too.

Not that he'd fixed things; not all of them. Not even close. But for then it was enough.

Ellie popped back out of the bushes. "The good news is that Wanda's okay as far as I can tell."

Then she grimaced, dragged one of her shoes through the weeds. "Darn, I've stepped in deer scat. Fresh, too."

In the moonlight she examined her other shoe; she was picky about her footwear. "That's the thing about preserves, if no one does anything with them there get to be about a million of the animals."

Wade plucked a clump of fuzz from a twig. "Yeah. One of 'em lost some hair here, looks like."

Then he frowned, rubbing the tuft of fluff in his fingers and sniffing it. "Blood. Deer is wounded, I think. Poachers've been out here again, maybe."

"Wouldn't someone have heard shots?" Ellie asked, glancing back at the campfire.

The men had sat down by it and were passing a bottle back and forth. Wanda sat with them.

Wade shook his head. "Not if they were bowhunting. But you need to be really good with a bow, drop the deer dead. Poachers," he added unhappily, "aren't always good shots."

"What's the bad news?" I asked, turning back to Ellie.

The clouds closed over our heads and the wind was picking up too, tossing the *GhOulIE gUrl* around where she rode at anchor.

"They're arguing, Mac and Joey. Mac's been here a couple of nights and he wants to stay a little longer." Ellie waved at the sky. "But Joey says another storm's coming in."

Wade nodded. "Yep. Heard it on the weather radio before I left. Worse than the last one, they say."

"There's something Mac's waiting for," Ellie went on. " 'Just a little longer,' he told Joey, 'and she'll do it.' "

"Do what?" I demanded. Out beyond the campfire, Mac and Joey Rickert were on their way back down to the shoreline again.

Wanda still sat. "Don't know," Ellie replied. "But whatever it is, once it's done and the storm passes by, he's going to move her. And I don't think it's going to be to anywhere around here."

"What makes you think that?" Wade asked as Joey sloshed back out to the *GhOulIE gUrl*.

God, but that water must've been cold. I winced in unwilling sympathy. "Mac said it was somewhere no one would *ever* find her, and Joey wouldn't see Mac for a while, either," Ellie answered.

"Oh, come on, then," I burst out, "let's go get her."

"No." Ellie put a hand out. "Don't you see what he's got?"

I squinted. Mac had stood up, and he *was* carrying something; I just hadn't been paying attention to it before.

But now I did: long and wider at one end, the other glinting bluish in the last shreds of light before the clouds thickened up entirely.

It was a shotgun. "Wade?" I asked.

"Yeah, I've got something."

A weapon, he meant. He wouldn't have come out here without one. "But I'm not going to start a shooting war here, Jake. For one thing, we're outgunned. And..."

And for another, he'd have had to pick them both off fast and by surprise, in a cold-blooded ambush: not his style.

Not in this lifetime. The *GhOulIE gUrl*'s diesel rumbled.

"Now that we're sure she's here, we'll tell Bob Arnold," Ellie said consolingly. "He can get a group together in daylight when there's not so much chance of something going wrong. They'll get her back, Jake. But now..."

Yeah, yeah. The boat noise was our cue to get out of here while we still could. Time and tide, and all that; pretty soon, we wouldn't be able to leave.

That was why I turned my back on Wanda Cathcart; careful not to snap telltale branches in the undergrowth–our flashlights on the way in had been risky enough, though the men hadn't seemed to spot them–we returned to the sandbar.

But at the edge of it I paused.

Wade went ahead on the slippery stones, now covered in water as the tide came in. Turning, he reached a hand back to me; Ellie had already gotten sure-footedly to the other side.

"Jake, if we try to do anything now, there'll be shooting and the result won't be good. Come on, take my hand."

So I did, clinging to the support he offered. But as I left Wanda I was leaving someone else behind, too, alone and unrescued.

Again.

• • •

"Turn here," I said minutes later.

"To the tenants' house?" Ellie was driving.

"Yes," I said, firmly. "We're going to tell Marge Cathcart her daughter's still alive."

It wouldn't be all good news. But it was something Marge could cling to for now, and that much I wasn't going to turn my back on.

In the moonless night the Quoddy Village houses looked smaller and meaner, some sporting jack-o'-lanterns grinning with orange malice, others entirely dark.

"Imagine if it was Sam or Lee. We'd be wild," I said. "We can't let Marge go on in the torture she's in. We just can't."

"Okay, okay," Ellie said, taking the turn. "I'm going."

Across the water a row of taillights on the causeway led out of town; it was Bingo night at the Youth Center and people were on their way home.

We drove slowly around the last curve. "Hey," Ellie said, slowing the car. "What's going on?"

Cherry beacons whirled in front of the rental house, one of them on Bob Arnold's squad car. In the drive an ambulance stood with its rear doors open; inside it the gurney was missing.

Ellie pulled in behind Bob's car and we all got out, Wade to talk with Bob, who was speaking into his radio, while Ellie and I hurried inside.

Greg Brand and Hetty Bonham were in the living room. "What's the problem?" I asked them.

Hetty answered. "Oh, it was horrible," she wailed. "Marge was in the kitchen, doing the dishes."

Sure she was, I thought. Probably she was still doing all the cooking, too. A burst of unreasoning anger for the sort of foolish woman who could get herself into such a bad situation in the first place at all washed over me.

But I cut it off because I'd gotten a good look recently at the sort of woman that was.

In the mirror.

"She had some kind of an attack," Greg added. "I told her if she sat down she'd feel better. But she wouldn't."

The EMTs brought her out. Marge was ghost-pale, what I could see of her under the oxygen mask.

"No, she had to start gasping and getting herself even more worked up," Greg added, gulping at his drink.

An IV bag hung over her and they were hustling her along in a businesslike manner. I followed them. "What's wrong with her?" I demanded of the EMT at the gurney's rear.

"Heart attack." A portable EKG machine bounced at the foot of the gurney. "Shocked her once." To the other technician he added tersely, "Come on, we gotta go."

They hefted her in, then pulled away with sirens howling.

"Did something trigger this?" I asked Jenna Durrell when we were back inside.

She shook her head impatiently. "No. She was a walking time bomb, is all. You could practically see her blood pressure going up, she kept forgetting to take her medicines, and..."

And I'd thought the last time I'd seen her that she wasn't well. We went out to the kitchen, where everything was spotless, only a single undried cup in the dish drainer indicating where Marge had been interrupted in her self-assigned chores.

"Where were you when it happened?" Ellie asked Jenna.

Meanwhile, in the living room, Hetty and Greg were arguing about whether or not they should go up to the hospital.

"You don't even know the woman," Greg insisted. "You just want to playact the role of the anxious friend in the waiting room," he accused.

"Out on the front steps," Jenna told Ellie. "Just sitting there trying to keep my head on straight. Because between Marge's anxiety and the gruesome twosome in there, it's been..."

She put her hands flat on the kitchen counter. "I could get a bus home to Massachusetts. Almost did it today. But then Marge would've been alone with them and I didn't quite have the heart for that," she finished.

Wade and Bob Arnold came in together, Bob wearing the "let's wrap it up" look his face took on when his duties were done but people still wanted to talk.

"What're you all doing out here?" he wanted to know when he spotted me. I wanted to tell him, too. But now wasn't the time, not when all three remaining tenants were listening.

"Just thought we'd come visit," I said.

Bob shot a funny glance at me and I could see him getting the notion that there was more, then deciding to let it go for now.

"Right," he said skeptically, not mentioning the message I'd left for him, either. Then he took off in the squad car, leaving Wade and Ellie to occupy the tenants while I had a peek around the house.

A *thorough* peek.

• • •

"At least we didn't have to explain to Marge why we'd left Wanda out there," Ellie said as we drove home a little later.

"Small comfort," I said distractedly. My search of Marge's bedroom had yielded a surprising result. "Ellie, when you have to take pills, where do you keep them?"

"Kitchen windowsill," she replied promptly.

Which was what I'd expected. Everyone I knew who took pills on a regular basis kept them somewhere like that, so they'd see them and remember. Only not Marge Cathcart.

Jenna had said Marge forgot to take her medicines, and that meant Jenna and probably the others as well had known of her need for them. Yet when I examined her quarters...

"I gave Marge's room a going-over." I held up two small orange plastic bottles. "And these were *inside* the base of her bedside lamp."

Wade turned interestedly. "So she was..."

"Yep. Hiding them." I tucked the bottles back in my pocket; when we got home I'd give the hospital a call, let them know what medicines she'd been on.

"Not at first, or Jenna wouldn't have known about them. But it looks like maybe once Marge got to know her housemates a little better..."

Ellie took the long way home, to Dog Island through Bayside Cemetery. On clear nights you could see up the Western Passage to New Brunswick, but tonight the only view was of clouds pierced by the strobing beam of the Cherry Island light.

"...she put them away," I finished. "Maybe she was worried about them, that someone might steal them or tamper with them?"

We drove between the deserted sidewalks and tall darkened storefront windows of Water Street, turned onto Key Street past the Happy Landings Café and Peavy Library, its big diamond-paned windows reflecting the yard lamps of the Motel East.

"Only now we can't ask her," I said. "I'm not even sure why I snooped around in the house in the first place, except..."

Except that there was still something important I wasn't getting about all this; something *missing*.

Like for instance an obvious villain. Because I'd had a good look at the way Mac Rickert behaved with Wanda on Tall Island. Their body language, at any rate: not predatory or threatening on his side, not frightened on hers.

For which there had to be some reasonable explanation. But I couldn't imagine what it was, and as long as I didn't know, I still feared for her.

Big-time. As I got out of the car at my house, the air seemed heavy with impending calamity and the fog drifting in the street didn't help; going inside, I wished I'd paid more attention to Marge when I'd had the chance.

I couldn't have consoled her; nothing could do that except her daughter's safe return. But I could've listened to her. If I had, maybe I'd know more than I did right now.

Because, I thought, feeling the pill bottles rattling in my pocket, maybe Marge hadn't been such a foolish woman after all.

• • •

The railing assembly for an outdoor stairway consists of the posts, the balusters between the posts, and the handrails. I knew this because I'd read it in one of the many how-to-build-it books I'd collected.

Reading them, unfortunately, was easier than following them. But the morning after we found Wanda on Tall Island, I needed a hands-on project.

Thus, after making some coffee and drinking it as calmly as I could, then taking the dogs outside–pausing to savor the pure, deceptively clear island morning with the air like spring water and the sun just now rising over Campobello, on the other side of the bay–I hauled my tools outside to the front of the house.

"Okay," Bob Arnold had replied when I'd called him as soon as we got home the previous night. He'd picked up the phone right away, not asking *how* we'd found Wanda or why I hadn't mentioned it to him at the Quoddy Village house, either.

Just: "I'll let the state boys know and they'll take care of it." *Click.* Which told me that one of those state boys was in his office right that minute, ears pricked alertly.

And that it was out of my hands.

The lawn's crisp frostiness showed my indented footprints as I walked on it; winter was coming. A border of clouds lay like cotton batting on the horizon, the edge of the approaching storm having drifted sneakily toward us overnight. In the neighborhood nothing moved yet, shades still drawn in the silent windows of the old houses around mine.

But loud nailing wasn't on the agenda today. Instead I opened the long red toolbox containing my ratchet kit, which was a set of tools for screwing or bolting things together.

So all right, now: the posts. These held up the handrails, or would once I'd bolted the posts to the stringers. I'd bought precut four-by-fours about forty inches long so I'd have enough to cut them at the proper angle. And George had drilled half-inch holes for the hex bolts, so my second task was simply putting bolts through the holes and tightening them one after the other; easy-peasey.

The *first* part was harder, though: holding the railing up at the angle I wanted it, then marking the sides of the posts to be cut so the rail could rest atop them. This did require noise, and a certain amount of terror as well, since the post cuts needed a circular saw: my personal old-house fix-up nemesis.

But the way I felt, I could either run the circular saw or roar on out right this minute to Tall Island, guns a-blazin': not a good plan. So I took the posts back off the stringers and laid them across a pair of sawhorses, and fired that sucker up.

Whang! There is nothing like the ferocious metallic sound of an operating circular saw, cutting either a four-by-four or the hand off your forearm, whichever it hits first. I cut the posts as fast as I could, before my bravery ran out and also before the neighbors started leaning out of their windows cursing a blue streak at me.

When I bolted the four-by-fours on, for a wonder they fit into their places perfectly, and they were cut at the correct angle, too. This I thought might have been my ration of good luck for the day, but never mind; now all they needed were the railings, which the book said to attach using galvanized nails.

I looked at the nails, and at my claw hammer, then around at the houses inside which people were just getting back to sleep after the racket of the saw.

On the other hand, at various ungodly hours I'd been woken by dogs barking, engines starting, and people summoning other people out late at night by leaning on their car horns.

Recalling those times, I gathered the claw hammer, a handful of nails, and one of the railings. There was no possible upside to the idea of driving to Tall Island.

None whatsoever, I told myself. Which was when Bob Arnold pulled up in his squad car and my luck ran out.

"*GhOulIE gUrl* turned up this morning," he reported. "Drifting. A lot of gear on her, camping stuff and so on. And a shotgun."

Uh-oh. "They found Joey Rickert's body floating a couple miles away," he added.

I put the hammer down. "What about Wanda?"

"No sign of her. Mac either. Looks like Joey fell over the rail. Hit his head, maybe–he's got a big scalp wound. Drowned."

• • •

"So you think Mac spotted you," my father said half an hour later at his place, a down-at-the-heels bungalow on Prince Street with a workshop out back.

"Must've," I said bitterly. The workshop was in what had once been a small concrete-floored garage, made over to include a woodstove, plenty of hanging tool storage, and a variety of old salvaged kitchen cabinets for the flotsam and jetsam guys with workshops always tend to collect.

"Ellie heard him saying he wasn't leaving. Not yet. So why else would he change his mind and get out of there so fast?"

Why, indeed. Because we'd spooked him, that's why. He just hadn't let *us* know we had.

"He must've taken off as soon as we were gone and the coast was clear. Dad, how did I let all this get so screwed up? Now the cops think Mac killed Gene Dibble *and* Joey, and Wanda Cathcart's more missing than ever."

"Hmm," he said, frowning down at the project he'd been working on when I arrived, under the set of hanging fluorescent lights installed over his workbench.

With the help of some of the town men who'd been working on the water pipe at my house, he'd taken home the big section of old foundation with the wooden box still encased in it.

"Things've got to get worse sometimes, 'fore they improve," he offered.

Old Maine license plates, glossies of classic cars, and cheesecake-calendar pictures of actresses from a bygone era were thumbtacked to the shop's interior walls, courtesy of the previous tenant.

"Thanks a lot," I said. "I've got half a mind to go down to Bob Arnold's office right this minute and tell the state cops the whole–"

"Oh?" he interrupted coolly. "Tell 'em you met with Rickert and his brother, followed the brother around, now the guy turns up dead? You do that, I can tell you what tomorrow's headline'll read, Jacobia."

Right. I felt my shoulders slump. *Drug House Owner Eyed in Pair of Suspicious Deaths . . .*

Not the news I wanted all my neighbors absorbing with their morning coffee. Also, once I started talking, it would come out *why* I'd been doing all that, and Bob Arnold's guy here in town would lose his kids.

"Chief Arnold hasn't brought you into it already, though? Not a word about your involvement?" my father asked. He got out his rock tools from one of the kitchen cabinets: chisels, a bunch of miniature pickaxes in various sizes, plus a hammer.

"No, he'd just have the same problem. Owning the rental house isn't enough reason to get Ellie and me snooping as hard as we've been doing, and with them being detectives and all, you know they'd tumble to the fact that we were doing it because *he* wasn't being allowed to," I said.

"So Bob said it was an anonymous tip?" my father concluded.

"You got it," I agreed. "That's exactly what he told them." If you didn't already know it was a lie, I supposed it was reasonably believable. Or anyway, it was working so far, according to Bob.

"At this point they think Joey was in on the drug deal with Mac and Gene Dibble, and Mac's been eliminating his partners," I went on. "But if you knew those guys at all, that wouldn't make sense. Mac didn't murder his brother, I'm really pretty sure."

"And you know this because . . . ?" His tone was skeptical.

"Wade says those two have been loyal to each other their whole lives," I explained. "And I believe it. Heck, all I did was badmouth Joey one time, and Mac jumped all over me."

But then I paused; no sense going into detail about exactly which time that was. My dad was as sensitive about my safety—or the absence of it—as Wade.

"Besides, Mac needed Joey's boat to get off Tall Island."

This notion seemed to interest my father. "Did he, then? Get off the island? Cops searched the whole place?"

He had a point. "Well, no, they didn't. They found the campsite. No one was there. Then I guess Joey's body turned up out on the water and that diverted them."

To put it mildly. And since the tip about Mac's whereabouts *had* been anonymous, they'd decided not to canvass the entire island's difficult terrain on the basis of it, turning their attention instead to the evidence they *did* have: another dead man.

"And Mac didn't actually need Joey to get off the island," I amended.

"Mac's own boat's big enough for around here. But to get clean out of the area, somewhere he wouldn't be recognized right off the bat, the *GhOulIE gUrl* was Mac's only option."

"And now it's gone." My father eyed the big chunk of granite and mortar now occupying his workbench, raised his stone chisel consideringly, and brought it down with a metallic *clink!*

A much bigger section of stone than I was expecting flew off it and whizzed across the room, tearing a paper chunk out of Rita Hayworth's left thigh before landing in the corner.

"Right," I said. Another chisel strike; a section of mortar cleaved off like an iceberg calving off a glacier. "You know, you really are pretty good at that."

He looked at me, amused. "I've had," he said drily, "a fair amount of experience."

Stone masonry being a fine way to support yourself while you are on the run; plenty of work, few questions asked, and payment in cash at the end of the day if that's the way you want it.

"Anyway," he said, eyeing his task again, "what I think is that if I was Mac Rickert at the moment, I'd be doubling back."

It was why I'd come to see my dad in the first place: to get his read on what an experienced fugitive might do under similar circumstances.

A successful fugitive. But now I just stared at him. "You mean you don't think Mac left Tall Island? That he's still . . . ?"

"Yup." He put down the chisel. "Because you said yourself his own boat isn't big enough to go far. And if I was a cop it's probably the last place I'd check again, at least for a while."

Where a tip *hadn't* panned out . . . it wasn't a great option but it was among the few available to Mac Rickert right now. So it made sense.

And it was worth a try. But at the door I paused, struck by a question that popped into my mind out of nowhere.

Along with the courage to ask. "Dad, do you think Mother would've forgiven you? I mean, if she'd known . . ."

If she'd known in advance that his radical activities would result in her death, in the explosion of a house everyone thought he'd blown up, accidentally or deliberately. That was why the Feds had chased him for so long; they'd thought he was responsible.

I'd thought so, too, until I learned different.

"Your mother," he said softly, "forgave me everything the first minute she laid eyes on me."

He hesitated, meanwhile testing the blade of his chisel with a callused finger. I guessed I wasn't the only one with memories too painful to scrutinize closely.

"Anyway," he said, "it's not other people forgiving us that's so difficult. Or us forgiving other people."

He examined my face. "When you get to be my age you might even start thinking it hardly matters who did the bad deed in the first place," he went on.

"Hard part's forgiving ourselves for not being smarter or stronger or . . . whatever fault we think we had, or we're afraid we had, that let the bad thing happen at all," he finished.

He glanced up at the bare hanging bulb over his workbench. "In my case it was lack of imagination, I guess. When I was a young man I thought I was a bad guy, the worst there was."

But he'd been wrong. There were much worse.

One of them had killed my mother, while trying to get at him. "You think about these things too much, they'll drive you crazy," he said, picking up his chisel again.

• • •

It was a long walk home past the old white clapboard houses of town, many with piles of autumn leaves already heaped against their foundations and plastic sheets stapled over their windows against the coming winter. But I was glad for it, thinking over what my father had said.

Mac Rickert ought to have been miles away by now. If he had any sense he'd have left Wanda behind to make his escape. But instead he'd stubbornly stayed here with her right up until last night.

If not longer. Which meant not just Wanda but something else about Tall Island was important to him.

Only...what? His reasoning seemed as impenetrable to me as the old well George Valentine had fallen down, back when he was a boy and the talents of Wanda's water-witching ancestor, Horeb Cathcart, had been required to locate him.

Too bad I couldn't call Horeb for help now. If the stories were true he might've sent a posse of animals to terrify Mac and escort the creature-loving Wanda to safety.

Instead the escort would have to be me. And if what my dad had suggested was true, probably the rescue had to happen pretty much right this minute.

"Mom?" Sam's voice came from the front parlor as I went in.

"What're you doing here?" I asked. The dogs appeared, galumphing down the hall at me affectionately, and Cat Dancing yowled a welcome.

"I needed to talk to you," Sam said as I bent to greet the canines. He followed me into the kitchen, where I'd begun mentally listing the equipment I meant to take with me: a life jacket, an outboard engine–in the cellar was a little seven-and-a-half-horse Evinrude that I thought I could muscle into my car trunk–and a gun.

A big one this time, the kind of weapon even a guy like Mac Rickert would be impressed by. Enough, I hoped, to do what I told him to, especially once he understood the deal I'd be offering.

But now here was Sam. "Listen, it's about Dad," he said.

And about the basketball games, no doubt; Sam still wanted my approval. Likely Victor had helped him come up with a slippery argument to try to get it, too.

"Sam, I don't like it but if you want to go I suppose it's your decision. I think your dad's just using you to try to get the better of me, but–"

"No," Sam put in impatiently, "that's not it. Mom, don't you understand? Weren't you listening to me the other night?"

Cat Dancing twined around my ankles. "Of course I was, but now I know your father didn't mean what you thought…"

He was shaking his head. "He's not at any seminar. He just said that so you wouldn't worry, or ask him a lot of questions."

Sam took a shaky breath. "Mom, he's at a clinic in Denver. They're going to try some new last-ditch experimental treatment they've got there."

I sat down at the table. What Sam was saying didn't compute. With Victor, it was always other people who got sick.

Always. And when they did he always fixed them. "Sam, are you sure about this?"

He nodded, and sat down across from me. "It's big, the tumor he's got, it's growing fast and it's in a place where you can't operate on it."

His forehead creased. "That whole thing about flying to the Celtics… I didn't want to do it. But it's like he needs a future to plan for, so he can go on right now."

Monday put her glossy black head on his knee; he patted her distractedly. "He tried to put a good face on it. But you know Dad, he always has. Even back when I was little and I'd have a birthday or Christmas was coming… he could talk a good game."

Right. *I'll be there,* Victor would always say. To blow out the candles, or open the presents… he could always convince me this time would be different. But an aneurysm, a blood clot, or a tumor would happen, and instead he would be away fixing it.

For somebody else. "Sam, if your dad thinks this clinic has a treatment that might work…"

But we'd both lived with Victor long enough to know that *might work* also implied another, darker possible outcome: *might not.*

"Listen, I told them I'd be at school soon but if you want me to stick around…"

"No," I said, getting up to put my hands on his shoulders. "It's okay, you should go. There's nothing that we can do about it right now but sit and worry, and your dad wouldn't like that."

My chest felt as if there were a boulder on it. "Did he say he would call?" I added. "Or how we're going to know if...?"

"Either way, he'll be home in a few days," Sam said. "He'll know then if he has to make more trips, to get more treatments."

He got up. "Otherwise..."

That word: "otherwise." Fleetingly I let my mind touch on the notion of a world without Victor. Half the time on those holidays he hadn't been in the operating room at all; instead he'd been in the bedroom of some pretty lab tech or X-ray technician.

But even though Victor wasn't the sun in my sky anymore, he was still the moon and several important stars. For one thing he was Sam's father. And...

Well, we'd known each other quite a while. I hugged Sam. "We'll talk more later," I promised him. "Try not to worry."

CLOTHES MAKE THE (WO)MAN

Put together a set of clothes and shoes and* always *wear them when you fix, paint, etc. This keeps your good clothes from turning into work clothes.

"Yeah," he replied, and after he went out I cried hard for a long time.

You might not notice the moon very much. White and silent, it shines a cold light that is merely a ghost of the beloved day.

But you'd miss it if it were gone.

A lot.

Chapter 12

I'm going to go out there and offer him the same deal as I meant to last time," I told Ellie determinedly when she showed up around noon. "Only *this* time, I'm not going to let him dump me in the water *and* I'm going to sweeten the pot."

On the table lay my cash stash: five grand. But it was worth it if it put an end to this mess.

"Mac's got to get away," I said, "and for that he needs real money. And I don't think he has any way to get it anywhere else. If he did, I bet he'd be long gone now."

I'd thought it over and it was the only reasonable answer to why Mac was still on Tall Island.

If he was. "What if something happens to you out there?" Ellie argued. "Then Sam will be left without you *and* maybe without his father, too."

She'd arrived just as I was pressing a cold towel to my eyes, and got the story about Victor out of me immediately.

"I'll be no good to Sam or anyone else if I don't do this," I said, getting a notepad out of a kitchen drawer. I'd promised to let Wade know if I was contemplating doing anything dangerous.

And this qualified. Next to the money lay an item I'd told myself I'd given up using, other than for target practice: the Bisley six-shot .45-caliber revolver with blued steel barrel and walnut checkered grip. It was an Italian-made replica of the gun that won the Old West.

If you can call what happened out there winning. Anyway, *I'm going to get Wanda,* I wrote; and then after detailing where I was going to do it, *I'll be home for dinner.*

I'd rather have waited for him but there was simply no time; he wouldn't be home for several hours. And if my dad was correct, right now there was a chance to bring Wanda home.

But Mac could be deciding to leave any minute. Signing the note, I lowered the loaded Bisley into my satchel.

"Jake," Ellie argued, "if he knew we were there last night he'll know it for sure in the daylight. And have you ever put an outboard engine on that little boat of yours before?"

"No. But there's a first time for everything." I slung the satchel over my shoulder.

"In that case, I'm coming, too." She pulled on her jacket and zipped it.

"No, you're not," I said. "You've got Leonora to think of."

Stubbornly she followed me out. I still had to get the outboard engine up through the bulkhead doors of the cellar, and there were only about four good hours left before dark, another reason I didn't want to waste any time....

Speaking of which, that daylight Ellie had mentioned was fading awfully fast. Looking around, I realized: The storm that had been forecast was here, clouds mounding in the sky like dark boulders.

Or almost here; an hour, tops. Any later and I'd need a miracle to get out to Tall Island safely. And I might need a miracle anyway.

"Jake," Ellie said insistently. Catching me, she turned me to face her by seizing my jacket and rotating it with me in it.

"You're right, there are some things I won't do on account of Lee. But going out in a boat certainly isn't one of them."

This, I thought, ignored important details about the trip. The fact that at least one Very Large Weapon might be part of the program, for example, didn't seem to be on her radar. And neither did the weather.

But it was also true that Ellie was nearly as comfortable on the water as on land. And that I wasn't. And although I'd loaded the Bisley, there was a chance I'd need to *re*load.

Possibly while on the boat. And for that, a helper could be... well, helpful. To handle the all-important steering portion of the program, for instance.

"Letting you do this alone isn't one of them either," she declared, backing away while holding up something shiny.

My keys. She'd plucked them from my pocket when she grabbed me. Now she dangled them at me, her face defiant.

"Oh, all right." I gave in. For one thing, I didn't have time to stand there arguing with her. "If you're coming you can help me get the outboard into the trunk."

"Nuts," she replied. "Are you crazy? Do you see that sky? If we're doing this we're taking my boat."

And there was no arguing with her about that either, so we got into her car. On the passenger seat lay the new issue of the *Quoddy Tides,* and as she turned the ignition key I picked it up and scanned it, hoping it might help calm my nerves.

It didn't. "Ellie, have you seen this?" I stared at the page of local obituaries, among them Eugene Dibble's.

"No, what?" She backed out of the driveway, headed toward the water.

"This... this..." I waved the paper at her. "Remember I told you that Bella Diamond knew Jenny, Gene Dibble's wife?"

"Yes," Ellie replied patiently. At the foot of Key Street she waited for a group of women in black pointy hats to cross, carrying refreshments; they were having a Halloween party for the kindergarten kids at the public library.

One of the women waved, cackling evilly at us. I scanned Dibble's obituary again. "And Bella said Jenny had a daughter by a previous marriage who was living on her own," I went on.

Threading between the cars parked in front of the library and a beer truck making a delivery at the Waco Diner, Ellie said nothing.

"The daughter," I said, throwing the paper down, "is Luanne Moretti."

That got a response. "Oh, man," Ellie breathed as we passed the post office. "So for a while at least he must've been living in the same house with..."

"Yeah. And what do you want to bet they didn't get along?" I said. "Gene and Luanne..."

"Or that *he* maybe wanted to get along with her a little *too* well?" Ellie said.

"Precisely." She took the turn into the parking lot between the boat ramp and the Coast Guard Station. "Damn," I said, angry with myself. "Why'd I miss this?"

"Because no one you were talking to knew it, and she didn't tell you," Ellie replied reasonably, shutting the car off. "Spilt milk now anyway," she added as we got out.

Yeah, and maybe disastrously so. Luanne's hint that she had a weapon seemed even clearer and more ominous, now that I knew her connection to Gene Dibble.

A connection she might've wanted to sever permanently. "And she can get pills," I said as we approached the metal gangway to the docks. "I don't know how she'd have gotten so many, but..."

"Doesn't matter," said Ellie, starting down. "It doesn't change what we're doing."

She was right again; it didn't. A few shaky moments later she was helping me board what up close looked even more like a rowboat on steroids: broad beam, high rails, and a big seventy-horse Tohatsu outboard engine that made my little seven-and-a-half-horse Evinrude resemble an eggbeater.

She hadn't forgotten how to run it, either. Bing, bang, boom and we were seated in the boat with the lines cast off and Ellie in the stern, her hand on the tiller as we slid past the mooring dolphin, the docks, and the fish pier.

The tall wooden sides of the docks echoed the engine's deep rumble, making talk impossible until after we'd cleared all the waterfront structures and were headed south, toward the thin line of the International Bridge to Campobello.

Beyond it a wall of dark clouds loomed on the horizon, even more ominous looking than the ones over our heads. Ellie angled her head at them. "Not much time," she mouthed.

But even now we were passing Treat Island, halfway between Eastport and North Lubec on the next long peninsula jutting out into the bay. As we slid past it a flock of eider ducks clad in sharp black-and-white plumage cooed their soft urgent call, and paddled away at our sudden approach.

The wreckage of an ancient wharf appeared, its massive weed-hung timbers studded with iron spikes dissolving to rust; a few minutes later we entered Tall Island's cove.

Here in the more protected water my fingers loosened their grip on the boat's seat. But the calm was deceptive; Ellie turned her head once more at the gathering weather.

"It's coming in fast," she said. "He must see it, too. If he really is here, he'll stay put for a while."

If, she meant, he hadn't cut and run already. My father's take on Mac Rickert was a prediction, after all, not a money-back guarantee.

She cut the engine to idle. "The weather report said gale flags are up all the way to the Carolinas. It's going to get nasty."

As we approached shore Ellie hauled engine so the propeller wouldn't break on the rocks. I'd have never thought to do that, I realized, glad she was there. We drifted toward the inlet where the night before we'd walked across to Mac's camp, and made shore.

"We were lucky," Ellie whispered as I clambered out. "The wind blew our engine noise in the other direction."

"Let's not say 'lucky' yet," I muttered.

Because we *were* on land again, a big plus right there in my opinion. And in theory, the rest could be easy: Mac might not be at the campsite, for instance. We might snatch Wanda and be out of here before he even had an inkling of what was happening.

But as I struggled through the brush toward a guy with a gun and a head trip about a young girl somewhere ahead of us, luck was what I wanted.

Not what I thought we already had. Ellie stopped. "There it is."

In daylight the campsite looked miserable, no more now than a clearing and a doused fire ring. No tent.

And no people. "Hey," Ellie said, pointing. "Over there by the rocks."

Tucked into a crevice nearly hidden from view was a pile of gear: a bedroll, a backpack, and a cooking kit of nested skillet and saucepan plus a coffeepot and a bag of canned food.

He was here, all right. But he didn't plan on staying much longer. I didn't see the shotgun anywhere. "I don't get it. Why now, and how's he going to . . . ?"

"Let's work our way around to the other side," said Ellie, "and see if we can spot them."

Just what I needed, more bushwhacking. What I wanted was a taxi, preferably one equipped with an electric blanket and a very dry martini.

Instead I struggled after Ellie until we reached a grove of old spruces whose massive trunks stood like sentinels in the silence, the forest floor softly carpeted with their tan needles.

Easy to walk through; easy to be spotted in, too. We hustled through as quickly and quietly as we could. Next came a barrier of wild raspberry cane bristling with what felt like hypodermic needles, then a bog of black mud.

Finally we reached the relative safety of a sweetgrass field, still wet underfoot but at least not threatening the tops of my boots, and the grass itself was tall enough to hide in.

"Which way?" All this freestyle tracking had spun my sense of direction around.

"Ssh," Ellie warned, parting the grass with both hands to peek through it. Squinting past her, I saw that we were on a narrow spit of land angling back toward Rickert's camp. And from here it was clear he'd chosen his location with skill.

You could've walked right past it on the beach and never known it was up there, and from the water it was curtained by the bushes so the campfire was hidden at night. Then:

"Oh," Ellie breathed. "Just look at her. Look at them both."

"Who?" But suddenly the camouflage of leaves, trees, and grass resolved, and I did see. Twenty yards off at the edge of the grassy clearing stood Wanda Cathcart, her hands at her sides and her dark head cocked slightly at an inquisitive angle.

But it was the thing standing there with her that made the breath stop in my throat: a big buck deer with a thick rust-brown coat, its huge eyes rolling in pain so the whites showed and its massive sides heaving with anxiety.

"Oh. My. God." The buck wore the biggest rack of antlers I'd ever seen that wasn't already mounted on a wall with the rest of the hunting trophies. And if it happened to toss its head in the wrong direction, Wanda would be skewered.

The animal pawed the earth with a powerful hoof and emitted a loud, unhappy-sounding snort. And now I saw why. An arrow was stuck in its neck.

Or rather stuck *through* it. The point had pierced its hide just above the animal's shoulders and come out the other side. Now it hung there as if the buck had sprouted long thin wings.

"That thing has to hurt," Ellie murmured as Wanda took a step.

"Don't do that," I whispered, "don't get closer..."

Because a scared buck was bad, but a pain-maddened one was worse. They don't call them *wild* animals for nothing.

"Ellie, what's she...oh, hell, we need to stop her." But we couldn't just jump out; it might startle the buck. "Any ideas?"

No answer. "Ellie, I'm not kidding, if we don't..."

"Mmmf," Ellie replied.

Not the reply I wanted. "Can't you be a little more–*mmf!*"

Something covered my mouth, spun me around. Ellie's eyes flashed, her own mouth closed by Mac Rickert's other hand. He let go of me, pushed me back hard, and backhanded the side of my head as I staggered, knocking me down.

Then he put his boot on my neck in a way that reminded me unpleasantly of spinal paralysis. "You move an inch and I'll kick you to death," he growled, and threw Ellie down beside me.

But he didn't take my satchel, either because I'd fallen on it and he didn't see it, or because he thought a foolish woman like me probably only owned one weapon and he'd taken that away from me a few nights earlier.

"So you didn't drown," he said with a glint of dark humor. Not the kind that made me want to trade jokes with him, though.

The kind that made me want to shoot him. Which I was going to do the very instant he gave me a chance; any deal notions I might have had were long gone.

His humor didn't last long, either. "Keep your mouth shut," he growled. "You too," he told Ellie. "The both of you've screwed things up enough already."

He shook his shaggy head at us scornfully. "You want to sneak up on someone at night," he added, "skip the flashlights."

So he had known we were here the night before. Which meant he'd figured out who sent the cops to try catching him, too; no wonder he was angry.

But his anger faded as he turned to watch Wanda again, only glancing at us often enough to prevent me from getting the Bisley from the satchel without him noticing.

"This is her last chance," he said. Wanda still stood by the animal, her body and expression passive.

Not coaxing, the way you might try to draw in a creature you wanted to feed or capture. Only waiting... but for what?

With my eyes I drew Ellie's attention to the satchel. She understood, nodding minutely.

Just then Wanda took another step. The big buck snorted once more but held its ground. "I told her what to do," Rickert said. "I told her, but if she can't..."

All at once I understood: Mac Rickert the outdoorsman, the well-known animal lover.

And a deer wounded by a poacher. Must've been, since no one was allowed to hunt on Tall Island. Rickert would've known what fate awaited the animal, doomed to die slowly and painfully over the course of a coming winter it couldn't hope to survive.

Not with that arrow stuck through it, and you couldn't just pull it out, because of the barbed tip at one end and fletching–that's what the feathered part was called–at the other.

If a game warden or veterinarian were here, he or she could simply dart the animal with a tranquilizer gun, remove the arrow, then let the deer wake up little the worse.

But Mac couldn't call anyone like that. Wanda took another step.

"See that arrow tip?" Mac whispered. "Not even legal the way it's barbed."

The girl stood beside the wounded creature. Her vulnerability gave me the heebie-jeebies, as did the wind, which just went on rising, bending the sweetgrass blades flat and clattering bare branches together over our heads.

Wanda was barely even tall enough to reach the arrow but she did it. Standing on tiptoe to reach the fletched end with both hands, she grasped the thing as the buck's hooves danced uneasily.

"Now's when you pray," Mac Rickert whispered, his eyes on the girl. His hands were pressed together in a worshipful gesture. "Pray that arrow's a cheap piece of crap."

I understood. A good new arrow was a high-tech item; Wanda wouldn't be able to break it even if that deer just stood there and let her try forever.

On the other hand, good arrows could run a hundred bucks, and most poachers weren't made of money. If they were they'd just take the bowhunting safety classes, pay for the hunting licenses, and buy legal gear.

Mostly. Thinking this, I watched Wanda's fingers close around the arrow's shaft, her brow knitting with effort. But then...

Her foot slipped. In reaction the big animal ducked its head, bleating with pain, and tossed that massive rack of antlers sideways.

"Wanda!" I lurched up as an antler tip grazed her cheek, just missing her eye. She touched the wound wonderingly with her finger, licked blood from it as Mac Rickert's big hand put me down hard again.

A jolt of pain rocketed through my shoulder, surprising me. I'd nearly forgotten the injury but now it was stiffening up again. Mac still hadn't noticed the satchel, though, too intent on the girl and the animal to pay attention.

The deer quieted; again Wanda strained to grasp the arrow shaft, but faster this time, and with a new glint in her eye that I could see and comprehend even at this distance.

If the arrow was breakable at all she didn't mean to fail on her second–and possibly final–try. A drop of blood slid down her cheek but she ignored it, seizing the shaft once more, straining against it.

Until it broke with a sharp snap, the feathered part falling to the ground as Wanda ducked lithely under the buck's muzzle, launched herself at the arrowhead end of the shaft, and *pulled.*

The animal bellowed with sudden anguish and fear, yanking its massive head one way as Wanda pulled the other. Then, her momentum carrying her forward, the girl landed hard with a cry of pained triumph as the buck reared up, its bellow one of fury and power.

The moment seemed to stretch on forever. Wanda scrambled to her knees, her eyes on the great beast. For an instant it stood outlined against the forest. Then it turned toward us, ears twitching alertly as if sensing us there. Finally its white tail flipped up and, with a snort, it bounded off into the woods.

Wanda came toward us with the barbed half of the arrow still in her hand. Halfway to us she dropped it carelessly, waded into the sweetgrass and through it until she spotted Rickert, then ran toward him.

Gritting my teeth against pain, I struggled up, thrust my hand into my satchel, then hesitated as Wanda sprinted the last dozen yards through the grass and into Mac's arms.

He held her gently, said something I couldn't hear. "How?" I demanded. "What just happened, how did she . . . ?"

He shrugged. "Don't know. But she's old Horeb Cathcart's kin, so maybe she inherited something."

I opened my mouth again but she interrupted me. "I'm cold," she uttered fretfully. Stepping away from Rickert, she wrapped her arms around herself, shivering espressively.

"I want to go home." Wanda–mute Wanda–was *speaking.*

I approached the girl. "Okay, honey. We're going to take you there. But Wanda, tell me if he hurt you, okay? If he bothered you, if he did anything to you, just . . . tell me now."

And get it over with. So you won't have to carry it around with you all your life.

"No," she said. "No, he–"

"You heard the lady," Rickert cut in harshly. "She wants to go. I think you two had better get up and get ready to take her."

Whereupon the skies opened abruptly and rain began pouring down by the bucketful.

• • •

"Here," Mac said when we got back to his campsite, handing me his pack to hold while he gathered up the rest of his gear.

Wanda's pills were in his pocket, he'd told me; he had made her take them, and he'd kept her diet as adequate as he could, he'd added gruffly.

"So I guess you really are kind of a Boy Scout," I said with as much lightness as I could summon.

No reply.

"What happened to the bat?" I asked, trying again. "Back at the house she'd made a pet of one of those little brown bats. She was keeping it in . . . gah!"

Something fluttered past my face in the gathering darkness. "Never mind," I said faintly, and zipped my windbreaker a little tighter up around my neck.

"Okay," Rickert pronounced, taking the pack back from me and hefting it. "We'd better go. There was somebody out there earlier scanning with binoculars. I saw the reflection."

He waved at the water. "And I don't think it was the cops back for another look. But I still don't think we've got a lot of time."

Fresh anxiety washed over me. Someone else scoping out the camp couldn't be a good development. "All right," I said. "You too, though. You're coming with us."

To my surprise Mac didn't argue, but I could wonder why later; at the moment what we needed was Ellie's boat.

"Listen, Mac," Ellie said as we made our way through the brush toward it, "what's going on? Because we don't think you killed Gene Dibble the way you said you did."

"Right, and especially not your own . . ." I began.

But then too late I realized: Mac probably didn't know his brother Joey was dead. By now that news was all over the island but Rickert wasn't in a position to have heard it. And the *GhOulIE gUrl* had foundered on the other side of the channel, where he couldn't have seen it.

"... anyway, if you didn't kill Dibble, someone else did and Wanda might've been a witness," I finished lamely.

He must have heard something in my voice, though. "What?" he demanded. For a moment there was no sound but wind and the patter of rain; the downpour had slacked off as swiftly as it began.

"What?" he asked again. "What happened?"

So I told him about his brother. "I'm sorry," I added, but he'd already turned away and I wasn't sure he'd heard me. I ran after him.

"Did Joey have the shotgun?" He didn't answer that either at first, his shoulders shuddering convulsively as he shoved through a stand of saplings. But finally he turned, his face fighting tears.

"He was just a harmless dope, Joey was." He tried to get control of himself. "Just... I tried to watch out for him, put him on the right track. He always... he always wanted to be like me, that's all."

He took a hitching breath, wiped his nose with the back of his sleeve. "And yeah, he had the shotgun. We loaded most of the heavy stuff I had here on his boat last night before he left."

Looking out at the water, he went on, "I kept the .22. He was supposed to come back here tonight after dark, pick up the rest of the gear. And us," he added with a glance toward Wanda.

We reached the stretch of beach where we'd left Ellie's boat on the gravel. The rising tide was beginning to lift the stern now, so we had to hurry; the currents would already be vicious.

Suddenly Mac spoke. "Wanda. Who killed that man? The one you saw getting shot, who... ?"

Her pinched face flattened at his questions; she shrank away and for a moment his eyes grew dark. Obviously, he wasn't used to being defied by anyone. Then his expression softened.

Ellie threw his pack in the boat. "Come on, it's not getting better out there, and with four of us, we'll be overloaded."

But Mac didn't budge. He just kept gazing at Wanda, and from the way he looked at her I suddenly knew I'd had it wrong.

All wrong. The girl stood helplessly, eyes frantic with the hopeless effort to get the words out of her mouth.

But she couldn't. "Okay," he relented finally. "You don't have to try anymore now if you can't. Maybe later."

Her face relaxed in gratitude. Whatever it was that had kept her speechless had descended upon her again, I guessed, at the memory of Dibble's murder.

"You go get in the boat," he told her, and as she obeyed he turned to me. "Look, I've got to tell you something. Maybe you can straighten this out once I'm out of here..."

Because he might be coming with us, but not all the way; not to the police. And suddenly I didn't want him to; this was all different from what I'd thought.

Way different. "...and get them to see," he went on. " 'Cause you're right, I didn't..."

"Make it fast." Ellie was already aboard and the clouds over our heads resembled a sack of anvils ready to drop; that earlier downpour had been only a preview.

"Gene Dibble said he had a deal, a big score," Rickert told me hurriedly. "But he had no way to get rid of that much stuff, so he got me in to be his man on the sales end of the operation. He thought I could dispose of it in volume."

I must've made a face. "Yeah, I know," Mac said. "But Dibble had some info on my brother that I didn't want spread around. He threatened to..."

I got it; a fellow like Joey could've been vulnerable to all kinds of blackmail. Rickert rushed on.

"The pills were supposed to be in the house but there turned out to be tenants in it so he had to sneak in. I agreed to drive his car there and watch his back."

Ellie was helping Wanda into the boat. She shot an impatient grimace at me; I waved her off. *One minute,* I mouthed at her.

"On the way, I asked where he'd gotten the money to do the deal," Rickert continued. "That's when he told me he didn't have any money, that he hadn't needed any. The seller was fronting him the stuff."

In other words, buy now and pay later. Even I knew this was not exactly standard operating procedure in the illicit drug business.

"When he told me that, I knew it was some kind of a setup," Rickert said. "Maybe cops, maybe something else, but something wasn't right. I tried to tell him but he wouldn't listen. A deal like that was once in a lifetime for Gene. He couldn't let it go."

"So you got to the house. You were behind the wheel. Then what happened?" I asked.

"He got out. The bag was supposed to be in the shed. But he took a long time, so I decided to go in, too."

His eyes narrowed regretfully. "I was outside the shed and looking right at him when somebody shot him. I couldn't see who it was," he added. "Wrong angle. But I saw..."

"Wanda," I finished for him, and he nodded.

"In the doorway. And from her face I knew whoever'd done it was there with her, somewhere real close."

"So then you ran." As I spoke, the air temperature dropped about ten degrees all at once; this weather really wasn't fooling around.

"Yeah. I had to. Whatever was going on, it was bad."

"You thought it had nothing to do with you." The wind had taken on a deep, ugly tone. "Dibble getting shot, I mean."

"Not if I could help it," he agreed. "But her face. The way she seemed to beg me with it, like I was her only chance. So even though I knew it was stupid..."

His eyes met mine. "I can't explain it but I went back there that night. And it was like she'd been waiting."

After she'd tried and failed to muster up courage to rouse me, to somehow ask me for help, because she couldn't do it while Jenna was listening. And because she hadn't *known* Rickert would return... but he had, probably soon after Wade and I left.

"Do you know why she hadn't told her mother?"

"Uh-uh. Don't know much, actually." His eyes met mine again. "I can't explain any of it," he repeated.

"You guys, come *on*," Ellie called insistently.

"You got her onto Joey's boat in the storm?" I asked.

"Walked her back the whole way. Freakin' gale, but she was a little trouper," he agreed admiringly, remembering it.

So the barrette could have been Wanda's after all. "Why didn't you tell me all this the other night?"

Instead of belting me with an oar and dumping me overboard, I thought but didn't add. Because his reasons for that now were pretty obvious to me; Bella Diamond had been right in describing Mac as looking like a mountain man.

Big, shaggy-headed, heavy-browed, and with muscles in places I hadn't even known people could have them... bottom line, he was a physical guy and he'd wanted me to believe that if I didn't do what he said, bad things would happen.

And when you looked like he did, it didn't take a mental giant to know how to play to your strengths. But we could expand *that* conversation later.

Mac shook his head regretfully. "Wish I had told you," he confessed. "But I didn't trust you and I wasn't sure what was going on myself. I mean," he added helplessly, spreading his big hands, "it was like she expected I'd come back. Come back and..."

Save her. Which in a way he had. "Okay," I told him. "Now I understand, I guess. But come on, we've really got to go."

He followed along obediently until we were nearly onto the beach. But there he hung back stubbornly.

"Listen, there's one other thing I want you to know. Maybe it's dumb for me to care what you think of me, but I, uh, haven't been actually selling anything for a while."

I turned. "What? Then why'd you even . . . ?" *Want the oxies at all,* I meant to finish. But he cut me off.

"Get Dibble off my back," he answered simply. "I'd built up quite a bankroll from when I was dealing, see."

Sure; all that good outdoor gear he'd had cost plenty. Ellie waved insistently at us.

He ignored her. "And . . . I know this doesn't make sense either but I felt sorry for Luanne Moretti. She's like . . . I don't know. A helpless animal. Made me think."

He took a deep breath. "So the truth is, I've been buying up the stuff myself, anyone who'd sell it to me, and dumping it in the ocean as much as I can."

Which also made little sense because all he was really doing was driving up the drug's street price. But I figured I could lecture him on supply-side economics some other time.

I did have to tell him one thing, though. "Mac, you know she can't go with you, right? Wanda, I mean."

He said nothing, his huge fists clenching reflexively at his sides.

"You do know that, though, don't you?" I persisted. "Wanda can't be out there on the run with you, wherever you're going. It's just not right for her."

For an instant I thought he was going to hit me. But instead he relaxed his fists with an effort, stuffed his hands defeatedly into his pockets.

Then an odd look crossed his face. "Just wait one second," he muttered, vanishing back into the brush and brambles.

Criminy, now what? Call of nature, I figured, hoping he'd be quick about it. Ellie swung the engine down over the boat's transom; hurrying to join her, I stuck my good hand into my bag for the Bisley.

I didn't expect to need it anymore. I just wanted to be sure it was there. Only it wasn't. That was when I realized he'd taken the weapon, probably right after he'd shoved me down. And–now what was he up to?

"Mac!" I called when he didn't reappear. No answer.

"He's got my gun," I told Ellie, wondering if maybe he'd been lying about where the shotgun was, too; had I had it wrong again?

"Get that engine started," I added, splashing into the cold water to heave myself into the vessel. But then a shot rang out.

I mean that's exactly what it did. It *rang,* the concussive *pow!* of the big firearm mingling instantly with a musical, just-like-in-the-movies *ker-whang!* of a projectile ricocheting off granite.

"Go!" I shouted, shoving again, but I hadn't reckoned on Wanda. At the sound of the gunshot she scrambled overboard with a howl of... well, I didn't know what it was a howl of, but it was damned inconvenient.

A second shot sounded. I made a grab for the girl, lost my footing on slippery stones, and went down hard, wrenching my arm yet again and letting out, I am reliably told, an impressive howl of my own.

By that time Wanda had made it to shore and was struggling into the woods. "Wait!" I yelled as Ellie leapt from the boat and we both ran after the girl, finally catching up to her in the clearing where she and Rickert had camped.

And where he now lay unconscious, bleeding from a head wound and from his right arm. Over him stood Jenna Durrell, clad in storm gear and holding the Bisley in her left hand.

"Hello, Jake," she said mildly. In her right hand was the .38 pistol she'd used to shoot Mac Rickert. It looked like he'd gone for the Bisley but she'd winged him and he'd dropped it.

And then she'd dropped him. I searched for words, couldn't find any. Probably she'd had the .38 on her ever since she'd used it to kill Dibble.

Good shot, too, from the way she'd turned Mac into a target. All that cop-job handgun practice she'd probably taken, I figured; another thing that didn't exactly make me feel confident about our situation.

"Fancy meeting you here," I said when my dry mouth had eased enough so I could speak.

Weak, but it was all I could muster. Jenna hadn't blown our heads off yet, but that only meant some other plan must be on her agenda.

Not a better one, though, as I soon discovered.

Much worse.

• • •

Jenna gestured sharply with the Bisley, gathering me, Wanda, and Ellie into a group around Mac Rickert's body.

He was breathing, but I didn't know for how long. "He needs a doctor," I said.

Jenna laughed, not a pleasant sound. "Sure, what do you say we call an ambulance?" she asked sarcastically.

Wanda dropped to her knees by Rickert, laid her hand on his forehead. But whatever odd powers of healing she had for animals, they weren't going to work here.

Jenna spared her a pitying headshake, then addressed Ellie and me. "You two have been a real pain in the ass, you know that? The rest of them, too, Marge and Hetty and Greg–if they'd just come back a little later I could've finished her. . . ."

Suddenly the whole thing spread out like a movie in my head: Wanda seeing Jenna shoot Gene Dibble. Then the others coming home so Jenna couldn't deal with the inconvenient witness.

And even though Wanda had been at the time utterly language-deficient, a killer wouldn't want to depend on that. Oh, no; the girl had to be shut up permanently.

"Why?" I asked Jenna, stalling for time in case one of us might think of something to get us out of this. But I wanted to know, too, and Jenna didn't disappoint; this was the only chance she would ever get to tell her side of it.

"Greg Brand screwed my mother out of every cent she had. But that wasn't the worst part."

"Dibble," I guessed. "When they were in jail together they'd cooked up a plan."

"You got it. Find a woman with money. One of them marries her, introduces her to the other one, who's supposed to be able to do all these repairs on the house. She'd never have gone for it if darling Greg hadn't said it was all right," said Jenna.

Another sad laugh escaped her. "That's what she called him. Gene was a little younger than Greg, all baby face and red lips. And his hands…"

Her shudder clued me in to the rest. "And he–"

She cut me off. "Let's not get into the gory details, okay?"

Rickert moaned. She didn't seem to hear it. "For a while I thought I'd gotten over it. Got to be a cop, working for other victims. I was good at it, too," she said.

I'll bet. Dealing with the wreckage of other people's lives probably distracted her from her own.

For a while. "I even started writing those how-not-to-get-screwed articles. A few of the smaller magazines bought them."

A wave of regret for her washed over me. She'd done so many of the right things: kept on going, made a life for herself. Trouble was, for all her energy and talent she'd still needed help.

And hadn't gotten it. "But I always kept track of Gene. Greg Brand, too," she continued. "And when Brand cooked up a witches-in-training scam and decided to bring it here, I knew it was my chance."

"You signed up," I said. "Stole the drugs from…where? The evidence room where you worked?"

She nodded agreement. "Right before I quit," she said. "To make it look more like a drug deal gone bad. A few weeks ago I came up here to set it up in advance, asked around, then put it together with him."

Her tone hardened. "And just like I thought, he didn't recognize me any more than Greg did. I found him in the bar at the Mexican restaurant and got him talking."

She paused, remembering. "When I told him he wouldn't even need any money up front…well. Gene always was a greedy bastard."

"Why'd you need the drugs at all? I mean, if you were going to shoot him the minute he showed up..."

I'd been right about the oxycontin tablet. She'd probably had the drugs hidden down in the crawl space, dropped one while transferring them to the paper bag. As for Dibble's body–well, just leaving it was safer than trying to dispose of it.

Wanda's too, probably, if it had come to that. Heck, Jenna had been a cop, she knew how to arrange a murder scene.

Including how to create the victims. "You still don't get it," she said impatiently. "Killing him wasn't enough. *He took my dreams.* I wanted him to be seeing that big stash, the score of his life, practically in his hands. And then I wanted him to *see* someone taking it from him."

She inhaled deeply. "It all had to be real. His dreams, like mine. I paid that son of a bitch back with interest. At last."

But once she did she'd had a problem. She hadn't realized the silent girl was even in the house. Still, Wanda was no *immediate* risk. Jenna would have to improvise... which she'd done.

Rickert groaned again, weakly.

"They'll know you rented a boat, they keep records," I tried. That must've been how she got here. "And when they find us they'll realize..."

But Jenna just laughed. "You don't think I actually signed it out, do you? Oh, *please.* I'm not stupid, you know. I copied a key, slid out of the boat basin.... I've been using that boat every day, no one's going to check the key rack if they even notice it's gone."

Her smile was triumphant. "And I can handle a boat without running lights at least as well as this dope," she added, kicking at Rickert's body.

"You did help me, though, Jake, for a while. Once you started snooping, all I had to do was follow you around. To that moron, Joey, for instance."

Poor Joey, I thought. About as attractive as a car accident, but still. "And he died because...?"

She shrugged dismissively. "Hey, he had a boat, too. I knew he could get the dynamic duo here out of the area. And I didn't want them skipping town at an inopportune moment."

So she'd murdered a little schmuck who'd done her no harm other than posing a mere threat of getting in her way. She pushed Wanda aside, then inspected Rickert's sheet-white face.

"How'd you do it? I mean he wouldn't have just let you..."

Jenna's grin turned scornful. "Faked being in distress. He let me aboard, I waited till his back was turned and put one in his head. Then I used a piece of gear you helpfully supplied."

"What? How did I...?"

"The ice-fishing stuff in the shed out at the rental house," she answered with a smirk. "Handy-dandy."

At first I didn't get it, but then I did. Ice-fishing gear, including... the auger. You could drill a good-sized hole with it. In, for instance, the bottom of a boat. You could even do it from outside, when you were back in your own vessel.

As she had. Mac Rickert's eyelids fluttered. "Guy's got a hard head," she observed, and waved the gun at us again. "Toss me that bag of yours," she ordered, and I didn't have much choice, so I did it.

Then, "You two drag him," she told Ellie and me. "I'll bring our witchy little friend."

And we didn't have much choice about that, either, so Ellie and I hauled the big man's limp body back to the boat, with Wanda following along disconsolately.

"Put him in," Jenna commanded. "And you, go get the cotter pin out of that engine propeller," she added to Ellie.

In other words, disable *our* boat; worse and worse. Ellie and I exchanged looks; somehow we had to slow her down.

"How would you know anything about cotter pins?" I asked, putting a deliberate note of skepticism into my voice. "From what I've seen you're no expert mariner, whatever you say."

As I'd hoped, Jenna took the bait. But her response was not what I was hoping for at all.

"I grew *up,*" she recited impatiently to me, "on *Nantucket.*"

Get it? her face added. *You dummy.*

Belatedly, the dummy did: island, water, boats...

"The beach club we belonged to when my dad was alive had boats, and lessons for the kids. Contests, too."

By now I knew what must be coming, the reason for her lean, athletic build and the same kind of easy grace I'd seen in my son Sam and his friends, all of whom were as comfortable on boats as monkeys are in trees.

But the details were even less reassuring than I expected. "I won my first sailing regatta division when I was seven," Jenna bragged, "and my first overall at eleven. We had a cabin cruiser, too, I tooled around in that a fair amount."

She gave me a smug smile. "So yeah, I guess you could say I'm fairly okay on the water. And considering where we are..." She waved behind her at the bay. "I had a feeling there'd be boating stuff involved sooner or later."

Her voice hardened. "And I figured it might work out better if everybody thought Jenna was a klutz. Now get him into the boat and get the damned cotter pin."

When we'd obeyed she snatched it from Ellie's hand. "You all get in, too, and sit there," she ordered. "I'll be back here in less than a minute and if you've moved I'll find you and waste three shots. Or," she added chillingly, "as many as it takes."

She vanished into the woods. "Now's our chance," I told Ellie when she had gone. "We'll take Wanda and..."

I was already half out of the boat, wincing at the cold raindrops blown stingingly into my face by the rising gale. But Wanda didn't move, refusing to leave Rickert.

No, her mute face expressed clearly. "Please," I exhaled in frustration. But she wouldn't. I couldn't even pry her arms from around him.

And we couldn't leave her. "It doesn't matter anyway, Jake," Ellie said when I'd stopped struggling with the girl. "There's no place we can go."

She waved at the wild water. Through the sound of the wind an engine was already approaching, even as Ellie held our useless engine's propeller in her lap.

That was what the cotter pin was for, to hold the propeller on. "Can we get anywhere without it?" I asked her, knowing the answer. And that it was probably already too late anyway.

She shook her head helplessly. "No. And the tide's too high now to walk across the channel, or even swim. That current..."

She didn't need to say more. By now the rushing water there was easily eight feet deep. It would have been like going over Niagara Falls without the barrel.

"We could still try hiding in the woods."

Ellie made a face, gesturing at Wanda, who remained crouched by Rickert's sprawled body, glaring up fiercely again at the bare suggestion of abandoning him.

And then it really was too late as the other boat came out of the storm at us, Jenna at the helm. As she'd implied, it was one of the day rentals from Quoddy Marine, a little smaller than Ellie's but with a bigger, more powerful engine; Deke Meekins didn't believe in underpowering his vessels.

Hauling the engine up in an easy, practiced way, Jenna hopped out and ran a heavy line through the eyebolt jutting from the prow of Ellie's craft.

"Seen the rest of it yet?" she asked conversationally as she worked.

Metal strands threaded into the line glinted dully. So much for the Swiss Army knife I'd slipped into my inside jacket pocket along with the five grand before we left home. Mac hadn't taken the knife or the money, either. But neither would help us now.

"What are you talking about?" I asked. "The rest of what?"

In answer she angled her head sharply toward the inlet we'd walked across the night before. Something white showed there on the other side but I couldn't quite distinguish what it was.

Jenna dug into her own jacket and came up with a small pair of binoculars, tossed them at me. "Have a gander," she invited.

So I did, and for an instant I thought it was as Victor had said at my kitchen table a few days–it felt like a few years–earlier: that they were all in it together. What else could explain the tenants' white van sitting there as if someone in it was watching?

But as I turned the focusing wheel on the glasses I realized it was worse than that. Greg Brand sat slumped over to one side in the driver's seat, and I was pretty sure he wasn't asleep.

"Are you crazy?" I asked Jenna in stunned disbelief. Because for someone who wasn't she was racking up quite a body count.

"Oh, no," she replied casually, putting a knot in the line and hauling it tight. "Just... careful."

Then she fastened something to the line, tightening it with a small screwdriver. I didn't know what it was, but from our point of view I doubted it could be anything good.

"For one thing, I don't want Greg to ever be able to testify against me about anything," she explained.

She finished tightening the gadget. "Aside, I mean, from the pleasure it gave me to finally put a bullet in his head."

She slid off the bow of our boat, onto the beach. "Best case," she added, brightening, "they'll blame the whole thing on him after I go back and put the gun in his hand."

I had the feeling it might not quite work out the way she expected; even for someone as well versed in the nuts and bolts as Jenna, what with modern lab techniques and so on, suicide's a harder thing to fake than it used to be.

But she was doing okay so far. And self-doubt didn't seem to be a big feature of her personality.

I let my breath out. "Jenna, you're a hard woman," I said.

Her face flattened until it looked barely human. "You have," she replied expressionlessly, "absolutely no idea."

With that she reboarded her own boat, lowering the engine and starting it in a brisk, confident series of motions.

Then we were *floating*. Jenna had our boat under her power.

And she was towing us out to sea.

Chapter 13

Jenna Durrell motored steadily into deeper water, towing us behind.

She'd taken our life vests. "We should just jump in anyway," I said as Tall Island receded behind us. "At least we'd have a chance."

"No we wouldn't," Ellie replied. "Please don't. It doesn't matter how badly you *want* to swim in it, Jake. It's just too . . ."

Cold. The memory of it won Ellie's argument; reluctantly I sat as Wanda uttered a mute sound of distress from where she sat by Rickert, her hand groping up for Ellie's hair.

It was coming out of its pins, red wisps flying. "It's okay, honey," Ellie tried reassuring the girl.

But it wasn't. A wave smacked the boat, nearly capsizing us as Wanda went on insisting, her small fingers fastening on two of the loosened hairpins and yanking them out.

She thrust them at Ellie urgently. "Thank you," Ellie began as if humoring a younger child, then stopped and stared at them.

"You know," she told the girl, "you might just have a..."

And then, carefully, she slid the hairpins together through the hole in the propeller where the cotter pin belonged.

Ahead, unaware of the navigational hazards, Jenna barely missed a clutch of jagged rocks local mariners called the Boar's Tits. My heart clogged my throat as she skimmed their tops.

But she probably wouldn't miss the next bunch, or maybe the ones after that. And if we were still tied to her when it happened, sooner or later neither would we.

"Okay," said Ellie decisively. Sliding into the stern, she stood up and reached out to the rear of the upraised engine, and fit the propeller onto its stem.

"Ellie, what're you..." Next she squeezed hairpins together and stuck their ends through the hole in the propeller stem, to hold the propeller on.

"...*doing*?" I demanded. A puddle of bloody water had pooled around Mac Rickert's head.

"I can't put the engine down," Ellie said, "while she's towing us. But in a minute..."

Finally I understood. The makeshift cotter pin wouldn't last forever, but it might just be enough for now. And now was all we had; once Jenna towed us far enough out to satisfy herself, she'd cut us loose. After that, the rocks around Tall Island would rip our boat's guts out, if the waves didn't overturn us first.

Jenna's boat slowed, came around facing us. The line went slack; we were effectively adrift. Instantly wind and currents captured us, slewing us sideways.

"Brace yourselves," Ellie shouted.

No kidding. But suddenly... *whack!* A hole sprang open in the side of the boat. A round hole, as if someone were...

Smack! Another hole, spurting water. "Hey, she's *shooting* at us!" I shouted.

"Bail," Ellie ordered Wanda grimly, tossing a coffee can at her.

Wanda complied as Ellie's green eyes narrowed coolly and in a way I knew very well. The rest was bad enough, that look said.

But now she was *mad.* "Whoa," she said, peering ahead. "Jenna doesn't know about the Nun's Head."

It was a boulder shaped like a head and upper torso, rising at low tide twenty feet over the surrounding water. Now only a low dark mound revealed where it lurked.

And only if you already knew where it was. Jenna's course aimed her straight for it. "Okay," Ellie said, "get ready..."

The prow of Jenna's boat lurched up suddenly. "Now," Ellie grated out. Dropping the engine down over the stern, she gave its ignition button a mighty push.

"Start, damn you," she implored it, and it roared to life.

Whereupon *we* were the ones under power while Jenna's boat, still tied to ours, zigzagged in a wild, impossible attempt to climb the Nun's Head.

"Yes!" Ellie shouted exultantly, and dropped the outboard into reverse. The gear engaged hard, drawing the line taut. In response Jenna's boat slithered at a sharp angle backwards into the roiling water, swamping the transom instantly.

The impact knocked Jenna off her feet. Her head smacked the rail with a dull, melon-thumping sound I could hear even over the rising storm. She went over the side.

Simultaneously Ellie cursed. "I can't get the engine out of reverse," she snarled, struggling with the shift mechanism.

Not a good development, because maybe we'd dealt with Jenna but we were still tied to her boat. If Ellie didn't get our engine back in gear in the next ten seconds it would seize up and quit and after that Jenna's boat would just keep towing us until it ran out of gas.

"Damn you, *move!*" Ellie screamed, throwing her weight on the shifter.

The lever popped free, the engine howl quieting and the boat nosing forward again under a steadily darkening sky, the clouds sullen purple and the wind snatching the whitecaps' foam off the wave tops.

Quietly, Wanda began to weep. Me too, but on the inside; the actual outward sobbing, I figured, would start any time now.

"Ellie, can you get us to . . . ?"

Shore, I was about to ask. But she just pointed at the eyebolt in our prow, where the line was still clipped.

The line connecting us to Jenna's boat. Which, it suddenly came to my attention, had begun sinking. And night was falling fast; soon we'd be lucky even to find Jenna's boat in the dark, much less get the tow line unhitched from it.

We could unclip it from our end, except that clever Jenna had put a line lock on the cable. That was the little gadget she had attached, I saw as I scrambled to it on my belly, the wind lashing my face. The kind of lock that took a key. . . .

I looked around wildly. No key. She'd taken it with her.

"Bail faster," Ellie snapped at Wanda, who struggled to obey, scooping up canfuls of the bloody water around Rickert.

By skillful steering, Ellie kept as much slack on the line as possible, postponing the moment when the other boat's weight would drag us under. Too bad this maneuver took us farther from land, the touch of which I now desired more than I craved heaven and more than I feared hell.

One of which I might be seeing in close-up, in the very near future. Ellie aimed us sharply to starboard.

"What are you doing?"

For an answer she just pointed, and in the encroaching gloom I spotted Jenna's face, her desperate hands clinging to the top of the Nun's Head.

Then a wave washed over her and she was gone. The boat, too, gave a swaying little shudder, then sank.

"Grab it!" Ellie shouted, waving at something. "Jake, get out there and..."

I didn't see what she meant but at her gesture I crawled out on the prow again anyway, then spotted a small plastic tackle box bobbing in the waves.

It had floated out of Jenna's boat. Tools, I thought. Maybe even the key to the cable lock. I scrabbled madly for it, the cold water numbing my hands instantly.

"Jake!" Ellie cried behind me. "Jake, please hurry!"

"I am!" I shouted. Or tried; all that came out of my mouth was the icy salt water that had just splashed into it.

And all I could think of was Wade reading the note I'd left. Not knowing–yet–that it contained my last words to him.

The prow was slippery, every roll of the vessel threatening to wash me off. My body trembled uncontrollably, partly from cold, partly in the kind of fear that turns your brain to mush.

But finally my fingers closed around the tackle box handle. I threw it behind me, sliding back desperately into the boat as the sunken craft's cable shortened inexorably. When it tightened, it would drag us down....

Fumbling with the latch, I got the box open. A small box of .22-caliber ammunition, a really quite enormous hunting knife...

I shuddered, not wanting to think of what Jenna might've had planned for that. Around it lay the usual snarl of fishing stuff that always litters the inside of a tackle box: lures, sinkers. But nothing I could *use*...

A light somewhere on shore caught my eye briefly. Then it vanished, and I was too intent on the box's contents to pay much attention.

"Get away, will you?" I told Wanda as she leaned in to where I rummaged in a mess of bagged hooks and other such small items. But she kept crowding me.

"Wanda, cut it out. Can't you see I'm trying?"

The boat jolted, stiffening as the last of the cable's slack went dangerously straight. The prow dipped abruptly. It was over; as Jenna's boat went down, we were inexorably being dragged under with it.

Suddenly Wanda's fingers shot out, dipped into the box, and reappeared with...

A key. Nimbly she scampered out onto the prow, now slanted down thirty degrees or more toward the water. As I watched openmouthed she dropped to her belly, slid forward, and grasped the cable with a small, utterly helpless-appearing hand.

Only it wasn't helpless. *You've got to stop underestimating this child,* I thought as she slotted the key into the lock, then turned it.... *Click!*

The cable loop snapped away with the mass of the sunken boat pulling on it, and it whiplashed nastily before sliding into the water like an evil genie vanishing back into its bottle. Freed, the prow popped sharply up again, nearly sending Wanda into the water.

But she clung on, sliding backwards to get her feet and then the rest of herself into the boat again.

I threw my arms around her. "You did it! Oh, you wonderful girl..."

She shrugged me off, dropping to her knees by Mac's body. I couldn't tell if he was alive or dead.

Dead, probably. Ellie brought us around, motoring us toward land, which was now barely distinguishable from the dark water...

...except for the light. It was there again, bright yellow-white, and moving. A flashlight, and as we approached the shore a car's headlights appeared. An ambulance was there, too.

Silhouetted against them: moving figures. A hundred yards off we began to hear their voices shouting.

I looked back, straining through the rain and wind to catch sight of Jenna again. But only the night and wild water were out there now, accompanied by a roar like a train bearing down on us.

The real storm had arrived. Rickert stirred, moaned weakly; Wanda bent to him again.

Then the makeshift cotter pin broke, the engine revving uselessly.

But the waves carried us in; moments later, stones scraped on the boat bottom. Faces appeared; strong hands reached out to us as we trudged ashore through the slippery shallows.

Wade lunged at me. "Jesus," he moaned in relief.

"I g-guess you g-got my nuh-note," I said into his shoulder. His head moved, his arms tightening around me.

"Yeah," he said. There were tears of angry joy in his eyes. "I got it, all right."

"Let her go with him," Bob Arnold ordered the ambulance guys when they'd loaded Rickert into the waiting vehicle. Even before he spoke, Wanda made a beeline for the open bay doors and scrambled in.

"Now, George," Ellie began as rain began hammering down. "It wasn't as bad as it seems."

The hell it wasn't. Everybody here knew that this time Ellie and I had pushed the envelope too far, us most of all. That we had gotten away with it–barely–didn't make me feel any better about it.

Especially when George opened the door of his truck and the cab light went on, revealing the infant car seat strapped inside.

"Mah!" Lee shouted gleefully as Ellie climbed onto the jump seat in back; then George closed the door, putting the light out.

"Wade," I began, intending to say *I'm sorry.*

He pressed my head to his shoulder. "Don't say it. Just...you screwed up, you and Ellie. But if you hadn't, the girl might be dead now. You'd have to live with that."

He held me away from him, looked into my face. "That you hadn't even tried," he said. "And anyway, if I'd wanted someone else, that's who I'd have married."

I leaned against him once more; it was all I'd wanted to hear. "The saddest thing is, I don't think Jenna ever once even asked anyone for help," I said.

Brief silence from Wade. Then, "Tell me about it," he said, his tone communicating perfectly his clear understanding of the relationship between pots, kettles, and the color black.

Whereupon I wisely decided to shut up, as the ambulance howled off toward Route 1 and the hospital in Calais. After that, George and Wade pulled Ellie's boat farther up the beach so the storm wouldn't carry it away, and Bob Arnold cornered me.

I gave him the short version, with emphasis on Jenna still being in the water. But squinting out over the dark roiling bay as he listened, his face confirmed what I already feared: that by now the waves had surely finished what her thirst for vengeance began.

"Won't have to arrest her," Bob said as if this were some consolation.

Which for Jenna maybe it would have been. "State cops checking on her found a warrant out of Massachusetts," he added. "Seems there's quite a collection of contraband missing out of the evidence room where she was on the job last."

"Right," I said inadequately. "Probably there is." Tiredly I finished summing up the night's events. Now that the adrenaline was draining from my system, my legs felt as if they were turning to water.

"Christ," said Bob when I was through. "What a sorry mess." He strode to his patrol car. "Get on home," he called over his shoulder. "I'll talk to you later, you and Ellie both. State cops will want to, too, I imagine."

No kidding; I felt my shoulders slump at the thought. But then he turned. "Jake."

"Yeah?" He didn't look happy, and he couldn't say *Good job.* It hadn't been. But...

"You really are the snoopiest woman I ever met," he told me finally, his mouth forming a grudging smile. "And by the way, I gave Victor a call. He's headed for the hospital to meet Rickert."

To do the surgery, he meant, if it turned out Mac was still a candidate for any. I felt a spark of hope, but puzzlement, too.

Victor had barely been gone a day; I hadn't known he was home. "And Marge Cathcart woke up," Bob added. "She'll be able to see Wanda when the ambulance gets there."

He started the squad car. "I sure wish winter would come," he finished with a touch of wistfulness. "Freeze things good and solid, maybe I could get a minute's peace once in a blue moon."

"Sure," I said carelessly, not thinking much of it. Wishing for winter was a chronic thing with Bob. His job became vastly less stressful when the last of the summer visitors departed and the rest of us were trapped inside by the cold.

But that time his wish came true, because the next day winter did come.

Along with something else.

Something I still haven't figured out.

• • •

The following afternoon, soon after I replaced the money in my cash stash–the envelope of bills looking lonely without the Bisley there behind the loose brick–my father arrived with the box he'd dug out of the mortar from the cellar wall.

"Here it is," he announced proudly as he carried it up the front steps.

The *new* front steps. Because as it turns out, what it takes me weeks to do can be accomplished in a few hours by a carpenter who's not following instructions out of a how-to book. One, for instance, like Ellie's husband George, who thinks of power tools simply as extensions of his hands, and uses them as easily.

Now the new wood glowed richly under a coating of ice; the cold front reaching down from Canada behind the storm was like a hand from a morgue refrigerator, gripping us by our throats and polishing the steps with a sneaky layer of slipperiness.

"Drain holes," George said. "I'll drill drain holes in 'em."

To keep water from pooling on them, he meant. But not right that minute; we were all too curious to see what the box held. My father brought it into the dining room and set it on the table.

"It's *beautiful,*" Ellie breathed at the dark cherry top and elaborate inlay figures delicately set into it. At the center was a rose, while fanciful birds adorned each corner and a checkered strip ran around the edges inside the raised trim.

"And you've cleaned it up so well. How did you get all that concrete off it?" Ellie asked.

He straightened proudly. "Steel wool so fine you could polish a baby's bottom with it, and olive oil mixed with just the right amount of... well, I ain't saying."

He waved a lean hand at Bella Diamond, hovering over the box there with us. "She came up with the recipe, deserves the most credit," he said.

"Oh, go on with you," Bella reacted gruffly, but with an interesting little glance at my father that I thought boded well for the future.

"That inlay's hand done," George said, admiring it. "Somebody spent a lot of hours on each o' them birds."

"And the finish," Wade agreed, "was hand mixed." In his gun-shop work he often concocted finishes so the repairs matched the originals. "Wish the guy had left us *that* secret recipe," he added with a touch of craftsman's envy.

My father took the top off with a ceremonial flourish. "And inside..."

"Oh," we said softly together. Inside lay a book bound in dark leather. Over the years the leather had dried but not so much as to crack or disfigure itself, and the golden curlicues stamped decoratively into the cover still gleamed.

"One hundred and eighty-one years ago, give or take a year," my father said reverently. "That's how old the house is, and they built the foundation first."

So the book was at least that old, too. "Age isn't the most interesting thing about it, though," he went on.

He lifted the volume, presenting it to me. Hesitantly I took it, feeling the surprising weight of it in my hands.

Whatever he had done to repair the little hole he'd drilled in it, he'd done invisibly. "Open it," my father said gently.

So I did.

Chapter 14

The dream was always the same, its events proceeding sim-ply and exactly as they'd happened in real life.

Exactly as they'd happened: Six weeks after Jenna Durrell died in the water off Tall Island, I sat in the rocking chair by Victor's bed in the guest room in my old house.

He opened his eyes. "Hello," he said thickly.

The clinic treatment hadn't worked and after that it was all downhill fast. The operation Victor did to remove the bullet from Mac Rickert's skull was the last surgery he ever performed.

"Hello, Victor," I answered, leaning forward so he could see me. If he could. Lately I wasn't sure. "I'm here," I said.

A faint smile touched his lips. After performing the surgery on Rickert, he'd arranged for Rickert's transfer to a rehab place in Portland, and referred Wanda Cathcart to some experts he knew in New York for evaluation of her language deficiency.

"Jake," Victor said, and closed his eyes again, his fingers plucking restlessly at the top of his linen sheet.

Outside it was snowing, white flakes swirling thickly past the window in the pale, bluish early-morning light. "I'm here," I said again, not knowing if he could hear me.

Only after Wanda had seen for herself that Rickert was alive and expected to make a full recovery had she agreed to go for the evaluation.

"After that," Marge Cathcart had told me of the bond between Rickert and her daughter, "we'll have to see." But it was clear she understood that Mac had saved Wanda's life, and that whatever else might be true about him, the unlikely pair loved one another.

"She was protecting me," Marge said of why Wanda hadn't told *her* about Eugene Dibble's murder. Wanda had known Marge was no match for Jenna, while Hetty and Greg would save only themselves if push came to shove. And how likely were the police to believe an odd girl with a bat in her sleeve, even in the event that she managed to make them understand?

"Edward Jenner," Victor whispered, then slept again.

If it was sleep. I leaned forward anxiously. His breath came at last, then another, lifting the blue and white quilt that the ladies at the medical center had made for him.

Blue for the sky, they'd said when they brought it; white for the summer clouds they prayed he would get well to see again.

But they'd known he wouldn't, and now cold winds rattled the storm windows as if trying to get in.

I sat back. Wade and I had agreed together that Victor must come here, and by that time he was in no position to argue. Sam spent most evenings here, too, and we had a hospice nurse. But she wouldn't be on duty for another hour or so.

Monday lay watchfully on the floor beside me, Prill in the hall. Astonishingly, Cat Dancing had stationed herself at Victor's feet, refusing to be moved.

After a while Ellie came to the door. "He's asleep?"

"I think so." Together we'd put the hospital bed in the room, Wade and George lugging its parts up the stairs for us. Now a tiny piece of white toast with quince jam on it lay uneaten on a plate on the bedside table.

"Bob Arnold called," she said. "He said you'd want to know a grand jury indicted Hetty Bonham for being an accomplice in more kinds of fraud than you can shake a stick at."

The poor-abused-Hetty story had been a lie, it turned out, along with all Greg and Hetty's supposed family history together. They'd been partners in crime, nothing more; why Hetty had been so vehement about Eugene Dibble's past–which *did* turn out to be true–was still her secret.

But I thought I could guess. Victor muttered something that I couldn't make out.

"Is Lee still wearing the mask?" I asked, mostly to distract myself.

As if I could. "Yes," Ellie smiled. "She won't take it off, or the rest of the getup, either."

For Halloween we'd had a record number of trick-or-treaters up the new front steps. To greet them, little Lee had been dressed as a baby goblin, and she'd fallen in love with the outfit.

The holiday had also conferred an unexpected benefit on me; at a party at the Happy Landings Café a pretty young high school teacher visiting our island from New York had suffered a costume malfunction so spectacular, so revealing, and so nearly certain to have been deliberate, it wiped me and my doings right off the map in the gossip department.

"I'll check on you later," Ellie said, and closed the door. Victor's eyes opened at the latch click, his lips moving without sound.

I reached out. "What is it?" His fingers closed around mine.

"Jake," he murmured. "Do you forgive me?"

And for once I knew just what to say to him. "Oh, Victor," I replied, letting a little impatience into my voice so he would be sure to believe me.

"Victor, you know I forgave you everything the first minute I laid eyes on you."

• • •

When the recurring dream ended I lurched up in bed. Wade slept beside me, sitting up with his reading glasses slipped to the end of his nose and his book splayed open under his hand.

Outside a blizzard howled massively, gusts of wind shaking the old house. When I drew back an edge of curtain to look out, I found the windows thickly plastered over with snow.

Tiptoeing to Wade's side of the bed, I eased his glasses off and plucked the book from his fingers, then snapped the light out and crept from the room. As I went I heard him slide down under the covers and turn over in his sleep.

Passing the open guest room door I looked in, unable to stop myself. But of course it was empty, the hospital bed dismantled and taken away weeks earlier. Downstairs the dogs followed me to the dining room, where I flipped the light switch without result.

The storm had taken the power out, and I supposed the snow made it difficult for the town men to get to the generator. So I lit candles and placed them around the room; then, wrapping my robe around myself against the chill, I sat down with the book my father had dug from the cellar.

The cover felt soft, smooth as skin. Hesitantly I opened it, fear and wonder stirring together in my heart. Inside was line after line of writing in a fine antique hand, each consisting of a single name.

Ship's captain James Waldron, for instance, was the very first inhabitant of my house; his was also the first name in the book, which had been hidden–there'd been no evidence, according to my father, of any more recent tampering with that section of the foundation–for nearly two hundred years.

I drew my finger down a page, one of forty or so bound by hand into the volume. A tiny hole pierced them–the injury done by that drill bit of my father's wasn't fixable on the inside, as it turned out–but they were all still perfectly readable.

Following the old sea captain's came more names, line after line of them. The ink and the penmanship never changed, though; all the entries in the book had been made by the same person.

Turning the last page I paused, once more unable to believe my eyes. In a volume written and hidden long ago by an unknown person, for reasons as mysterious to me as the dark side of the moon, the final entry was as familiar to me as my own two hands.

Or my face in a mirror. A dreamlike feeling seized me but this was no dream. I put out my finger and traced the old lines of antique ink; so odd, so utterly impossible.

But the book was real, lying open before me.

And my own name was in it.

ABOUT THE AUTHOR

SARAH GRAVES lives with her husband in Eastport, Maine, in the 1823 Federal-style house that helped inspire her books. She is currently at work on her next Home Repair Is Homicide mystery, which Bantam will publish in hardcover in 2007.